BE SAFE I LOVE YOU

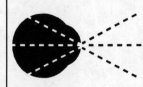

This Large Print Book carries the
Seal of Approval of N.A.V.H.

BE SAFE I LOVE YOU

CARA HOFFMAN

THORNDIKE PRESS
A part of Gale, Cengage Learning

GALE
CENGAGE Learning·

Farmington Hills, Mich • San Francisco • New York • Waterville, Maine
Meriden, Conn • Mason, Ohio • Chicago

LIBRARY OF CONGRESS CATALOGING-IN-PUBLICATION DATA

Hoffman, Cara.
  Be safe I love you / by Cara Hoffman. — Large print edition.
    pages ; cm. — (Thorndike Press large print core)
  ISBN 978-1-4104-7042-3 (hardcover) — ISBN 1-4104-7042-3 (hardcover)
  1. Veteran reintegration—Fiction. 2. Depressed persons—Family relationships—Fiction. 3. Large type books. 4. Psychological fiction. I. Title.
PS3608.O4775B4 2014b
813'.6—dc23   2014009847

Published in 2014 by arrangement with Simon & Schuster, Inc.

Printed in Mexico
1 2 3 4 5 6 7 18 17 16 15 14

For Eli

Even from ten or fifteen miles away you get a good view of a burning village. It was a merry sight. A tiny hamlet that you wouldn't even notice in the daytime, with ugly, uninteresting country around it, you can't imagine how impressive it can be when it's on fire at night! You'd think it was Notre-Dame! A village, even a small one, takes at least all night to burn, in the end it looks like an enormous flower, then there's only a bud, and after that nothing.

— Louis-Ferdinand Céline,
Journey to the End of the Night

PART ONE

PROLOGUE

January 6
Jeanne d'Arc Basin, Northern Canada

She had been naked for less than ten seconds when the snow began to feel hot. Her body, pale and lean and strong, biceps and thighs banded with black tattoos, lay basking against the glacial ice; a snow angel overcome by shadows and lights, calm and awed in whatever seconds remained.

The tower scaffolding from the rig flickered, and she could barely make out where the dark stacks cut into the white sky. Just shapes and brightness. And she thought of a silent shower of frozen sparks. And the *shhh* and *hush* of sand and desert blindness; how it was here too in the snow where everything shone. Where everything refracted and blazed and brought the world back to the simple material of itself, of its beauty. This was all she had ever wanted.

It was his breath she saw first, then the

11

red of his tongue and gums and black fur. He panted and cantered painfully, lifting his frozen paws and wincing, and then he bowed and pushed his face against hers. She felt the impossible heat of his tongue against her skin. The condensation from his breath had crystallized into tiny bits of ice surrounding his muzzle. He huddled down and curled his small warm body beside her, and she slipped her numb fingers beneath his collar, rested her cheek against him.

The lights of the rig burned and bled to white, and before she closed her eyes, she could see the dunes out in the distance. Placid and silent and stretching on forever.

DISPATCH #216

Bad News Sistopher Robins,
Sebastian anti-froze to death and by that
I don't mean he overheated. He drank
anti-freeze and died. The most clichéd
ending possible for a dog — like vomit-
choking for a rock star or heart attack
for a Teamster. Dad found him and at
first held it together. He didn't know the
cause of death was poisoning and came
to my room telling me our dog lived a
good long life etc. Using my forensic
senses I accidentally stepped in a puddle
of bright green dog vomit and put two
and two together. I was dumb enough
to tell our Dad who then freaked out
because he's the one that spilled the dog
poison on the garage floor. I tried to
make him feel better by saying that dogs,
like pregnant women, know what their
bodies need. Grass for dogstipation, just
like pickles and ice cream for whatever
that treats, and that maybe Sebastian
was on his way out anyway. But Dad
thought I was just being a smart ass.
Anyway, he was a good dog and at least
he was old. We're getting him cremated
— good he drank anti-freeze instead of
gasoline — and then putting his ashes in

his favorite spots in the yard. Dad wants to save some until you get home but I am sure you, like me, think that's weird so I'll just do it myself. I can't wait until you get home.

Be safe, I love you.

Danny

ONE

No one was waiting at the airport for Lauren Clay because she had told no one she was coming home. She called a cab from the car rental at the front desk and then waited by the luggage claim for her duffel, which was more than half full of presents for her father and brother; things she'd bought at the FOB PX and things she'd bought out in the street, in the cramped and sweltering little market just outside the forward operating base where she'd been stationed for the last nine months. She checked her watch, readjusted the bobby pins in her hair. And thought about the promise of relief that would come from doing everyday things like washing dishes, gazing out the window at kids playing by the duplex next door, taking Danny to the movies or going through the *National Geographic* with him, or ordering Chinese food and sitting by her dad while he watched TV and slept.

She couldn't wait for them to open presents, to surprise her brother. Sebastian had been one of those surprises, and the look on Danny's face when he saw the dog made up for a lot, maybe everything. Sebastian's fur was still brown and as soft as a rabbit's when she brought him home years ago. He had ears like a kitten's and his eyes were shiny and black and alert. He looked like a baby wolf and lived in a cardboard box in her room. Sebastian was the sweet helpless thing she wanted Danny to raise. Something he could train. Somewhere good to focus his attention. The kind of thing she knew could save a life.

The dog lived in their house for two days before they showed him to their father and he wasn't angry. He sat up in bed and held the puppy and laughed. And Sebastian snorted and licked him, fell over and rolled around, chewed on his knuckles with his needle-sharp teeth. His belly was round and taut and pale pink. Jack Clay held the dog and looked into its face.

"He's a nice pup," Jack said, smiling, pulling his hair back from his shoulders so the dog wouldn't nip at it. "He's a good boy," he said in babytalk. And then Danny picked up the dog and cradled him. And she felt good because they were happy and she was getting their lives in order. She was getting things done.

Lauren hadn't thought of Sebastian since getting Danny's letter, but now in the calm and safety of the terminal she found his memory was the first to vividly greet her, to lead her thoughts to the neighborhood and the house she hadn't seen in two years.

The dog had followed Danny around, sat on his lap, and, when he got bigger, accompanied them on treks through back lots and out along the river where he would hunt squirrels and swim and snap his teeth at the water. He was a strange-looking animal, and the woman who sold him to Lauren said he was a schipperke mix, told her they were bred to be miniature watchdogs and made the grandiose claim that during World War II schipperkes were used to deliver messages between Resistance hideouts. She and Danny tried to train him to do it, tying notes to his collar to carry between their rooms, but he tore them off and raced through the house dangling the shredded wet paper in his teeth, his head held high. When he got excited he galloped back and forth between their rooms growling, gums drawn back, teeth a gleaming white crescent amidst his fur.

She looked around the terminal and smiled. She had nothing that could replace Sebastian in her duffel, but she'd made it home, cruised right by what could have become a month's worth of useless talk back on post, and made it home for the holiday. And now she had a week of relaxing before she headed out to finish things up. Meet Daryl, tie up loose ends.

Christmas music played from speakers mounted near the cameras beside the baggage claim. Beyond the sliding-glass doors rain baptized those who ran from the curb to meet their friends and relatives in the roped-off lobby beneath a faded blue and white sign reading simply: ARRIVALS. They came in dripping, disheveled, their faces shining or makeup running as they embraced and balanced packages and bags. People regarded her in her uniform; her black hair pulled up into a bun, her dark eyes and deeply tanned face. If she weren't in desert camo, if she were wearing a light jacket and high boots over skinny jeans, she could be returning home from school in California, or be some rich girl coming home after a year studying abroad in Greece or Africa.

She was back but didn't feel so far away from Iraq. Home was closer to the wider world than she had realized as a girl. Watertown was a base town, the home of Fort Drum, and the place reverberated with its presence. She felt it now more than ever, bodies training and bodies deploying and the vast interconnected system of sleepy faraway places that housed and built soldiers to send out. They were everywhere. And from every lonely FOB or smoldering rubble-strewn corridor, she could feel their readiness now as if they were one.

When her bag arrived she slung it over her shoulder and walked out into the freezing rain to wait. She was giddy from the freedom and the space and the strangeness of returning. The streets were black and slick and reflected the yellow lights flanking the entryway, and the hiss and hush of cars speeding past made her anxious to get going. When the cab arrived she surprised herself by giving the driver Shane's address. Shane, who she'd stopped emailing months ago. Shane, who hadn't received a paper letter from her since the first mad lonely and exhausted weeks she'd been away. Her most recent, most consistent correspondence was with Danny. His dispatches. The full report and at least a page of jokes every time.

The last letter made her laugh out loud and when Daryl asked, "What?" she got to say, "My dog died." Lauren loved that kid. She loved Daryl too because he was smart and did things right but not too right. He liked hearing Danny's letters. And when he showed her pictures of his kid they were always action shots: the kid doing a head stand, jumping off the top step of the porch, standing on the seat of his tricycle in little red cowboy boots holding a long spindly stick. The kid was a daredevil, had a buzz cut like his dad and the same sweet face. Daryl'd had him when he was nineteen, and, like Lauren, enlisted so he could provide better for his family. Daryl got it. There was no explanation needed between them.

Shane she wasn't so sure about. His letters were serious and obsessed with the future. Graduate school, cities, traveling, and always "when you come home . . ." Something made her stop emailing and she didn't know what. When she thought about it, all she could come up with was ancient history, a thing he'd said back when she decided not to go to school. Like everyone else he'd been genuinely surprised. She was in most of his classes, studied with him. They'd sat in the library together beneath the fluorescent lights, heads down, his glasses glinting, reflecting the pages they were reading, their feet touching beneath the table. Shane had gone to her recitals, he knew who she was. But his words were an echo of the same stupid question she'd heard from all her teachers, and she was still amazed anyone had the balls to ask her. Amazed she had to clarify yet again how dinner gets on the table.

He said: "Half the fucking kids from this neighborhood are doing the army 'cause they can't get into college. And after all the bullshit you went through you're going to send yourself to the same place as those white-trash fuckwads."

It meant nothing to her at the time. She'd actually laughed about it. Knew she was right, Shane was wrong. But later, dust covered and weighted down and baking in the heat, with every pothole on what wasn't really a road making her shoulders and back work for her living, sitting just two feet from some brand-new killer who couldn't shut the fuck up on the day's journey back to the FOB, she would long for a reprieve. She would try for the music in her head but sometimes she just got Shane's voice, and

21

those were always the words he was saying. One more reason on a very long list you shouldn't have anything to do with the Murphys. Because they're smart enough to know not to say a thing, but they're always mean enough to say it anyway.

The Murphys were Shane and his mother and the big crucifix in the kitchen and his three bald and blue-eyed uncles, Patrick and two others, whose arms were branded with terse gothic directives in black ink. They came together every Sunday dinner and at one time every one of them could have gone to college like Shane but they opted for bartending, carpentry, and the occasional visit to County instead. They were men so indistinct from one another Shane referred to them collectively as "the Patricks." He couldn't stand a thing about them and neither could Lauren. Whatever they were, Shane wasn't. But he couldn't escape the fact that they'd helped raise him, given him the confidence and wit to live in the body of a thin, soft-featured, almost pretty man. And he'd inherited their look — the bright, expansive calm that assured you he was paying close attention, assured you that Shane Murphy, slight and myopic and often hidden behind a book, was not the kind of boy who experienced fear, was in fact capable of anything.

Lauren knew his drive to change and escape and how the specter of becoming his uncles had ridden his heels all the way to the lush gardens of Swarthmore. She loved him, had loved him since tenth grade. But it didn't matter. She'd never had the luxury of taking off like he'd had, never even indulged in the fantasy for too long. She had to take care of Danny and make sure they were ahead several mortgage payments, make sure there was money in the bank. And enlisting was a good plan overall. She didn't just get smart in basic, she got strong. And when people came home for break with their freshman fifteen, and drug stories, and gross soft, self-centered plans, she saw them for what they were — and so did Shane, and he respected her.

Now it seemed like that had all happened to another girl. That mind, that decision, belonged to another girl. He'd go to graduate school and he'd be a teacher or a professor, and she was back home to do god knows what. To fix things. To do what good women do.

Six months into her tour she didn't feel like telling Shane anything. Didn't feel like discussing her plans, didn't have the energy for "when" or "if" or "afterward," so she just stopped. Reading one less letter, picturing one less face or having one less dream that wouldn't come true felt like a good decision in the new war economy, the new austerity plan she had instituted in her soul. But Danny was a different story. Danny wrote her letters like dispatches, pretended that home and middle school were war zones and she was on vacation in sunny, exotic Iraq. He was dark, that kid. And strong and smart. And if there was any "when" or "afterward" it belonged to him and she would make sure he got it.

She looked out the window of the cab as they passed through empty streets, the remains of snow on yellowed green and muddy lawns and houses strung with colored and white and blinking lights. Outside Lourdes Church a nativity scene rose from a puddle, the camels knee-deep in murky water. Red bows and candy canes decorated the streetlamps, and the place rang with quiet. Quieter than anything she'd experienced in fifteen months.

Lauren watched the rain on the window and started at the sound of the cab driver's voice.

"Don't you guys usually come into Drum on a military flight or a bus or something?"

"Well, yes sir, that's often the case. I could

see why you'd think that. However I came into Fort Lewis in Washington." Lauren pushed the earnest lilt of hick into her voice. "I'm unna be seein' my folks today after quite some time."

"You'll make their Christmas."

"Yes sir, I sure do hope so."

The cab driver nodded knowingly and looked at her again in the rearview mirror. She smiled back at him. Straight teeth and smooth skin and kind dark eyes.

"I got a nephew over in Afghanistan," he told her.

"Is that right?" Lauren asked, leaning forward and resting her arms on the front seat. "Who's he with? What unit?"

Lauren wanted the streets of her hometown and silence to be her only welcome, but she talked to the driver instead. Words, stories, expressions, the lax, entitled way of soft civilian life. She was making him feel at ease and proud of his sister's kid. And she heard that voice that she couldn't stand coming out of her mouth. Some kind of camouflage in itself. The constricted encouraging tone of a liar. The modesty and gentleness and ignorance, the unassuming pose. It was a linguistic costume for a woman who'd never really felt these things in her life. But she was patient enough to listen, to know it was important for the cab driver to speak.

He answered her and she began talking quickly. Felt herself suddenly animated when she'd intended to say nothing, to see the town, feel the pull of the streets and the homey memory of places she'd driven past with Shane on their way to park somewhere where they could sink down in the seats and talk and kiss. This place held her life. It was an empty cup, an empty clip, a place from which she'd slipped, but it still fit her form. She surveyed the uneven sidewalks she'd raced down as a girl, the yellow diamond signs of the dead-end streets that led to the river where she'd played with Holly at the edge of the abandoned, graffiti-tagged industrial park. They skateboarded on the smooth concrete of the loading docks, gliding down the slope of the ramps and up into the arc, the cradle, of the half pipe. In that place they were alone and alive, and sometimes set small fires to let the flames hypnotize them. Stood sweat-worn and thirsty after exerting themselves, dropping wooden matches onto piles of newspapers and scrap wood.

They watched the fire grow until they almost couldn't put it out. Gauging their abilities against its size, the direction of the breeze, the time of year, what some boy had said at school. When Holly would move to snuff it Lauren would hold her back, make her wait for the feeling, the rush and strange false calm of watching it grow and then the panic that it was not their fire anymore. She'd wait for the quick efficient intake of breath, the flooded dilated feeling in her chest, before they'd dash to stamp it down, or in worst cases blanket the flames with their sweatshirts and jackets. Lauren always made sure it wasn't smoldering before she left, taking the feeling of terror and virtue with her like the good girl she was, the good girl she'd always been.

Afterward they didn't talk about these fires. About how they were learning to be patient with fear. How there was no such thing as undoing, and that putting out a flame didn't mean it hadn't burned.

By the time she got out of the car at Shane's she felt like she was floating, still watching herself from outside. She ran up the narrow back stairs and pounded on the door while cold rain cooled her face and hair. It was lovely after all the dust and heat, after the feeling of ash in the air settling on skin; the hot granulated ground turned to powder kicked up and blown against lips, into her mouth and nose and anyplace sweat-soaked and exposed, whipping in a sharp crackling static against her glasses and the heavy ceramic plate strapped high and tight across her breasts, there to protect the soft flesh of organs beneath her rib cage and to keep the estuaries of blood inside of her, instead of bursting and pouring over the dry ground.

Rain was a relief. To shiver a luxury. That feeling of hovering not so strange beneath the gray diffuse light of the quiet Watertown sky, low close clouds and no smoke, no sound, no sun beating and burning her flat. She waited, looking around the small, square muddy plots of land that made up the back yards of the neighborhood. Kids next door had spray-painted a marijuana leaf on the plywood backboard of their garage basketball hoop, and plastic toys were strewn across their driveway, left there before the snow — or brought out now in this false spring.

The yellow checkered curtain covering the back window moved, and Shane's face stared blankly for a moment while she smiled. Then he gasped and shouted her name and the chain slid, the lock clicked, the door swung open, and he rushed out onto the narrow concrete step to hold her, bent down around her, squeezed her, and she pushed herself against him to feel all of his body and so she wouldn't see surprise or sadness on his face. She closed her eyes, kissed him on the mouth and he held her tight to his chest, crushed their thighs together, and she felt his warm skin, the flood of pleasure and joy and safety to be in his arms. He put his hands on her shoulders, her arms, her back, as if making sure she was all there. Then she stood on his long feet and walked him backward, until they were in the low-ceilinged kitchen.

"Is your mother home?"

He laughed. "No. She's over at Patrick's."

"Can I have some?" she asked.

He raised his eyebrows slowly and grinned at her. "Sure," he whispered, then put his hands on her shoulders and pushed her back so he could look into her face, look for something, some explanation. She met his eyes and smiled because he was so pretty and because she didn't want to worry him.

He said, "You know, I've been calling your dad for the past six months to find out if you're okay."

"Did you find out?" she asked, and he made a short breathy sound and stared at her, his eyes wet and shining with relief. He hadn't changed, didn't look a day older than when they were in high school. Still had those beautiful teeth, the flushed and hollow cheeks and full lips and long straight nose, his wavy messy hair and his little wire-rimmed glasses; the white T-shirt and stupid sweater vest, the way he filled out his jeans, all the things that gave her that hollow hungry feeling in her stomach and constricted her breath.

He looked overwhelmed and like he was trying to be careful with her, but that wasn't what she wanted at all. She moved close to him again and inhaled his scent. Put her hands at the base of his spine. Feeling his body made the hair on her neck stand up, made her heart restless. She wanted to bite him through his shirt, she wanted a mouthful of his skin. When her hands touched his belt she could feel his breathing change.

"Well?"

He was trembling slightly when he picked her up and she wrapped her legs around him. He walked quickly upstairs, slammed his bedroom door open with her back and kept walking until he pressed her into the metal-framed twin bed that creaked and cradled their weight. He put his lips on her. She tasted him, held his face, his head, her hands in his hair.

"You've been haunting these sheets," he whispered against her cheek. She didn't want him to talk. She grabbed his shirt and pulled it over his head and was crushed at once by how beautiful his chest was. How familiar and gentle. His long thin torso, smooth skin and the subtle ripple of muscle, a body like water, no knots that rose or cuts in flesh. No tattoos. Not frozen solid beneath the skin of his stomach and chest, but strong and supple. He touched her with his soft hands, his long fingers on her face and in her hair, and his smell was so clean, unspoiled. He unbuttoned her camouflage top, pulled up the T-shirt beneath, tore at her pants, and then stood before the bed looking down at her.

"Take this off," he said, "take all of this off, please. Take it off."

Her body had changed. Her skin was tanned, taut, her shoulders and back, her hips. And she could feel just how different she was built now that he was seeing her, touching her. Her stomach and legs, everything like an animal now. She felt his desire for her war body, almost curiosity at her hardness, and then she watched his face as he saw the rest of the tattoos, saw his look of distress and then hunger. He ran his fingers over her arms and legs, and she felt the difference between her inked and bare skin, the desensitized numbness of the black bands on her shoulders, biceps, forearms, thighs. His strength and delicacy and smell were overwhelming and everything he was doing was beyond familiar. A taste she'd forgotten she loved drew her into her body, and then out into nothing but breath upon breath.

When it was over her head was clear and she got up and put her clothes back on. Left her hair unpinned and hanging tangled around her shoulders. Shane smiled and she looked at his relaxed face, his high and hollow cheeks, lips swollen from kissing. Lauren heard the sound of the rain on the windows, felt the gutted, senseless floating feeling again, and she wanted to be outside with cold water on her face.

He asked, "What are you doing tomorrow?"

She bent down to lace up her boots and felt no air in her lungs with which to answer him. Couldn't make her voice work. Felt that if she spoke at all some understanding she had with herself, a thing with its own logic and language would come undone. She took a breath and found her camo shirt buried in the blankets at the foot of the bed, looked at him again, at his long legs, the curve of muscle and vein at his hip bones, and smiled.

"I have to be back to Swarthmore by next Thursday," he told her. "Otherwise I'm around. I could even put off going for maybe another week." He said eagerly, "Maybe we could go somewhere."

She didn't say anything — kissed him on the cheek and began walking downstairs. After a few seconds Shane got up and followed her in his bare feet, buttoning his jeans as he walked.

"Lauren, baby," he said, and his voice was placid and gentle like his body. "Are you okay?"

She looked at his face and did not like what she saw: the concern and confusion and, worst of all, the pale light of his eyes searching her.

"You okay?" he asked her again, holding the back of her hand against his lips as she stood at the door.

She gave him a quick nod, smiled. She needed to get outside. "I'm good," she told him as she walked down the back steps. "I'm good."

Two

The Clays lived in a bungalow-style building that crouched between a small, unkempt
lot plastered with mottled-yellow leaves and
a row of identical duplexes. Steam rose from
a vent near the back door, and Lauren could
smell dryer sheets, laundry being done. The
walk from Shane's had left her body feeling
refreshed and strong, her joints loose and
humming. Now she had a clear head to
think about what she'd have to do at home.

She stepped up to the back door and
pushed it open, instinctively putting her
hand down to stop Sebastian from jumping, then remembered he was gone. To hear
the door creak and no barking felt like missing a step. His round blue dishes were not
on the floor beside the closet, but his leash
and collar hung on a hook by the coat rack,
along with Danny's jacket, her father's plaid
scarf and puffy coat. It smelled like home; a
damp autumnal smell of leaves, musty old

books, and some kind of citrus cleaner, or maybe someone had been eating an orange. Things she forgot existed made her smile in recognition. Wallpaper, linoleum, the vintage microwave with the analog clock on the front. She was shocked at how clean the kitchen was, dropped her bag in the corner and took a few tentative steps toward the living room.

"Hello?" her father called, and the sound of his voice caught in her chest and made her want to laugh, suddenly calm and giddy at once. She heard the squeak of the ottoman being pushed away from the couch but kept quiet, stood grinning by the kitchen table, waiting for him to lay eyes on her, excited to see his face after so long.

Jack Clay walked into the hall, his hair pulled back into a shaggy gray ponytail. He opened his mouth and shook his head, blinked quickly, then smiled. He was wearing faded jeans and beat-up slippers and a red sweater that looked brand new. His chest expanded and he held his breath, his face at first confused; and then, filled with relief, with joy, he stretched out his arms and then, overcome, began crying.

"Dad," she said tenderly. He rushed into the kitchen to hug her, choked with emotion and laughing. He looked well.

"Dad," she said again, patting him on the back. He kissed her on the cheeks. "Oh my girl," he said, and his voice was hoarse. "It's my girl." She squeezed him tight and rested her head on his shoulder, then heard the race of Danny's footsteps pounding heavily down the stairs and he burst into the room — six inches taller — he hadn't been kidding, as tall as she was now.

Danny threw his arms around her and their father, and he rocked them back and forth. Jack let go so that he could give his sister a proper embrace. "Whooooo!" Danny yelled. He high-fived her. Then hugged her again. She rested her head against his shoulder and they stood that way close to tears. He still felt like a baby to her. Taller and thinner but no muscles. She pulled back to look at him. His once round face was now longer and defined, making their resemblance clear, the dark hair and eyes and something in the expression. Some abiding tough sweetness.

"The two of you," Jack said, wiping his eyes, the smile still there. "Look at you."

Danny picked her up and walked in a little circle around the kitchen, humming some cartoonish victory song. And their father started laughing, really laughing from his gut, a sound they both loved.

"When did you get here?" Jack asked. "You didn't walk all the way from the airport, did you? We'd have picked you up!"

She and Danny stood side by side, arms around each other's shoulders, leaning into one another, a force now twice as strong as yesterday, smiling indulgently at him.

"I took a cab."

"Oh sweetheart, you're soaking wet," he said, shaking his head. "Danny, run down and get your sister some clothes."

Danny headed down to the basement, and she heard the hollow clang of the dryer door. A sound that proved she was home. That this was real. She had left the FOB, left Amarah. She had not dreamed this. She and Sue Godwin and Specialist Gibbons had driven to the airbase where they'd boarded a flight that had taken them back to the States. Less than three days ago, hours ago really, she'd been out on patrol. Now she was standing in the kitchen. Done with it. All of it.

"Look at you," Jack said to her. "Look at you." She worried he would start crying again, but instead he turned to the refrigerator and pulled out several deli bags: ham and turkey and cheese, then mustard and vegetables. He set them on the table, then went to the sink to peel carrots, fill the tea kettle. Lauren was surprised to see how relaxed he looked, how the refrigerator was stocked. For a moment she was afraid she was dreaming.

Danny shut the basement door, handed her an old plaid shirt and a pair of his Levi's, and she held them, watching their father. She glanced at Danny incredulously, and he gave a quick nod in their father's direction, smiled. "Dad's been making a mean turkey pita lately," he said.

His phone buzzed and he pulled it from the front pocket of his jeans, read the text and clicked back a quick reply with his thumbs.

Something seemed wrong, a little too well organized, too normal. Why had her father been up and in the living room when she arrived? "Did you guys know I was coming home?" she asked, hungrily watching her father make sandwiches, marveling once more at the amount of food in the house.

"We knew you were coming home this month," Jack said, his eyes filling with tears again. "Because you said December but I was beginning to think it wasn't going to happen. There was bad news yesterday and I knew you weren't in Fedaliya, but I never really believed we knew where you were or what you were doing." He said this last part bitterly, glanced up at her for just a second.

"I was in the same place for the last nine months, Dad."

"Clown College," Danny said, finishing the sentence in her same earnest tone.

Lauren burst out laughing and their father shot him a disapproving look. Danny smiled to himself and she could see him as he was at eight, back when the comfort of their secret world unfurled around him.

When Danny was little she would bring him piles of *National Geographic*s she'd got at the library sale and they would sit together for hours cutting out pictures: giraffes, single-sailed boats, churches made out of bones. And, thanks to his foresight, eating raisins and crackers and salami and drinking warm juice. Danny had made his closet into a kind of pantry. In case of emergencies, he said. One more way he was smarter than she was. Better prepared.

They papered every wall of his room with photographs of different places. To make a whole new landscape. *National Geographic* provided them with a bigger, more interesting world to replace the one they'd been born into. Cherry blossoms and Eskimos and animals from the Galápagos. Houses on stilts and miles of lush forests and people with strange faces and beautiful crazy clothes. *Our whole life is out there,* she told him, looking into his dark eyes, *and we will get to it. Nothing that happens here is real.*

She shook the memory off and breathed in the intoxicating smell of home. Things had been hard for a while, but she should be happy. Compared to where she'd just come from, they'd had riches. Their childhood was fine. It didn't matter what happened before when they were small or when their dad wasn't well, they were fine. They were safe.

When she thought about all the freedom they'd had, it came to her as a pile of books. Flannery O'Connor, Vonnegut, Ivan Illich, Carl Jung, Joan Didion, and the autobiography of Lenny Bruce. Textbooks on family therapy and early childhood education, instructions on how to administer and grade IQ tests, and the not so incongruous combination of Samuel Beckett, R.D. Laing, and Baba Ram Dass. The house was full of shelves and shelves of poetry and stacks of albums that had been abandoned like the relics of some conquered tribe. And they were alone to discover it all, free to read the gentle prose and listen to Charlie Parker and David Bowie and the Beatles, forage in the cupboards for canned soup and drink from mugs sporting the Cornell seal like urchins squirreling away the still-useful items from some ruin.

Every corner of their house had a worn-out paperback or library-sale classic waiting to be read and she craved them now — the feel of the bindings, the yellowed pages, the hours alone lying on the living-room floor with Danny, their feet propped against the wall, reading.

Eventually they rearranged all the furniture, reorganized cupboards, screwed the frayed outdoor hammock into the living-room ceiling so it could be a swing. They'd also replaced the bottom of the glass-top table with an old aquarium they'd found in a free box on the street and bought two large goldfish for three dollars to live in it. She and Danny had thought this was a huge improvement, but their father's friend PJ came over one afternoon and put the table back together because they hadn't been cleaning the fish tank; he looked alarmed by what they'd done to the ceiling but just shook his head. She didn't want to know what he'd think of her now that she was back from Amarah.

Like the images of fires, or songs she had practiced, these memories amassed over decades were now dwarfed by things that had taken seconds or, depending on your perspective, centuries to unfold.

Her father smiled and touched her cheek. He handed her a plate piled with sandwiches and vegetables and a steaming mug of black tea with milk and sugar.

He said, "Welcome home, Angel."

She took the cup without touching the handle so it would burn her hand.

THREE

The tree was fat and had long soft needles and smelled so good she wanted to eat it. It was carefully decorated with familiar baubles; a white ball with tiny red hearts, pine cones spray-painted gold, a gingerbread house. A delicate string of glass cranberries wrapped around the tree and multicolored lights glowed against the ceiling and across the white carpet, which was littered with crumpled red and green and white wrapping paper. She was happy to see there'd been presents this morning. She'd sent them money last month so they could get what they needed for Christmas. And aside from the fact that there was no dog to eat the paper or monopolize part of the couch, and that the dust on the bookcases made it clear they hadn't been touched since she left, it was as cozy as that house had ever been.

She set her dish on the coffee table and

ran quickly up to her room to change her clothes and pull gifts from her duffel. Suddenly the gentleness, the ease of her family and the shock of seeing her room made her feel uneasy, like she was returning from a place that was outside of time. Shane's body had made her feel that way too. She stood in her room trembling, sat on her bed for a moment and breathed. She took off her boots and fatigues and slipped her arms and legs into Danny's warm clothes like they were a disguise. She was home alive, in one piece and in this moment fighting a desire to wash her eyes out with lye.

The duffel offered some distraction. She'd bought her father a classic black and white kafiyah, the traditional head scarf guys like him always associated with radicalism and "people's resistance."

She'd bought a SEAL pup knife for Danny. Now that she'd seen how much he'd grown she wished she'd gotten him the full-size knife. She also got him Swedish mittens with liners, a first-aid kit, six silver emergency survival blankets, waterproof matches, a box of twelve sure-pak MREs, a mess kit, a flask, a compass, and a crank flashlight that didn't require batteries.

Danny was a scholar in disaster — the coming ice age, to be specific. Something he'd fallen in love with in third grade after watching a documentary on the Discovery Channel in the school library. It had been hilarious and beautiful to listen to him, a skinny, four-foot-tall kid lecturing on what happened to the woolly mammoth and what would inevitably happen to humanity. But even in third grade, the prevailing wisdom pointed to global warming, not ice age, and so Danny's research on topics like hypothermia, treating frostbite, and snowshoeing gave way to reading about impending disaster from floods and droughts. Still, he was never as captivated by these things as he'd been with glaciers. Never stood in her doorway at one in the morning worried about a heat wave. Never rattled on the way he had back when mammoths roamed his imagination, and he was compelled to describe the creeping ice and the darkening sky. Or stand in the kitchen, his gaze distant and glassy, as he detailed William Parry's fearless expedition to the North Pole.

She brought the armload of presents down to the living room and set them around the tree, then settled into the beat-up futon couch to eat.

Danny handed her a little box wrapped in glossy paper with a picture of a sea lion on it. Inside was a silver bracelet with a working compass for a charm. She laughed as she put it on and then handed him a brown paper bag, which he opened to find a red and black military compass attached to a lanyard. He put it around his neck and high-fived her.

"Great minds . . ." their father said, and he handed her a slim rectangle wrapped in white and covered with silver script reading PEACE ON EARTH.

She tore the paper: It was Robert Frost's *North of Boston;* she flipped to the poem "Mending Wall," her favorite, and smiled at her father, felt the book crack as she opened the stiff new binding and slumped lower on the couch to get lost in it again. Jack went to the closet, retrieved an old plaid blanket and put it over her lap, then handed her the mug from the table so she could drink and read. It was a gesture from so long ago, she didn't know if it had ever happened before. A gesture from a ghost's life.

"Open more presents!" she shouted, and she threw the green plastic bag covered with Arabic script to her father. He slid the kafiyah out, held up the checkered square of woven tasseled fabric, the tag still hanging from the side. She reached out and snapped off the cardboard sticker. He pretended not to notice. "Whoah!" her father smiled, "this is pretty cool."

"Put it on!" she told him. "That's going to look great with the red sweater." And for a moment, when she saw her father's smiling face she was happy like she'd never been down range.

Danny opened his pile of boxes and bags, laughing in delight and holding up each new thing for their father to see. He put on the mittens and then flipped the tops down so he could use his fingers to send a text message. Then he cranked the flashlight, waiting for his phone to buzz in reply. He sent another message and opened one of the silver blankets, putting it around his shoulders like a cape, studied his new knife.

After everything was opened they were content together around the tree, not saying much of anything. Their father sat cross-legged on the floor in front of the couch, his new head scarf wrapped around his neck and face. Danny opened one of the MREs and read the contents of the sealed packs: pork ribs, pound cake, and grape drink. He sent another text message. Lauren watched him, saw how his mannerisms had changed, saw how they fit now in his bigger body, how the culture of middle school, the urgency of connections had overtaken him.

Even today with her home, sitting right in front of him.

"Well, Low," her father said, "maybe we should sing some Christmas carols, huh?"

She smiled at him, shook her head no, then turned away before she had to see his disappointment.

Danny's phone buzzed again and he flipped it open.

"Are you in chorus?" she asked Danny. It was obvious he wasn't doing any sports, so maybe he was singing and hadn't mentioned it in his dispatches.

"There is no chorus," he said distractedly, still looking down at his phone.

"Really?"

"No chorus, no art classes," Danny said.

And her father nodded in confirmation. "No budget, no tax base," he said.

Danny put his phone away and then looked through the MREs again with a satisfied grin.

"Those things have a ten-year shelf life!" Lauren told him excitedly. "The vegetarian lasagna is actually pretty good."

Then he looked right at her. "This is what I always wanted," he said, entirely serious.

"That's why I got them."

Danny cut the pound cake with his new knife and handed a piece to his father, who

48

lowered the scarf to take a bite, and then they heard PJ's voice calling from the kitchen.

"I didn't even hear the door," Danny mumbled through a mouthful of cake.

"Oh, he's stealthy," Lauren whispered sarcastically.

"Peej," Jack called. "We got a surprise."

They heard his boots in the hall and then he ducked his head around the corner and raised his eyebrows, looking at all of them sitting together happy, relaxed. He was genuinely shocked to see Lauren, started laughing hard, then held out his arms to her. His beard was nearly white, and the sides of his uneven afro had gone smoky gray and almost silver. He smelled like coffee. She stood and hugged him, and rested her cheek against his chest until the sound of his heartbeat made her step back.

"Yeah! Oh yeah! This is our soldier," he said, clapping her on the back. "Boom. There she is. Just. Like. That. That's right." He looked down at Jack Clay, who again had tears in his eyes, and nodded. "That's all right. Good time to cry. This is what we humans do."

Then he squeezed Lauren's shoulder, leaned down to speak quietly into her ear. "Please tell me you got that head rag from somebody still breathing."

She laughed for real for the first time since she'd landed, and her father asked PJ, "What do you think of our girl?"

"What I always think," he said. "Beautiful. Needs her hair combed." Then, "What's all this? C rations? Oh shit. That brings me back."

"They're MREs," Danny corrected him.

"Nah, we had the C rats," PJ said. "What's that, a SEAL?"

"SEAL pup," Danny told him, brandishing his new knife. "Wait, check this out." He shined the flashlight in PJ's face and PJ squinted, put up his hand.

"Yeah! Okay, I can see it. Sister's making sure everybody safe and prepared," he said. "That's cool."

"It's chill," Danny corrected him.

"Nah," PJ said, "it's cool. Just like you got MREs and we got C rats." He sat down on the futon and folded his hands behind his head. Jack passed him a piece of military-issue pound cake and he ate it, nodding at Lauren. "When d'you get Stateside, baby G?" he asked her with a mouth full of cake.

"Couple of days ago," she said.

He furrowed his brow for a second, then looked at her and nodded. "Now, you need to worry about stop-loss or what? They gonna send you right back or are you good to go?"

"No sir. I am on terminal leave." She smiled as she said it. "Got outprocessed at Lewis. I'm telling you I could not wait to get that shit done. I was so ready to hand my stuff over. I got in and out of the PDHA in less than two hours, man, packed up my gear, and that's that." She laughed. "That is fucking that."

"What's 'PDHA'?" Danny asked.

"You get a physical and they ask you a bunch of questions," she said.

"Like what?"

"A bunch of screwy shit."

"Like, are you going to go to the mall and shoot people when you get home? Do you plan on becoming a drug addict and robbing pharmacies? Have you ever eaten a baby?" Her father and PJ gave Danny a look but she laughed.

"Yeah. Yeah," she said, in a quick deadpan, "stuff like that."

"You tell me all about it later," PJ said, and she nodded, but that was the last thing she would be doing. She would not be wasting one more second talking about acts that shouldn't be described and couldn't be undone.

"We'll go out for coffee," he said. "Don't

want to bore the old man."

Jack laughed. "Would you listen to this guy, two years older than me, and he's calling me 'the old man.' "

The phone rang and Danny jumped up to answer it, the silver emergency blanket still wrapped around his shoulders. She heard him telling a joke, then talking about her being home, and then he called to her. "Lauren, Mom!"

"Who?"

He laughed. But she sat and took another bite of her sandwich. Did not get up to get the phone. PJ and Jack looked at her expectantly.

"Lauren," Danny called again from the kitchen.

"Tell her I'll call when I get settled in," she said. But she knew she wouldn't.

She could hear the soothing sound of rain, a relentless hushing on concrete and quick hollow taps against the windows and metal gutters. The glow of the Christmas lights played over the walls and ceiling. She snapped on the lamp beside the couch and sank beneath the rough wool blanket that smelled faintly of dog, opened her new book, and began to read, shielding her face from scrutiny behind the cover.

She'd made it home. If things could have

gone differently, if she could have had any other life she wanted no reminding now. Her mother's voice was the last sound she wanted to hear.

Dear Sistopher,

How's your vacation in Desertown going? I've been trying to get a second to write you, but our Internet connection is unreliable out here in the middle of Watertown, and I have to keep morale up, otherwise I won't be able to rely on Sebastian to bring you this message. When he gets there please feed him some socks and send him home. My class is planting a hydroponic victory garden, which should help some with all the rationing. Pip-pip, what? We're growing sugar cane, and tobacco, and whiskey, and ladies stockings, and other things that have been hard to get. Like intelligent conversation.

You must be really sick of all the surfing and sailing and guy supermodels by now. Maybe you could come home or I could come visit you and get a little bit of the good life.

Dad seems okay. (This part is serious. He really does.) He's talking about getting an office in PJ's building and he's gotten a few calls for clients. (I'm not kidding, people are actually calling him to get help with their problems.) OMG,

WTF, LOL, ETC . . . ETC . . .
   Don't wear yourself out at the spa.
                          Be safe I love you,
                             Daniel Clay

FOUR

The books were there but it was like someone else's room. Some girl she could barely
remember. A girl who had painted everything yellow, including the ceiling. Who had
hung blue curtains. What seemed like a
sophisticated idea when she was seventeen
now felt claustrophobic. Childish. The
shelves that were not filled with books
housed trophies and pictures. A photograph
of Danny as a baby wrapped in a blanket in
her arms, while she looked eagerly up into
the camera. A picture of her and Holly
before prom. They'd bought their dresses
together at T.J. Maxx. Holly's was yellow
and shiny, and Holly's mother babysat that
night so they could go out. Holly didn't
drink because she was still nursing, but
Lauren and Shane had a bottle of schnapps
and Uncle Patrick's station wagon — which
was still filled with newspapers Patrick
hadn't delivered. They sat in the parking lot

behind the gym and drank quickly right from the bottle. The air was warm, and she remembered the sweet burning feeling in her throat from the liquor. Holly laughing at them, showing them a new picture of Grace. They stooped over her flip phone as it glowed in the clear night, squinting at her standing up in her crib, four tiny white teeth visible in a smile that took up her entire face. It was just the three of them together at prom because Asshole had already broken up with Holly. But they were happy and they drank to getting out of school.

They shared Shane for the slow dances and watched the girls from their neighborhood leaning drunkenly against boys from Fort Drum whom they'd brought as their dates, boys who'd already graduated high school back in their hometowns and looked interchangeable in their high and tight crew cuts. They were fun and good dancers, had fine bodies and exchanged ironic knowing grins. She remembered how much she loved Shane's way in contrast to them. How proud she was of him that night. He'd just heard from Swarthmore and they were paying for part of it and for the rest he took loans. Lauren would be finding out within the next week about school too, and they were exuberant that night. It was their last

party and you could see it in the photograph. You could see how happy they were,
because they were almost gone.

Lauren looked at the other pictures in the
room. More unsettling proof. A face she'd
once had and would not be getting back.
Here is what you were and what you won't
be again. Here are people you loved in
funny clothes and different-fitting skin;
there she was at graduation with Danny
wearing her cap. And there as a little girl
standing on her father's shoulders at a
music festival, tents in the background, trees
and a long green lawn — flowers painted
on her cheeks, one of her front teeth missing and the one beside it half grown in. In
the photograph Jack looked relaxed. Happy.
His wavy unruly hair down to his shoulders
and a string of green, black and yellow
beads hanging around his neck. He looked
younger than she could remember him ever
looking.

Somehow at this moment the idea of
keeping or even taking photographs seemed
to her grotesque and clinical, like evidence
gathering.

She sat on the bed and let her focus
soften, blur. Rain was hitting the bedroom
window, and downstairs the refrigerator
hummed. From across the hall she could

hear the staccato tones of Danny's phone receiving and sending text messages and the bright *ping* of incoming chat on his computer. Every sound seemed heightened, an annoying intrusion on her concentration, though she had no idea what she was concentrating on. When Danny was little he used to fall asleep singing to himself, songs from the radio or songs he'd heard her practicing. Now the house was filled with sharp noises and distracting unnerving clicks, not the languid sounds of living.

She unpacked the rest of her gear, setting it on the bed. Opened a fake leather box and looked at the cheap metal chunk inside, the ribbon, the pin like a trinket from Claire's Boutique at the mall. Everyone likes jewelry. But no one likes to think about what the army has in common with a group of middle-school girls. If Sebastian were alive she would have pinned it to his collar. She snapped the box shut and put it in the bottom of her top drawer, took out her cosmetic bag, took out her pistol, wrapped it up in a T-shirt, and stowed it under her pillow. Finally she turned the duffel upside down and let whatever was left fall to the floor. Socks, pens, an envelope full of paperwork signed by Captain Parker when the 15-6 happened back at the FOB, and a single sheet of lined paper with the words *Daryl Green* written on it, and beneath that *Camille Bartolette, 2149 Lake Darling Road, Hebron, Canada.* She held the paper and it made the world quiet. Her thumbs on either side of his firmly printed script. "This is where we'll be for sure," he said. "We'll go out ice fishing when you come. We'll get good work out there. We can build a motherfucking snow skyscraper and then knock it down with remote-control planes."

The phone rang and stopped and then her father called her name.

"I'm not home," she yelled. Then pressed her fingers into her ears in case he had something else to tell her.

She didn't remember taking a shower and coming back to the room, but she must have because she was lying on her back now wearing an olive tank top and sweats. Her hair was wet; the soapy smell of her own clean skin hovered around her. Jack was at her door, dressed in pajama pants, his hair whiter than it should have been. He smiled and sat on the edge of her bed. If he was alarmed by the number of tattoos she'd gotten in Iraq he didn't show it. Only a deep calm kindness, a patience and respect radiated from him. It was, right then, as if he was her dad from the picture. The dad who could carry her weight on his shoulders.

"I'm just taking the laundry down. You need any done?"

"No thanks."

"That was someone named Dr. Klein who called earlier," he said.

"What did she want?" It felt hot in the room, and her clothes were uncomfortable, itchy.

"She wanted you to give her a call," he said. "I left the number by the phone. You still don't have a cell?"

She shook her head. "Nah, I'm an analog gal, you know that." Cell phones were expensive and she'd rather save the money or spend it on Danny.

He held her chin and smiled, his eyes clear and calm. She turned to the side, worried he'd start crying if he looked at her long enough. But he didn't. He just smiled.

"Uncle P.'s really happy you're home. Said he's got someone to talk to now."

"Like PJ ever had trouble talking," she said.

"Oh, I know it," Jack said. "More trouble to get him to stop. But I remember when PJ came home. It was hard for him. He had a tough time hanging out again. Wouldn't take off his jump boots, for one thing. He wore those damn boots everywhere. That fool would wear them swimming. He'd be there in his American flag bathing suit and army boots. I mean, come on."

She laughed.

"Believe it," Jack said, nodding. "There was a time when he was walking around — I should say *stalking around* the neighborhood like some kind of angry, I don't know what you'd call it, angry . . . one of those guys from a kung fu movie. He wore the boots and he always wore this black headband and Wayfarer glasses. Ridiculous."

"Oh my god." She laughed. "I don't remember any of that."

"All before you were born. But he was really a different guy."

"You hippies were a bad influence on him, I guess. Now he's hugging everyone and eating vegetables and shit like that. He won't do anything the army way now."

"You bet. You bet we influenced him."

"That's just 'cause he was worn down," she said, suddenly annoyed at her father's ignorance, disgusted at how bad it must have been for Peej. The insufficient boot camp they gave people back then, getting sent over with a bunch of fucking unprepared civilians, coming back and having no job and being a criminal in your own heart at twenty.

"It was harder for those guys back then," she said. "They didn't have the training we do. Different army. They were more susceptible to your bullshit. They weren't as squared away as we are now."

He laughed, shrugged. "Yeah, maybe so," he said. "I just want you to know if you need to talk I am right here, sweetheart. I really am."

She nodded at the sentiment. Looked at his guileless face.

"PJ said there's a group of folks that came home who meet over at his space in the Neighborhood House," her father told her. "Couple times a week."

"That's called AA, Dad."

He laughed. "Wise guy. You and your brother, the two of you, I swear. Seriously, Low. They seem like nice folks if you ever want to go over there."

He got up and kissed the top of her head, said, "I'll see you in the morning." But she held his hand and was frightened at the thought of falling asleep in her old bed.

Jack sat back down beside her and didn't say anything. She was afraid of insomnia or something worse. Her thoughts turned to Daryl up there in the cold, not being able to sleep either. Spending the night with visions of rising dust and black rigs in their heads. A shared dream viewed through crosshairs, heard through the sound of blood rushing in their ears.

Her father patted her hand and said, "Everyone has jet lag after a long trip, babe. Everyone feels a little wired and out of sorts when there's a transition." He looked relieved to be sitting with her, so confident that it was really her, confident for both of them, and his words brought her back to herself for a second. So what if she dreamt, or laid awake? At least she knew what was happening, knew what it was called. The significance of nightmares was not lost on Lauren; she knew all about the scenes that repeat themselves, the feelings of "hyper-vigilance." And that's why none of it would get her. She knew what was coming and she knew how it would end. And, after all, hypervigilance was not such a bad thing. It helped you understand. You in your yellow room; you with your good grades, and your pretty voice, and your chores all done, you are not special. You are not inviolate.

Lauren was familiar with vigilance because she'd felt it for most of her life; been gifted with the ability to read the air in a room, a hair out of place, a single sentence for the wealth of information beneath it. For the

64

premonition it will give you. The sound of the lipstick case snapping shut, a bag being zipped, a throat being cleared, the clink of a light chain against the mirror at 4 A.M. These are just some of the little things that mean you might be a soldier one day.

"I'll see you in the morning," she said, squeezing her father's hand. And made herself believe it.

In the dream she was running with Danny in the snow. The sky was blue, the sun was shining, the air was clear. Large snowflakes were falling, tall pine trees rose up all around them. Danny's face was flushed and rosy, his breath visible in the cold pouring from his mouth and nostrils as he ran. His face made her smile. Made her remember his little hands and arms and shoulders, his baby fat, his happy face. She thought about how he talked so fast she had to tell him to slow down. Lauren looked past his shoulder into the distance, and powdery gusts of snow rose like dust on a road. Something was traveling toward them, fast and erratic. No, she said. She slapped herself in the face, Daryl and Walker weren't there. It was just her and Danny. So it was a dream. But she could hear the sound of a helicopter.

Just to be on the safe side she raised her

rifle, made sure she could see the target clearly through the scope. She needed to do it differently this time so things would work out right. She took a breath, pointed the gun down at her feet, determined not to do it. But gusts of snow still rose. There was no way to know who was in the car. She couldn't risk it, not with Danny there. In one perfect motion she raised her rifle, spotted the mark, pulled the trigger, and then before the pop and shatter, before the silence and the relentless empty din that rushed to fill it, she broke through the surface of the dream sweating, gasping.

The room was dark and still and Sebastian was curled beside her, tucked in behind her knees where he always slept. He looked better than when she'd left. His fur caught the dim light and she could see that he still had the soft brown undercoat he'd had as a puppy. His eyes were shining. Deep black and compassionate. So black the pupils looked lighter. It was a relief to see him, and she reached down to touch him. Let him lick her hand, then closed her eyes for a few more minutes while her heart beat against her chest.

When she opened her eyes again it was to a yellow ceiling. The reading lamp was still on and she felt hungry. Got up and sat with her feet hanging off the side of the bed. The red numbers on the digital clock read 333 and she looked away in case it was a bad omen. She felt like crying and for a moment was gripped by a cold terror that Danny was lying in his room dead. The rain beat heavily down outside and she was frightened that she'd awakened again into another dream.

FIVE

Eileen Klein signed her name on Sergeant Clay's Post Deployment Health Assessment, Form DD-2900, on the afternoon of December 23. The soldier had filled out the form online and Dr. Klein saw no red flags. Clay had not been concussed or injured or suffered an amputation. She had not been sexually assaulted or gotten pregnant on her tour, and she had no medically unexplained symptoms.

Based on Clay's answers on the form, Dr. Klein felt she was not at risk for major depressive disorder. She did not appear to have signs of PTSD or markers for addiction, suicide, or committing acts of domestic violence. Klein scheduled an in-office meeting to discuss factors related to combat and operational stress: normal stuff, expected issues for returning service members. And also so she could lay eyes on Clay, make sure the soldier understood that not reporting health problems meant practical concerns later, like not getting psychiatric health coverage or even getting routine counseling paid for.

Lauren Clay was a model soldier. She described herself in the PDHA interview as a "returning warrior" and said she'd been well prepared for the stressors of command. She said Army Resilience Training for post deployment had helped her understand what to expect at home. Which is why she had plans to keep busy, including applying to school and a possible new job at a site in Canada with Daryl Green, one of the men in her command. Lauren was already stamped, sealed, and delivered back to Watertown when Dr. Klein came across Green's name again, this time as she was assessing a medic on his third tour of duty who presented with ten specific risk factors, requested extensive counseling on base, a referral for someone specializing in combat-related psychiatric issues for home, and knew exactly what pills he'd need prescribed to get him through the next several months.

Eileen Klein had made a mistake when she signed Lauren Clay's Post Deployment Health Assessment Form. And she needed to correct it quickly, because, contrary to the folk wisdom of families and spouses and others who never make it down range, home is not always the safest place for a returning warrior.

Six

Lauren walked across the hall to Danny's room. A gray light washed over the walls, distorting the magazine cutouts that were taped there into a series of unfamiliar shapes. She stood and looked at him — the rise and fall of his breathing relaxed her. Then she sat on the bed beside him and put her hand on his back. After some minutes he woke and gently smiled at her.

"I can't sleep," she said.

Danny moved part of the pillow out from beneath him and extended it to her, and she lay down beside him in his narrow bed, resting her head next to his. Her eyes adjusted to the darkness and she looked at the pictures.

"It's vacation now," he told her, his voice heavy, coming from some warm deep place. "You don't have to sleep."

She looked at the walls. He'd taped up more pictures while she was away. Right

above them hung a series of frozen landscapes, a map showing William Parry's
expedition route; then icebergs and glaciers,
one that looked like it was engulfed in a
waterfall. She knew why he surrounded
himself with these things. They were a
comfort. Like knowing that one day the sun
would explode. A comfort like the plans
she'd made with Daryl for when they got
home. She pointed to the photograph of
rushing water.

"Greenland," he said. "I bet it's much
smaller now. Probably a quarter of that ice
shelf is gone."

"It's so beautiful," she said.

"It is. People think maps don't change, or
they change just because of wars." He
sounded drowsy, like he was talking in his
sleep.

"Like Mesopotamia," she said. Then
turned on her side and closed her eyes.

"Right," Danny whispered, alive beside
her. "But the land changes too, not just the
name or the border. And when the land
changes, then it's for real."

Their mother, Megan Clay, had always been
good at seeing beautiful things. She could
make plain or ugly surroundings sink beneath the weight of a single red-tipped leaf.

You just had to look at things closely enough to make the rest of the world go away. Gasoline spilled in a shallow puddle by the self-serve pump formed a swirling metallic rainbow, a skin upon the water.

"Look, look!" She would breathe excitedly, crouched by Lauren's shoulder, her cheek against her daughter's, trying to get low to see what she saw, to direct her gaze.

"Right there." She'd point. "There!"

A baby bird or a snail or someone's round-cheeked child, a place close to the bank of the Black River where a fish jumped and might jump again. She'd grab Lauren's arm or nearly shove her suddenly. "Look! Someone let go of their balloon, look at how red it is against those clouds."

Lauren did look as they stood in the parking lot of the strip mall watching it until they couldn't see it anymore, until it was part of the sky.

"Do you sometimes feel like everything is really weird?" Lauren asked her mother, lying upside down on the couch in her Pokémon pajamas. "Like a word when you say it over and over and you don't know what it means anymore and then you're not sure it really is a word?"

Meg nodded, preoccupied behind her book.

"I mean like that but with the way things look," Lauren said. "Or like other stuff, just the way things are. Like what the heck is a clock really? Who thought of making up something like that, they just made it up! And what did they do when there wasn't one?" Lauren hung her head off the edge of the couch and looked at her teacup, upside down on the table.

"Yeah," Meg said, peering over her reading. "I do occasionally think everything is a little weird." Piles of notes and other heavy books with library numbers on their spines were spread across the living room. Danny wasn't born yet and her mother still wore octagonal-shaped glasses, and she carried everything anyone could need in a school backpack, including a Ziploc bag full of half-broken Crayola crayons. Meg took out her pen and drew two eyes on either side of Lauren's chin while the girl lolled on the couch, then she started laughing, riffled through her pack for her compact mirror to show Lauren. It looked like her mouth was on upside down, like it belonged to another face. Lauren laughed so hard her stomach hurt. Every time she looked at her own face she started again. Tears rolled out of her eyes and into her hair. Meg smiled at her, picked her up while she was still humming with laughter, and her belly felt good.

"Eight o'clock," Meg said. "Bedtime."

"No. Wait wait wait," Lauren protested, still giddy, her head resting on her mother's shoulder. She could smell the perfume she wore, and linked her finger gently into the loop of her thin gold earring. "Wait," Lauren said. "It can't be bedtime. Clocks aren't really real."

Meg laughed and headed up the stairs. She said, "I'm afraid they are, my dear. Tick. Tick. Tick."

Danny was still asleep when Lauren woke again a few hours later. She went to her room to change, then sat in the kitchen for an hour drinking coffee. As it got lighter a pale mist rose from the ground and fog hung about the windows like the house was engulfed in a cloud. She stood and gazed out the back door into a thick bank of white air and then stepped out into the quiet yard.

It should have been much colder. The rain-slicked driveway disappeared into nothing before her. She turned and squinted up at the windows of Danny's room, the house at once exalted and shabby in the muted morning light. She went down to the end of the driveway and stood in the garage kicking little holes into the gravel floor, digging the toe of her boot into the dirt beneath it over and over. She picked up a handful of the small smooth gray stones and whipped them hard against the wall, then did it again. And again. And again. Hard enough for them to ricochet back and hit her. But not hard enough at all.

When she finally walked back out into the mist the great mass of the neighborhood was looming, closing in on her. Invisible but closing in.

Winters were never like this when she was growing up. There were snow days and frozen mountains to play on. The sound of plows on the streets before daylight. The nights clear and star-filled shining down on the lots and yards made beautiful from the blanket of sparkling snow, pinpricks of icy light shining and flickering up from the white banks. Branches thick with it. Snowmen and forts in the front yards. Sledding down by the river. Ice-skating with Holly out at the park.

She'd imagined all the things they would do on Danny's Christmas break: sledding, maybe even camping somewhere outside in the snow, they could've built an igloo and she could've made a fire inside and they could've sat in there and drank tea.

Everything was different now. As if the heat of Amarah reached through time and erased her childhood. The future she'd been destined to live had caused this somehow. Her future. Her decisions. It was nearly warm in Watertown on December 26 because of the things they were fighting for. The things they were unearthing that would see them all burn. It was hard not to think of oil as blood, real blood, not the trite symbol of soldier or civilian blood. But some deep blank coursing system, meaningless on its own. The cellular history of great bodies long devoured by the land and resurrected, an obsidian fat made from corpses. Winter had been stolen from the future. Like everything else, the past had risen up and taken it away.

She wouldn't let this happen to Danny. All his days inside on his computer staring into nothing. And outside, more nothing waiting for him. He needed to see things that were beautiful, feel the snow and cold instead of dreaming about it. Be able to leave his chair and run and leap and burst forward instead of living in a flat world. She could fix it. She'd fixed harder things. She had more than enough cold-weather gear for both of them. They could camp and trek and go to Hebron, go to Daryl's. She could easily bring him along. Danny and Sebastian too.

Back in the kitchen she left her father a note, then set off in the blighted light to Our Lady of Lourdes, hoping the doors would be open. She called on the memory of Danny's face and his baby-fine curly hair to keep her company on her walk. The image she'd been calling up for months to remember why she wanted to go home. His laughter. His round cheeks turning red.

It must have been sometime just after the first Gulf War and Fort Drum was welcoming troops home. She was maybe nine or ten and there was a parade, there was music and people hugging and a big inflatable bouncy castle that was red and gray and had four corner towers with pointy roofs that shook and swayed from the ruckus inside. She didn't know where her parents were that day. Maybe PJ had taken her and Danny to the parade, or maybe it was just the two of them, and someone dropped them off for a while.

She held his hand and they watched other kids playing. He looked up at her, raised his eyebrows and laughed as the children inside bounced high like they were flying. Even some big kids almost her age were playing.

She picked Danny up and walked over to a sturdy friendly guy in desert camo who'd been helping kids in and out of the castle. Someone's dad maybe. She asked if it was okay, was Danny too little to go in? She set him down and he almost came up to her chest. Danny looked up at her and at the nice soldier with his big dark eyes. And the man smiled the way everyone smiled at Danny when he was a baby. She always thought he looked like an animal because his eyes were too big for his face and they were so shiny, so alert. It made you want to carry him around and read to him and build him forts. The man put his hands on his hips and stood in front of them nodding, with his eyebrows knit like he was making a big decision.

"That is a good question, little gal. What-deryer folks say?" He looked more awake than any adult she'd ever met. And his clothes fit the way clothes fit a mannequin. He smelled like soap and she noticed that his skin was very smooth. He had blond hair on his forearms and raised veins that snaked like rivers on a map across his hands. She wanted him to pick her up and hold her. She liked the light goofy sound of his voice. The way he talked seemed to imply that what her "folks said," if in fact they were around to say anything at all, was just one opinion, something to weigh before taking matters into their own capable hands.

She shrugged and then she watched him scan the crowd over her head for a moment. He gave her a couple of rough pats on the shoulder.

"Don't you want to go in there and play too?"

"I have to watch Danny," she said.

"Gotcha," he said, and he gave her a quick nod. "You're in charge."

She took off Danny's shoes and the soldier picked him up and said, "All right, little dude! Let's see how high you can jump." Then he set him inside the castle.

Danny put his arms out at his sides, took a couple of tentative steps, fell over, and was immediately tossed into the air from the impact of a heavier kid landing next to him. He squealed and started laughing, a throaty belly laugh. Stood up and looked back at her, grinning so wide she could see his gums, rocking on the taut inflated plastic, his hands balled into fists in front of his narrow chest. His eyes so bright and excited, and she felt her face mirroring his.

He hopped, fell on his knees, bounced in the air, and then flopped flat on his back, his curly hair light about his face. Two little kids in jeans and T-shirts bumped into each other and fell on top of him and he started laughing again, his head back, his face red. They all struggled to get up, a scrambling tangle of limbs, socked feet slipping against the shaky foundation. Danny made his way to the middle of the castle by scooting on his knees, stood and jumped over and over, threw himself down on his stomach, flopped over on his back, giggling. She hunched and dodged where she stood on the pavement as other children knocked into him. If she had seen anyone as happy as he was right then she couldn't remember it. He staggered, dizzily elated, his light body flew and landed, he rolled and struggled and convulsed with laughter, and she could feel how it must be to be so small and soaring inside a safe cocoon. She hadn't ever played in a bouncy castle like that, but watching him she could feel how it must be. The pleasure of falling and rising. His face made her laugh, his eyes made her laugh, everything about his tiny body made her laugh, and she stood transfixed. Danny's smile, Danny's face, the way his eyes lit as he was lost in a fit of absurdity. A cord of joy was tied so tightly between them, all she had to do was see his tiny square teeth and she felt it, felt the world order itself in the sound of his voice, his throaty baby laugh.

This was the thought she called upon in training, in transport, in the emptiness of waiting that would never again be called boredom. It was with her the whole time, that sound. And there was no way she would have come home without it. No place outside that sound where she could live. No home, no country, no body to inhabit. It was the last breath of music she still felt in her belly, a little fire that she needed to stoke and carry.

SEVEN

Lourdes Church was a simple stone building with a slate steeple that rose and disappeared into the fog. Across the street the strip-mall parking lot was empty, but the glowing lights of the Rite Aid sign shone dully through the mist, like the lamps around the blast walls during a dust storm.

The doors were open, and she went in and sat in the dark cavernous chapel on the creaking pews amidst the smell of wax and pine cleaner and frankincense. The stained-glass windows were dimly lit and she looked at them pane by pane; the long slow journey of Jesus, dragging his cross from window to window, until the Roman soldiers crucified him. It was a storyboard, she thought, like the kind you have to make and go over with your CO when you get back from a capture or kill. The stations of the cross were so everyone had their story straight, created agreement and uniformity in reporting the event.

She'd spent nearly every afternoon in that church since she was fourteen, and loved the windows, the acoustics, the empty haunted feeling, the freedom of her voice rising and filling the space. But this was the first time she'd thought about the stations of the cross. Insurgent Jesus. Another pretty thing put into its proper context. Like the way running wasn't the same anymore, or sitting in the sun; the way washing sand out of her hair would probably never feel the same, wouldn't remind her of nice things like waves lapping against a beach. The stations of the cross made sense now, one more common war story hiding in plain sight.

Lauren had no compulsion to pray and didn't want to acknowledge the exhibition-ism of the crucifix with a glance. And this was also new. She'd never cared much one way or the other about looking at wrecked Jesus with his crown of thorns. It was religious art, and it had been beautiful like the stained glass. But now it made her think of bodies, real naked tattered bodies and real blood. And the strange phenomena of seeing soldiers break and become religious so they'd have someone to blame or some-one to forgive them the unforgivable.

Few things were as unsettling as a person

getting combat-induced religion, rambling about ghosts, life after death, being surveilled by some all-powerful thing. Nothing was quite as baffling as a hired killer, a soldier, a person from the very profession that killed Jesus, saying what he fought for was Jesus. But it just got crazier from there: They were fighting for a man who'd died thousands of years ago but actually wasn't dead and he wanted you to love your enemy, and not to kill, and not to be greedy. His dad's God and his mom's a virgin. It was like a nonsense song from kindergarten: "It rained so hard the day I left / the weather it was dry / The sun so hot I froze to death / Susanna don't you cry." People loved this religious stuff because it actually made no sense. Just like the war made no sense. And she knew now for certain that feeling of mystery, that impenetrable false logic was necessary to make people do stupid things.

Of all the things Lauren had seen that she didn't want to see, battlefield baptism was among the worst. She could feel it rising in her again, just looking at the stained glass. "God's grace" settling over someone's face and the relief they radiated once they gave into the unreal, and it was too much for her, actually horrifying. Created a thick knot in her stomach. The hypocrisy. The cruelty and terror it was meant to wash away, absolve. She didn't care if it made people feel better. It was fucking retarded and incredibly dangerous. Serving with men and women who believed in God and Jesus and Mary made her nervous. Why would it make anyone comfortable to be around a soldier who thought they'd be getting God's reward after they died? Those were the people they were supposed to be fighting, not standing beside. She wanted to be with folks who knew that all you got, you got right now. Everything else was make-believe, stories to tell and stories to keep straight. Daryl had put it best: Anyone who came away from what they'd been doing in Iraq believing in God was a total cocksucker.

She shivered in the pew and folded her arms across her chest, looked over at the rows of memorial candles flickering by the feet of the Virgin in her blue robes. The smell of wax was strong and the lingering scent of smoldering wicks from prayers that had been extinguished by chance, or snuffed out when she opened the heavy door, gave the place an air of fixed melancholic nostalgia; hopeful birthday cries of "make a wish" and the faint odor of wreckage.

She stood and walked quickly through the church and into the chantry and then down a flight of stairs into the basement, passing storage rooms filled with holy hylics: clear plastic sacks of Communion wafers, not yet transformed into the body of Christ; boxes filled with candles; stacks of hymnals and Sunday school supplies.

The corridor was cloying and almost dank but not unpleasant; the cement floor, the brick and paneled walls were welcoming in their humbleness. At the end of the hallway a red exit sign hung above an ornate wooden door that let out onto a cracked and weedy parking lot littered with small, Ziploc glassine baggies. The lot was home to garbage cans and a basketball court where she'd played sometimes when she was little; beyond that, a bent and sloping chainlink fence guarded an ancient playground, metal climbing bars, swings and a slide and a teeter-totter.

Lauren stopped at a small white door between the exit and the boiler room and knocked lightly, then took the handle and pushed, peeking her head around the corner into the room.

Troy looked up from his desk. And then gave a quick, startled, "Ha!"

The room was just big enough to fit his desk, a file cabinet, and a living-room chair upholstered in yellow and orange flowers that had long ago lost its springs and showed its stuffing at the seams. Every wall of the office was taken up by bookshelves filled with binders and folders and sheet music, and there were no windows, just a desk lamp glowing hotly in the little windowless space.

Troy was thin and pale, his wavy black hair shot through with strands of white. His blue eyes bright behind the thick black-framed glasses he'd had for twenty years. She knew they were military issue, that he'd been wearing them since his tour ended back in the '90s, but they looked like Buddy Holly's, hip, of an era. He knit his eyebrows and then smiled, revealing the gap between his front teeth, stood up to greet her as she came in and closed the door.

Troy shook her hand heartily, then went back behind his desk and sat facing her in a kind of awkward mock formality as she sat down in the beat-up chair, hanging one leg over the side.

"I have to go up and play in two hours," he told her, rearranging some papers. He spoke quickly, his voice resonant and overly clear, perfectly articulated like it was coming from a radio. His eyes were downcast, but he was smiling broadly, seeming to take in everything about her. She liked that he didn't say "welcome back."

"I figured," she said. "I wanted to stop by and see if you were here early."

He nodded vigorously. "I have time right now and no one else is here if you want to go up to the choir loft."

She shook her head. "I just wanted to see you."

He smiled, the corner of his mouth twitched, and then he looked down. "Or you could come after mass or before vespers," he said. "I still have your score here. I have it in the cabinet and we could start where we left off."

She shook her head again. "I'm out of practice."

"Well exactly," he said nervously, almost angrily, his smile vanishing in an instant. "You need to get back in." He looked up at her with something bordering on contempt or incredulity. "You haven't missed a thing, really. I mean you missed all those years while your voice would be ripening, so to speak. You have to get back in. I don't see any other option." Then he said, "Have you been in touch with Curtis?"

"Man, fuck Curtis," she said.

He looked taken aback, gave a short offended laugh through his teeth.

She just wanted to be there with him. She

did not want to talk about Curtis or her voice. The truth was, she wanted to smell the church, sit in that chair and look at Troy across his desk. Maybe after a few months of doing just that they could talk about something else. Not that she still measured time in months. Second to second worked best if you wanted to feel like you were going to make it.

"Well what do you think you'll do? Get a job? What did you learn to do? I think you should come upstairs and practice now. I mean, what else are you going to do?"

She cringed and put her hand over her eyes. Get a job was exactly what she was planning on doing. A good job, one that could support her whole family; any other idea was just a dream. "Have you been outside in the fog?" she asked, changing the subject.

He smiled and nodded emphatically. "Yes," he said, "it's mythic."

"How was midnight mass?" she asked.

"It was beautiful. I played Arvo Pärt's *Annum per Annum.*"

"You're kidding me. With that beginning? What's next, Schoenberg?"

"I'm not! I'm not kidding you! That's why I like it here. I can play whatever I want."

Lauren looked at Troy, his face open yet

completely impenetrable, unreadable. Most people accepted that the line between crazy and genius was blurred, but few people thought about the line between genius and retardation until they met Troy. She loved him. Every awkward honest sentence. His dandruff. The reserved, repressed way he carried himself and then the way that carriage shattered into a languid, confident coordination, his whole body suddenly engaged when he played or listened or began talking about music. She tried to imagine the congregation at Lourdes listening to the silences and dissonance of Arvo Pärt on Christmas Eve instead of Handel. Musically the choice made sense. Minimalists, sacred music. But one was still alive, denied what he wrote was sacred and composed music that was so stark, so spare and clean and desolately beautiful she'd wanted to hear and sing nothing else. She knew she was biased, felt this as a person who'd been trained to hear by Troy, and she didn't care. Her ears, her mind, her mouth, the sinewy bands of flesh that vibrated in her throat, better that he had shaped her than anyone else.

Troy had been accompanying Lauren since she was fourteen and her ninth-grade music teacher brought her to meet him.

He'd been playing organ at Lourdes for ten years before she showed up — and he was nothing like any teacher she'd had. He was distracted and then suddenly hyperfocused on things she couldn't even hear. He talked to her almost like she was a peer, and apart from one small, slightly confused-looking smile he gave when Ms. Heimal brought her in to sing for the first time, he acted as though he wasn't remotely impressed with her voice.

Now Troy was someone who knew her deeply, knew a part of her she didn't like very much. Some useless part she was embarrassed to talk about. Still she wanted to be nowhere else that morning, was compelled to hear the acoustics of her own footsteps in the hallway and to see his face, if nothing more.

"I read that Arvo Pärt's not a Holy Minimalist," she said.

Troy's face broke into a huge smile and he laughed, nodded vigorously. "If we can take the man's description of his own work, then yes, I guess it's true. He doesn't like the term, says no. It's just fascinating!"

"Why did he say it?" she asked. "I mean, the *Magnificat*? *I Am the True Vine*? Come on."

"Sure sure sure," Troy said impatiently.

"You realize of course that's not what makes it sacred music." He tapped the side of his pen nervously on the desk a few times. "You know, what is the spirit in the work? You have to ask yourself. What is the ghost in the work? And what is the holy thing we're trying to impart when we play? It's not the words, for God's sake. Words are just gibberish, just empty bodies for the tone to inhabit, right? I mean when you hear something in Latin you are often more transported, right? The mystery of it. Or the meaninglessness of it, something with no meaning is the vehicle that carries something with all the meaning. Listen." He said, "Seriously, listen, listen."

Then he sang, full throated and with such rich timbre she felt a surge of emotion, felt lifted. He sang, *"My soul doth magnify the Lord, and my spirit rejoiceth in God thy Savior for He hath provided . . ."* Then he stopped abruptly.

"Now listen," he said, and in the same radiant tone he sang, *"Blah blah de blah de blah de blah eggs and bacon wooden nickels, fox in socks, ski trip tornado."*

She laughed. "Beautiful."

He nodded. "Right," he agreed. "I often want to get rid of all the words, you know? They're so silly. So hollow. They're like a house for the tone and nothing more, some kind of intent, you know . . . or words are a wish, you know, part of the flat world but meaningless without the voice. The sound, or the resonance of this kind of human sound, rather, is divine on its own. Entirely on its own! And oh! This reminds me, I've been listening so much to *Cantate Domino.* Perfect for your voice. You should come up and learn some of it right now. Right now, actually." He set his pen down and began to stand. "Now is the time."

She shook her head.

And he shook his head back at her, leaned over his desk, his eyebrows raised in question.

"No? I say yes. I say yes, you do it." He quietly hummed the beginning of Pärt's *Cantate.* Again, his voice was so clear, the tone rang from his belly, from the strength of his gut and lungs, and each phrase was punctuated by perfect metered quiet. The absence of tone, a silent counterpart that gave the sound its power. He smiled at her. She felt her body resonate, a coda of the sounds he was making. She caught her breath, felt her throat constrict suddenly as if she'd been struck by something, then she bent and covered her mouth in a fit of coughing.

Troy offered her a mug half filled with ice-cold black coffee, and she drank it, realizing after it was in her mouth that it'd probably been sitting there for days. Her eyes watered, she swallowed. After some silence she said, "I just wanted to let you know I'm home."

"Well, I can see that. You're home in form, anyway, and I'm glad. I'm really glad." He stared at her for a few more minutes and they said nothing. She wanted badly to go up into the choir loft with him. Wanted to become embodied; to become good. But she'd already said no and didn't want to start herself on the path to some dumb fantasy. She was not going to call Curtis. Nothing would come of it.

Troy was unchanged, or maybe he'd been changed long before she'd ever met him. She remembered riding her bicycle home from practicing with him. The light strong feeling in her body like she could rise up and out of there, out of Watertown, out of that life. The autumn air and the dead leaves in the gutter scuttling and fluttering like pages in a book as she pedaled through them. She would ride no-handed. And the sun would be low but still warm. It was twenty minutes maybe — twenty minutes a day that she carried nothing but the sounds in her head and the crisp, smoky smell of fall. A high precise line of melody now committed to the twin bands of membrane that stretched at the top of her trachea, a muscle memory, a melody committed to her lungs, committed to her mouth, to her gut, to her mind.

Only moments before this ride she would have been standing with him in the cold choir loft, straight shouldered beneath her sweater, hair tucked up into her black wool watchcap, a hand-me-down from PJ. Standing and singing the same phrase until there was no way to do it wrong.

"Again," Troy would say, his eyes trained on her mouth, his head bowed slightly. So close she could smell the woody, unwashed medicinal scent of him.

She would repeat it until the impossibility of the notes became itself an impossibility.

"Again," he would say, placing his index finger on the hollow at the base of her throat.

And she felt his touch still. Felt it now, cool and smooth as a stone.

When the lesson was over she would stand and talk to him, tell him about boys or ramble about her classes. He'd listened to the things she said, but had no advice apart from how she should sing, how she should hold her head and shoulders and expression, how she should focus on solos; choir was not for her, would not give her what she needed. But choir was more beautiful, she'd said, and he'd insisted, "Not for you. Not for your voice." The older she got the more she wanted to blend, to be transparent. To make it so she was singing as clear and silver a sound as possible, and yet be completely hidden, make it so no one could hear her voice, no one could know its sound alone.

"You know," he said. "You know, ah. I went to conservatory right after I got home."

She looked up at the ceiling. Of course she knew. Troy, fresh from the dull trial run of the real war from which she'd just returned, went to Oberlin when he got back in 1991. The myth of flight at the end of the tunnel, that led to fellowships and accompanying real opera singers and the Met and then one day, inexplicably, his own office in a church basement in his hometown upstate. Now that she'd done her own tour she could see a little bit of the war in him, his familiarity with silences, his drive, a reconciled sorrow that lifted the corners of his mouth in a kind of mocking self-abnegation. The weight of being alive, being a victim of the killing you've done. She smiled, thinking about the music they loved and how one day the government would pay for their funerals. They might even be buried in the same cemetery.

Lauren handed back his mug without speaking and headed to the door that opened onto the blacktop, leaving Troy to his work. An abrupt exit wasn't rude in his mind, and if she stayed she might start talking like she'd done when she was a girl, only this time about the war, and she didn't want to do that. Didn't need to measure the width of another gulf that had grown while she was gone, or glimpse more wreckage; some blackened sky, some keening sound that is far from sacred, some fire neither of them could put out.

Jack Clay had fallen asleep reading and the book was still open on his chest. For the first time in years, the rousing sound of the house phone did not constrict the world into a blinding knot, a concentrated moment of dread and sinking, flailing anticipation.

He let it ring and knew his daughter was safe in her bed. He'd slept well because of it. Nothing mattered the way it had just two days before. He opened his eyes and gazed at the ceiling for a moment before rolling over and finding the phone tangled in the bedspread beneath some newspapers and a water-damaged issue of *Harper's* he'd been using as a coaster.

The voice said, "Hello, is Sergeant Lauren Clay there?"

He sat up and swung his feet off the bed, found his slippers. He said, "Yeah, she is, can you hang on a minute?"

The feeling of calling his daughter to the phone pleased him. He walked back to look into her bedroom, then went into the kitchen and found her note, picked up the downstairs extension.

"Looks like she's gone out to run some errands," he said. "Can I take a message?"

"Yes, thank you. This is Dr. Klein calling again. I'd like to go over a couple of things with her when she gets the chance." There was no urgency in the woman's voice, but she gave him three different phone numbers this time.

"All right," Jack said. "Sounds good. I'll let her know, Dr. Klein. You take care."

He sat and looked at his daughter's precise delicate handwriting on the paper, then folded up the note and put it in the pocket of his robe.

He put water on for tea, opened the front door and got the newspaper off the porch.

The air was lush with a bite and mist curled around the base of the crabapple tree in their neighbor's yard. It felt like spring. He half expected the day to heat up, the sun to come out and burn off the fog and dry the streets.

By the end of the week, he thought, the mist would lift and it would be sixty degrees out, warm enough for shirtsleeves. And the neighborhood would suddenly be alive with kids testing out their Christmas presents, playing basketball, and riding their bikes and scooters in the street. Danny and Lauren would be playing in the driveway, coming home with mud on their boots. He didn't have to worry about either of them now. She'd be singing again. Danny's face wouldn't grow solemn when he thought Jack wasn't looking. His children were home; for all the ways he had failed them, they were together now. Like some myth, Lauren's return had uncurled April's green tendrils in December.

He could eat breakfast today without thoughts of where she was and what she was doing hollowing out his day. He could answer the phone. He could make dinner for his children. She was alive and he could live.

■ ■ ■ ■

Outside the church she thought again of Shane and how many times she'd left there after lessons, had gone to his house before his mother got home, eager to touch him. She imagined his smile, his body, the smell of his skin. She used to love to lie on the couch with him, in that way that made everything right; the cheap, brown particle-board paneling became cozy and the water-stained drop ceiling looked like an antique map of the continents.

The Murphys had always lived in that neighborhood, but you couldn't tell from the way he was. She'd known him since fourth grade. He lived eight blocks away and played on her Little League team one year. But she hadn't remembered that until high school, when he was in her geometry class and sat next to her in the back row by the windows. The first words she'd remembered him saying to her were, "I hate it here."

"Here in class?" she asked. "Or *here* here?"

It was an important distinction, and if the answer was school she didn't fucking care. Who didn't hate school?

He smirked, looked around and raised one eyebrow. He opened his mouth, about to say something, then stopped and looked back up at the blackboard, and she saw the interest return to his face. She felt at once like she'd known him forever and like she'd just discovered something entirely new. In that moment he became visible, not just a figure that walked the same route home every afternoon. He was like her. Nothing would make him belong there, and he was on his way through.

She'd had that same feeling again last year when she met Daryl. But Daryl wore a ring.

She thought about the vows people made and the claims laid upon bodies, then climbed over the chainlink fence at the edge of the playground, where rainwater filled the foot-dragged wells beneath the swings.

Lauren opened her mouth and breathed. She opened her mouth to sing one clear note. But her throat closed and her eyes watered and she sat there waiting for some time, waiting for the low clouds, the white sky, the wet earth. Waiting for all of it to rise up and leave her behind.

Sistopher,

Everything is fine, really, but I don't want to tell Mom or PJ that I need a few bucks because they'll make a big deal of it. I've pretty much outgrown everything I had in my closet. I've been borrowing jeans from Dylan but I'd like to get a pair that I can wear most of the week and maybe some shirts. Nothing special. I could go to Salvo. I can't mention it to Dad because he'll say it's all his fault and you know how it goes from there, and if I tell Mom she'll either make it into a thing or will forget about it. I'll pay you back once I'm famous and you're home from vacation. But seriously it's not a big deal and I'm fine. PJ takes Dad shopping every week now and we have toothpaste and stuff so you don't have to keep putting it in the packages. I just don't want any bullshit about me to make anyone A) upset or B) talk to me. You know what I mean. I have a feeling Mrs. Princiato is going to say something to me at school by the way she looks at me. All "oh no, poor thing" or whatever.

Be safe there in your hot tub or ski

chalet or whatever five-star hotel you're staying at. Things really are fine here, especially now that we've got the Internet. Mom's paying for it so we can keep in touch. Everything's fine.

BSI ♥ U,
Danny

EIGHT

The Patricks drank the way animals will eat things that are slightly poisonous in order to purge their guts. The Patricks used one kind of spirit to release another and they were doing it now at three P.M. in The Bag of Nails.

Lauren was there to see Holly, but as soon as she came in the Patricks shouted her over, had already ordered her a Guinness. They smelled like tobacco and beer and the stale sourness of work clothes that had not been washed for several days. Tony Bennett's Christmas album was playing and white Christmas lights framed the mirror behind the bar. She rested her eyes on a corner of the beer cooler and let the whole place disappear.

"Shane'll be here," his Uncle Shamus told her. Gerry and Patrick patted her on the back, drawing her into the room again, telegraphing varied states of crazy. She could feel something in them that envied the violence she'd come from, like they felt it on her and wanted to rub up against it.

"It's homecoming for you and Gerry both," Shamus said, his eyes glassy, the whites darkened with a broken brocade of red. He smirked and gave her a quick wink. Gerry raised his glass. "Released yesterday morning," Shamus explained, "picked up for breaking and entering, wunnit?"

"For walking a dog," Gerry said. "It was for walking a dog, let's be honest here."

"For *breaking* into a nice little house on the northside, *entering* it, and walking a yuppie couple's dog," Patrick explained to Lauren.

"Which they'd irresponsibly left alone for who-the-fuck knows how long, barking and whining," Gerry said.

"And when he was done with the walking," Shamus continued, "he brought the dog back and watched some television. Which startled the young couple when they returned home."

"They were just paranoid," Gerry said, laughing. "They could see I wasn't doing nothing, they didn't have to get so pissed off about it. I told them I was helping them out."

"And then he threatened them with a

steak knife," Shamus concluded.

"All right, enough now!" Gerry said. "It wasn't a steak knife. It was a steak-knife sharpener."

"Do they make such an item?" Patrick asked quietly.

"And *they* were threatening me," Gerry said, all his humor gone. "I took care of their animal and they were threatening me. I should've just taken him to my place. You don't leave a dog whining like that."

Lauren had started disliking the Patricks the week she met them. She was a sophomore in high school and had watched Uncle Gerry eat a piece of glass on a fifty-dollar bet. The blood in his mouth. The sound of him chewing it. She was angry that the image had become a part of her memory, and by virtue of that memory part of herself. She would lie awake sometimes thinking about how to erase it. Probing the insides of her cheek with her tongue and succumbing to a breathless queasy feeling, the cut within the protected flesh of the mouth. She didn't like it. And she didn't like them. But the Patricks didn't care. They were going to like her no matter what. And this she hated the most of all — that they seemed to possess some kind of wisdom, something tribal and suicidal tied tightly to the neighborhood, a kind of smirking anarchic spirit that would see them burn like monks to prove that nothing could touch what they were.

"So," she said, ignoring the dog story as if they'd never told it, "you guys expecting Shane?"

"Fuck yes," Patrick said, "and we haven't yet got the quality time we would have liked with him."

She put money on the bar to pay for the beer but Shamus handed it back to her. His skin was bad, a fine web of capillaries blooming around his nose, but the unmistakable gleam of intelligence in his rheumy eyes. "Everybody in this fucking place owes you a drink," he said. She stared blankly at him, then around the bar. She thought for one brief moment that she could buy The Bag of Nails with her combat pay and just have it torn down. Then, having had an idea worthy of toasting, she raised her glass to the Patricks and drank the smooth and bitter pint in several long gulps.

"Everybody," Shamus said again, and his brothers raised their glasses and looked menacingly at the small group of people who were spending the midafternoon of December 26 sitting in a bar. No one looked up. And it wouldn't have mattered if they did. In her jeans and flannel no one else would understand where she had been. They wouldn't take up the sentimentality the uncles wanted to see catch on, and that was fine. She wasn't interested in being the idea they tried on for meaning, or righteousness, the new vessel into which they poured all the excuses for their intemperance.

As she put down the glass she saw Holly coming out of the kitchen, wearing a white shirt with poofy shoulders, black polyester pants, and Converse sneakers. She was a short, slim-hipped, coltish woman with a long neck and broad shoulders. A body that had been made fun of in elementary school, at once stubby and blunt but long armed, fit.

Holly took a breath, smiled, said nothing, and walked directly to her — as if she'd just seen her yesterday — put her arms around Lauren and squeezed her hard, rested her head on her friend's shoulder. She smelled like fried food and Prell shampoo and coffee. They stood that way long enough for some drunk to call them dykes. Uncle Gerry turned and slapped the man hard in the face, pulled him by the shirt until he broke free and hunched his way to a back booth to sit with his drink. Had it been later in the afternoon the drunk's response wouldn't have been good enough and the uncles would have followed him to his seat to discuss it.

Holly stepped back and smiled. "You look good," she said simply. Lauren grinned and admired the spaces between Holly's teeth and the one twisted incisor that she'd wanted for herself when they were girls. A smile that was pretty and messed up at the same time.

"Thanks."

"You here to meet your boy?"

She shook her head. "I came to see you. How's Grace?"

"She's over at Asshole's parents'. I'm picking her up in a coupla hours. I seen Danny walking the other day — from the back I thought it was you for a minute, he's so tall now."

Lauren smiled proudly. "I know it. Boy's a champion."

"How's your dad?" Holly asked.

"He's been replaced by an impostor while I was gone," she said, and for a hundredth of a second felt it might be true. There was nothing about the way her father behaved in the last day that she could recognize.

"Prolly should get a blood sample."

"That might be hard — he gets up and does stuff now. You'd have to catch him first."

Holly's mouth twisted into that crooked smile. She shook her head, trying to stifle a laugh, and hunched forward a little. "Shouldn't joke about it," she said. "Your father's a good man." Then she looked into Lauren's eyes and laughed. "He still wearing that robe all day?"

"No, I'm telling you!" she said. "The robe's gone, he apparently has an office over at the Nabe with PJ, it's weird. He's all doing laundry and shit. How's Gracie?"

"She's good, she's good. She's real good." Holly put one hand on her hip and turned her foot out to the side, lost in thoughts about her daughter. She nodded to herself. "Asshole's paying for her to take some karate lessons, so . . . that's one thing. I got her signed up for soccer comin' up this year. You'd be proud of her, Ren."

She pulled out her phone and opened it, scrolled to a picture of Grace.

"No way!" Lauren shouted at the screen.

"Way!" Holly said, smiling with reluctant pride, rolling her eyes. "She tore right into everything at four in the morning. She woke up at three and came in to tell me Santa'd been there and I managed to keep her in bed a little longer. Course, I'd gotten back from here around midnight. God knows Shamus and Gerry and Patrick gotta have

111

somewhere to spend their fucking Christmas Eve, right?" she yelled over to the bar.

"You want to ruin a sacred tradition?" Gerry asked her.

Lauren laughed again at the picture.

"Let's see it, now." Shamus turned and gestured for her to bring the phone over to the bar and then they all peered at Grace on the tiny screen, exhausted in her footie pajamas, clutching red Christmas ribbon, struggling to keep her eyes open.

Holly laughed again. "She was so tired by the time the sun came out she could barely keep her head up. By the time Mom and Dave finished making the pancakes she was out."

"Ah," Patrick said. "Look at her, she looks like yer mother."

"Now that was a beauty queen if ever there was one," said Shamus.

Holly smiled and flipped through more pictures, and they all stooped eagerly around her, quietly watching Grace's Christmas morning unfold.

"You got your Aunt Jean's looks," Patrick said, giving Holly a little squeeze, and she smirked so he gave her a quick kiss on the cheek. "That's a compliment," he said. Lauren watched the soft way he looked at her friend, the quiet comfortable way he talked to her. "You didn't know her in high school. You think we all looked like we do now? We didn't. We were just like you," he said. "I was just like Shane. I was handsome like Shane. I was taller 'n Shane. I tell you what, I got better grades 'n Shane, and that's a fact."

"And you worked," Gerry reminded him.

"*And* I worked," Patrick said.

"National merit scholar," Shamus said, putting up his empty to be refilled.

"And you served this country in the armed forces," Gerry said.

"Just like little Lauren Clay." Patrick laid a hand on her shoulder until she shrugged it off. There was nothing about Patrick that was just like her. His Gulf War was not hers.

"But the real thing is I had civic pride," Patrick said. "Which noneayuh have."

"Noneayuh," Shamus said in disgust.

Holly shut her phone and walked back toward the kitchen and Lauren followed her. She took a big white cake out of the walk-in cooler, cut a slice, poured mugs of coffee, adding a shot of Jameson's to each, turned on the ceiling fan, and offered Lauren a cigarette. They leaned against the counter sipping the hot bitter drink in the glow of the warming light and eating cold Christmas cake. White butter-cream frosting and sparkly red sugar sprinkles sweet and salty in their mouths.

"So what were you doing over there?" Holly asked.

Lauren shrugged. "Hanging out," she said.

Holly nodded respectfully. "Hanging out in a city or in like a desert place?"

"I was at a FOB outside an oil field."

"What's a FOB?"

"Forward operating base," Lauren said.

"So is that like way in the middle of nowhere?"

"Kinda."

"Do people live around there?"

"Yeah."

"Did you get to save anyone's life?"

Lauren smiled. It was the opposite of what people wanted to ask when you came home, the opposite of what everyone thought.

She shook her head and then sipped her coffee to wash away the sugary taste. "I saved millions from the inconvenience of taking public transportation," she said. "And I saved a bunch of fucking money in my own bank account."

Holly said, "Well, the last part's good, right?" She punched her in the arm. "The first part's kinda good too." Then she pointed to the door. "Who's that skinny nerd?"

Shane walked into The Bag of Nails wearing a rain-spattered windbreaker and carrying a plastic Stop & Shop bag filled with mail, which he handed to his Uncle Gerry. The Patricks patted his shoulders and back like they were checking for weapons and the bartender put up a beer, but Shane turned to leave and that's when he saw her and Holly looking at him and laughing. She put her hand out for him to come hold, but he hugged Holly first before taking it. The three of them stood together like no time had gone by and they weren't just some castaways from eighth grade honors biology. Like Shane hadn't become someone, and she and Holly hadn't become two kinds of no one.

"Gerry's this close to fighting Marty 'cause he called your girlfriend a dyke," Holly told him.

"Lovely," he said.

Lauren handed him her fork and he took several hasty bites of cake. Raised his eyebrows and nodded and then took another. He said, "Let's get out of here," with his mouth still full.

"To where?" she asked him. It was pointless. He was trying to stay ahead of the boredom and depression of being home, and even she knew that was futile.

His phone buzzed and he pulled it out and looked at it. Hesitated a moment before silencing it and putting it back in his jacket, then he shrugged. "Let's go ice-skating. Let's go get Danny and go ice-skating."

A flicker of resentment passed over Holly's face as he said it.

"We can drive up to the rink," he said. "You want to come?"

Lauren shook her head at the casualness of his question, and Holly raised her eyebrows and smirked. "You want to cover my shift, college boy? So me and L can go?"

"I would," he said. "Yeah." Lauren knew he meant it and also that it was insulting. Like anyone could come in and do Holly's job, like it wasn't a real job.

"I'm just fucking with you," Holly said. "Somebody's gotta stay here, babysit your uncles."

"Wait, we should wait until later and then we can bring Grace," Lauren said.

Holly's look softened and slid into guilt. "No. No, you go now with your boy. You just got home. I was just fucking with you, seriously."

Lauren didn't want to get in the car with him, was suddenly sick from the very idea of it. But there was nothing more to salvaging this day. She was not living side by side with the rest of them anymore. Something had propelled her into the future. She could see what people were thinking and what they were going to say before they said it. She'd been like this before she left for Iraq, but now it was excruciating the way she knew every little thing that would happen. The way she could see people thinking things about her they wouldn't say. The filthiest secret of all is hiding in plain sight all over the world; they put up monuments to it and have parades. But when it's just you, just one person alone in the same room with them, they stare, watch you like you'll do something wrong now. Because deep down they knew you were doing something wrong in the first place. All that training was not for rescuing kittens from trees. She squared her shoulders. Soon she'd see Daryl again and be with someone who got it. Someone with whom she could be quiet.

Shane didn't try to hug her or kiss her in the car, and she respected him for it. He smiled at her. He said, "I missed you."

She nodded, said, "I just need to settle in, babe." She wanted to tear his shirt open and bite him, wanted to pull his face down and shut his mouth with hers. But she sat looking at him, waiting patiently for him to

117

say the exact thing he said:

"I'm kind of going nuts being here. I can't believe I agreed to stay two weeks this time. My uncles are . . . I can't even talk about it. I keep seeing people we went to high school with that still fucking live here. Live with their parents or whatever. It's fucking crazy. It must be even weirder for you."

She nodded, but it was irritating that he was talking about her and didn't realize it. She was still there with nowhere to go and so was Holly. And most of the friends she served with had gone back to their home-towns too. She knew she just needed to leave it all for a while. She'd take it up with Daryl when she saw him. They'd both find good work up north. She could bring Danny with her to check things out. She had skills now and she didn't need to take three steps back, follow a plan she'd set up before she'd ever been down range.

She said, "I'm going to walk home."

He looked at her like he had just woken up, like he realized he'd been talking to a stranger, and it was a relief to see, made that tight sick feeling in her chest go away. And for a moment it made her love him like she used to. How quick he was. How he could see the way she was gone.

There was no reason why he should know

her anymore. Shane was depressed running into people from high school because of what it said about who he was and where he came from. Now Shane lived among people who read like he did or talked about books, who went to parties that weren't in parking lots or half-burnt warehouses. He was grieving for having lived here now that he'd been found. But as far as she was concerned Watertown wasn't a place at all.

Watertown was like some imaginary landscape in a movie she'd once seen and now she had to go visit the set. See how the buildings were just facades propped up with pieces of plywood. It wasn't just her father that had been replaced. Shane was trying to act like Shane, but he hadn't aged a second or changed his clothes. Holly seemed like she was in some kind of hostage situation, forced to work as a waitress so Asshole's parents would help her out. The Patricks had clearly been that way forever. Cartoon construction workers chewing on fat cigars claiming they'd ever had a chance to leave, lying to themselves every day at the bar.

And the town looked wrong — all high definition but flat like she was watching it from somewhere inside herself. Like she had no eyes anymore, just a scope that she stood behind, not even searching or aiming but watching, seeing everything a few seconds off — seconds before it really happened — and that removed the feeling of surprise or empathy you're supposed to have. It was as though she was living ten seconds in the future and could tell before anyone else that nothing mattered. She'd already read the fairy tale this life was based on and it ended badly, the birds eat your trail of bread crumbs, children are beheaded while peering into old trunks, idealistic suitors fertilize the roses on which they're impaled with their blood.

The rain was falling heavily on the car now, and it sounded like they were being buried in gravel.

"Sit here awhile until this lets up," he said. She held his hand and watched the empty street succumb to the deluge before them. It was like a summer thunderstorm in the middle of winter: bare trees and naked muddy concrete and no wind.

Shane looked strong and lost at the same time and he was about to say something to her, but she pressed her palm to his face and pushed her fingers into his mouth. Cupped her other hand over the front of his jeans. He sucked on her fingers as she undid his belt, then reached in with her warm wet hand and felt him. Put her mouth on his mouth and straddled him, pressing her body against him. His glasses fogged and she took them off and put them on the dashboard — his head was against her chest and he looked up at her and she kissed him while he put his hands in her hair, guided her face down to his and kissed her perfectly, hungrily. Her back was against the steering wheel and she kissed his neck while she stroked him. So familiar and so much better than familiar in its distant dislocated newness. She could feel how tense he was, pulled tight and lovely, blood straining against delicate skin and filling her hand. The hum of their intent filled the little space and she felt for a moment the happy rush of living alongside him, not watching from outside, not far away. She held firmly to his flesh and beating blood and slid her hand along him in the cramped car on that chilly empty street beneath the hammering rain, hoping that if he could not bring her back this way, he could at least make her disappear.

NINE

When she was done she rested her forehead on his chest, her hand slick and limp against his sticky tender skin, the car thick with the smell of him. She felt like she'd woken up, felt sobered. He leaned his head back and breathed while she adjusted herself and stepped out of the car. Stood in the rain, stretched. When she came around to the driver's side he put the window down, looked into her eyes. She watched him uneasily as he loved and studied her, then she leaned down and kissed him.

"What the fuck, baby?" he whispered against her mouth.

She stood again and looked at him. "Nice language," she said.

"Seriously, girl," he said, smiling.

"Don't call me 'girl.' "

"All right, bad lieutenant," he said, his face confused, reconfiguring itself. "What d'you want me to call you now? 'Sar'n

Clay'?" He said it in a southern accent, and she saw again that thing college had done to him that she didn't like at all.

"You want to fight outside The Bag of Nails like one of your fucking uncles?" she asked. She had none of the warm feelings she'd had for him thirty seconds before.

He looked at her in surprise and his eyes changed slowly, like land growing lighter after a cloud passes. He was naive, and it infuriated her the way he still possessed the luxury of disappointment.

"My intention was to take you ice-skating, not to have sex or fight," he said.

"So you've not achieved your goal and accomplished two things you didn't want. What does that feel like?"

"*You're* asking *me* what that feels like?"

Shane laughed through his teeth but stopped abruptly as her hands shot through the open window. She grabbed the collar of his shirt roughly in one deft movement and he jerked his head back, shocked. He was weak, and she put a stop to his flailing immediately by putting the heel of her palm right beneath his nose and pressing up. He tried to turn but was forced to tilt his head back against the seat. She scrambled farther into the car and pressed her other forearm against his throat. Her face was close to his and the car still thick with the smell of sex. He made a sick sad grunt as he struggled to turn his head, a frightened echo of sounds he made when she was touching him or in his sleep. It turned her stomach. The cartilage in his nose began to give and it revulsed her, a sickening, enervating jolt ran through her joints. She dropped her hands as if her tendons had been cut, stepped back, and shoved them deep into her jacket pockets to keep him safe.

Shane sat upright again, confused and disarranged, and looked at her. He was furious and hurt and didn't realize those feelings served no purpose at all. Like everyone else, he simply had no idea of how easily he could be dispatched.

She was soaking wet and her tears were hot on her face, crying for what just happened to him. She hated all the intelligence behind his eyes, pitied him and was ashamed by his knowing look — as if he'd been studying up on her while she was gone. Now she was just doing what he expected, what they taught him about people like her at his smug liberal school. Thought he was seeing what war did but he had no fucking clue. Thought he was seeing trauma up close but he was seeing it from a remote distance, might as well have been seeing a glacier melting, an ocean dying, an oil field set on fire.

"I'm sorry," he told her, looking steadily into her eyes. "I'm sorry I said that. But not because you tried to push my nose up into my brain." She leaned down and he put his hand against her cheek, pushed her soaking hair back from her neck. Her clothes stuck to her body and she could feel their weight.

"I hate it here," she said. And she did not mean the bar or the town or the country in which they lived.

TEN

Shane wasn't angry until after she turned and walked away. She'd messed up his face and he could feel the heat of blood swelling in his nose and upper lip. He should not have apologized to her after she did that. She was not all right, and god only knew, in her house nothing would be done to help her and no one would say a thing. Lauren could breeze through her whole life, doted upon or ignored, left to figure it all out for everyone else. Even when they were in high school she kept things to herself, protected her father, pretended for her brother. Shane punched the steering wheel with the side of his fist. He touched his face where she had hurt him, the skin hot and sensitive, beginning to swell.

Holly smiled when he walked back in, then stopped abruptly when she saw his face. "That was a quick trip to the rink," she said.

"You okay?" She was standing too close to Patrick, and his other uncles were playing dice.

Patrick winked at him. "Lauren all right then?" he asked, pointing his chin in the direction of the door.

Shane shrugged, nodded.

"She didn't look herself, did she?" Patrick asked, a knowing smirk spreading across his face.

"Oh for chrissakes," Holly said. "She's been home twelve hours. You don't look yourself after a day of delivering that fake newspaper."

"Sure I do," Patrick said. "I look better than myself, got plenty of time to reflect while I'm driving around. I'd say I actually have one of the most relaxing jobs in town. Makes me feel fantastically myself. I get to take part in the life of the proletariat. I get to cruise around and think about what I'm reading or what I'm going to read next. You know what I'm going to read next?"

Shane and Holly said nothing, just looked patiently at one another.

"I'm reading *Wilderness and the American Mind*," he said, answering his own question. "It's next on my list."

Shane looked up at him for a minute and Patrick nodded. "That's right," he said.

Shane didn't want to hear his drunk, delivery-boy uncle say intelligent things because all he could picture was the man borrowing money from his mother. Borrowing money after she'd worked all day and cooked dinner for three grown men who were perfectly capable of feeding themselves or getting real jobs. It made him want to elbow Patrick hard in the face. He wondered why he was so short tempered today, then clenched his teeth thinking about the force with which Lauren had grabbed him. Recognized how eager he was to pass that treatment on to someone else. Someone who deserved it.

His mother had gone to college for two years, had Shane, and then went to one year of professional school — secretary school, they called it then — and she was supporting all of them, happily. As if her brothers' sweet faces still shone for her. She still saw them as boys, ignored or denied the things they had done, took on the weight of survival for their family name or some hereditary poetic tendency that was carried on a coffin ship and made it alive, only to be delivered this century to The Bag of Nails, the department of social services, and the Jefferson County jail. In fact Shane wanted to hit Patrick hard in the face just for standing there, for just looking at him. He wanted to break something, to clear the bar with a baseball bat. But instead he nodded at his uncle. Said, "It's a good book, though dated."

"Though dated," his uncle repeated, winking at Holly and laughing, then he reached out and put his hand on his nephew's shoulder — shaking him back and forth a bit. "All right, easy there, take it easy, boy. Think I can't read your mind but I can." He looked at Holly and grinned. "I can read yours too," he said. Then he turned his attention to his brothers who were shaking dice inside a plastic dessert cup and spilling them upon the tacky grime-darkened wood of the bar.

The bartender put up a beer for Shane and he stood and drank it this time. He had another week in Watertown. Every bit of it was worse than he remembered, and the way Lauren had blown back in from nowhere was tearing down everything he'd built. He was spent and sticky from her touch, snared by the relief and grief of seeing her. Inhabited by her even as she seemed disembodied herself.

He drank the pint and ordered another, and Holly watched him from a booth across from the bar where she sat sending texts and rolling silverware into paper napkins. She smiled at him and then pointed to the seat across from her. When he brought his drink over he said nothing, touched his nose lightly to feel if it was swelling. His phone buzzed and he looked at it guiltily, then hit SILENCE again.

"I guess this throws a wrench in your Swarthmore romances, huh?"

"I've seen her twice in three years," he said of Lauren. "But once I get around her I can't think of anyone else, or I can't even fucking think."

He shook his head and smiled sadly, looked up into his friend's wise, wry face.

"What happened out there?" she asked. "She mad at you? Why's your nose all red, you been crying?"

"Doesn't mean anything." He shrugged, amazed at how inarticulate he'd become in just a week. How he didn't even bother. Right now he was drinking in the same bar with the Patricks. He was sitting with a woman who'd been his peer in every way, and whose life had been tanked six years ago by some jackass party boy and she was still trying to make good. He shook his head and started over. "I think Lauren may be having some real problems," he began, then Patrick crossed the bar with a fresh drink in his hand and stood beside Holly, resting his other hand on her shoulder.

"Anyway," he said to her. "Getting back to my point before we were sidetracked by this romantic tale of woe, you have to engage them especially if you think they are looking down on you. I've had conversations with professors in houses where Gerry and me were working odd jobs and they are blown away by what I'm reading, by the thought experiments I'm undertaking. You should see their faces."

"We're talking," Holly said to Patrick, giving him a shy smile and gesturing at Shane. But Shane couldn't tolerate another of his uncle's interruptions, couldn't stand the things he said.

"That's just great," Shane told him. "Of course the people whose garage you're cleaning out are shocked you're reading things from their freshman seminars. You were a national merit scholar, now you're a newspaper delivery man, how many of those do you think there are?"

Holly said, "Prolly more than you think" at the same time Patrick said, "None." And Shane shook his head at both of them.

"No, none," Patrick said again, taking no offense at all — as this was all clearly part of some fundamental case he was making.

"Or not too many. I've had conversations with these people and they say I should be teaching their class. You know I could have done that if I'd actually wanted to." He shrugged and took a gulp of his drink. "It was my choice. But I just didn't want to. I got offers to go to St. Lawrence and George Washington." Patrick laughed mockingly, shook his head and raised his glass to his lips again, smiling to himself. "People think if they hold out a bone you have to sit up and beg."

Shane's rage roiled again and his uncle watched with amusement.

"What are you going to do about it?" Patrick asked him belligerently.

"About what?" Shane asked tightly.

"This great weight upon you whenever I talk about having the things you never had."

Shane looked genuinely startled. "Excuse me? Having what I never had? You seriously think I'm angry because I'm *jealous* of you? You never had a fucking thing, Paddy. You never had a thing."

"You're mad because I got freedom and you don't," he said, slowed by drink and whatever grand vision it provided. "You all care so much about what people think and how they see you. All of you." He waved his hand in a dainty circle and spoke in a

132

falsetto: "All the little sheep, little college sheep, grazing along." He dropped abruptly back into his normal speaking tone. "I've got riches up here. I've got things they can't imagine." Patrick straightened his shoulders, raised his chest expansively; he breathed deeply, smiling a wistful self-congratulatory smile, and Shane knew they were about to be the audience for one of his drunken soliloquies.

"Here's what I have that you don't. That you can't get — can't even begin to get. I wake up at four in the morning amidst this beautiful decay, this city that's an object of your scorn. I get to smoke and read and drink coffee and then load the car, all simple but complexly transcendent pleasures. I get to feel my muscles working. I get to see the faces of the grotesques that do this job — they're real people, you know. People your kind don't want to know exist because they've got nothing, not even books. But they're beautiful, dressed in their dickies and thermal underwear, smoking generic cigarettes, pulling the bundles off the great filthy truck from the printers and heaving them onto the loading dock."

"Patrick, *shut* the fuck up," Shane told him. "Enough with the Herman Melville of the loading docks routine."

"What you can't stand, boyo," he said, invoking his father's accent, bringing on some pugnacious, bred-in-the-bone fury that had no place in this country or century, "is that I love this life and I *want* this life. I can live in my little room and read Nietzsche and have more wealth and depth than you'll ever have following orders about what you're supposed to think and learn. You just keep lapping it up and maybe you'll be a good little professor one day and perpetuate the whole sycophantic monstrosity all over again."

It was a mistake to have told him to shut up and Shane knew it. Patrick's competitive nature would guarantee a longer monologue, and Patrick had an advantage over normal people because he didn't care if what he said made sense or not; it was more about the cadence of the language and the emotion it carried. Shane had seen this his whole life. Regardless of his high-school glory days, Patrick didn't actually know much, didn't retain information for very long at all. He rarely finished anything he started reading and couldn't articulate concepts or follow more than a basic plot, but he did read on occasion, he did remember the names of titles and authors and memorized big words he liked the sounds of, and the uncanny nature of these acts where they lived was enough to convince himself he was intelligent. Patrick was versed in nothing and because of that he was doomed to perpetual audience, perpetual awe, everything a mystery. He had placed himself on a pedestal — he was his own high-school sweetheart.

Patrick was so ignorant he didn't even understand the fundamentals of his own poverty, had created a mystique and heroism around it, made it about being looked down upon by professors who were suddenly shocked to learn of his genius, exploited by some phantom elite, even as he was paying the Guinness and Marlboro empires for his own death on credit. Shane concentrated on not responding.

"I'm a loser to you!" Patrick went on, and Shane stopped himself from nodding in agreement. "Home from college just a few days and you can't even *pretend* you want to spend time with us. I'm a loser to you? Guess what? Nine tenths of humanity is losers. *You,* my friend, are outside of real life! You're the freak. I'm not ashamed to be what I am. I'm closer to real brilliance and transcendence and all the things you worship down there at your dainty little school than you'll ever be. I can go home and read

Cormac McCarthy and Faulkner and Heidegger and Husserl. All. Goddamn. Night!" He viciously enunciated the *T* in *night* and jabbed a finger into Shane's chest, leaving it there while he took a trembling, menacing step forward. "I'm closer to them than you'll *ever* be."

At that point Shane actually laughed; he could see the sweat on his uncle's upper lip and smell his inky, dirty clothes. The man had just shouted the name of Husserl in a dive bar, as if it was part of some incantation to bring him power.

"Let's just take a break here for a minute," Holly said, trapped in her seat at the booth. She put her hand on Patrick's arm.

"No," he said, choked with emotion, buoyed by drinks. "Hon, this is just what we were talking about the other day. Just exactly what we were talking about."

He turned to Shane. "I'm not keeping my little foot in line to make sure my interpretation is correct. I'm reading masterpieces in the white-trash wilds." His face was red now and he was shaking his head emphatically. "*You,* you just *degrade* people like me — poor people, you look down on me and the joke's on you because I get the real meanings. I get what you never will. In MY way, not the way that keeps the world all buttoned up tight. I get it in MY way. In MY way!"

Shane sighed and shifted in the booth. He was trying not to speak because it would only make it worse. There was a certain tone Patrick took, halfway through the grandstanding, where it became entirely comic, one of those rousing speeches from the end of a '60s-era movie. Some hushed and grandiose pronouncement. He whipped himself up into a rage, his body tense, almost bringing himself to tears at the thought of his own bravery in the face of the struggle for authenticity.

"I'm the last wild animal in this region," he said, teary eyed and grinning defiantly at his nephew. "All the rest of you are afraid," he said, and raised his voice to falsetto again: "Like your poor little mother, pinching every penny, terrified to do the slightest thing for herself because she's so —"

At this Shane stood up and punched his uncle hard in the mouth. Holly leapt from the booth and stood in front of Shane, putting her arms around him to block whatever response might be coming, but Shane pushed her away, trembling with rage. Patrick staggered back, put a hand to his face but managed to keep hold of his drink with the other. He smiled and his teeth were slick and red with blood. He took a frightfully calm step toward Shane, his eyes dancing.

Gerry and Shamus were standing now, looking at them. Gerry laughed and folded his arms across his chest, waiting.

"Go," Holly said, turning to Patrick, pointing to his barstool. "Go. Enough. Enough."

"Sit down now, Paddy," Shamus said. "You'll get us thrown out before suppertime."

"How does it feel?" Patrick asked his nephew thickly through the blood pooling in his mouth. "You thought you left this place, you thought you belonged out in the suburbs at a Quaker school. You'll be here the rest of your life no matter where you go. Your polo pony friends aren't in a bar today beating the souls that raised them, are they?"

"Enough," Holly said again. "Shut up, now." She pulled some napkins off the pile on the table and pressed them to Patrick's mouth, to his split lips. He closed his eyes and took a breath, relaxed, almost relieved, as he held her delicate hand to his face.

ELEVEN

After vespers Troy went back into his office and riffled through his filing cabinet for Lauren's CD. Something he hadn't thought about for four years. It was packed up with the music he'd photocopied for her, parts of librettos and heavily marked four-page arias, a repertoire he'd chosen for her voice and for her temperament. Her neat narrow writing annotated the margins of the piece.

He'd asked her to return all the music before she left, for safekeeping and for other students who might need it — not as a punishment; her decision was her decision, and as far as he was concerned, it wasn't terrible. He still had his insurance paid for by them, what little he had left was due mostly to military benefits. And service is temporary. All those things you see and do over there, temporary. A small price for what it enables you to do later if you're smart.

"You have no other students," she'd said, looking up at him plaintively, her dark brown eyes darker still for the circles beneath them. He laughed at her. There was that. But it would do her no good to feel special. He had to compose himself or he would start laughing really hard at her. That ratty watchcap she wore, all she needed was some coal rubbed on her cheeks. The little match girl shivering in the icy air from all the stark holy music she insisted upon singing, thinking he was angry at her, not aware she was Maria Callas at eighteen.

"Someone else might come along," he'd said. "Some boy or girl who might not be able to buy his or her own score."

He knew it wasn't likely though. When she sang for him the day Ms. Heimal brought her in, he had to drown his first thoughts. Which were that he could almost taste the timbre of her voice. He listened to the little art song she'd prepared and then asked her to sing some scales. She had a three-octave range, comfortably extending beyond high C. Her voice was clear, smooth and sweet and rich. It was bell-like. Drinkable. About to spill over the rim. Filled with a natural exuberant power, untrained, wavering between release and restraint.

But where the voice was light and strong

the girl looked tired. Even back then, wiry and tired, her long hair pulled back in a ponytail, she wore ripped jeans and a flannel shirt, generic sneakers.

"Lovely," he said, purposefully, professionally. Not letting her hear his excitement. "Can you come in after school?"

"I have to do chores and then pick up my brother," she said, not what he'd asked and too much information. "But I have a study hall like fourth period so I can ride my bike here before lunch."

"Fine." He nodded. For the next two years she would come during the day. After that he added some late-afternoon practices. She would show up in a track uniform and sometimes bring a distracted little boy who had a hard time keeping quiet unless he was playing with those plastic blocks that snapped together. They were both thin, sleepy, ragged-looking children. They reminded Troy of himself.

He had never met her parents. They did not come to her recitals. Once he'd suggested in passing that her mom take her to Knapp's music store out by the mall. The little boy's head whipped around from where he was playing to look at her. And she'd said simply, evenly, "I can ride my bike there," but did not look up from her score.

It was hard not to think about Lauren. She was a serious student and high on what came naturally to her and she had a rare focus, could be entirely in the piece for the minutes it lasted, be transported. She was the kind of musician who is alive as the vessel for the voice, whose discipline was created by a desire for discipline itself and the physical need to sing, to leave the material world, leave the body. It was his job to teach her that the voice is the body. It was his job to break her of reliance on her innate abilities so that she could actually use them. She was attached to little but the praise of teachers and the chattering ragamuffin she dragged around with her and doted upon. And Troy knew better than most that those things would get her nowhere.

It wasn't just talent or drive, though, she was simply a good student. She did what was written and did what he told her to do, and she came in wanting to know things, technical things, things that mattered. The great mistake students make is to ask how a piece is supposed to feel or sound before they've mastered it. She never did that. She respected what was on the page and tried to live up to it first before daring to ask a question about it.

"What was that?" he asked her that day, pulling his hands abruptly away from the keyboard.

"What was what?" she asked, looking toward the door as if she'd missed some noise from outside.

"That *sound.*"

She looked confused.

"Pick up to rehearsal G, second system," he told her tersely so she could find it in the score.

"An F sharp," she said.

"An F sharp," he repeated deadpan. "Sing from rehearsal D." And she repeated the phrase, airy and with ease, up through her belly and into her head until the high note where she pushed the sound from her throat.

"Do you hear that?" he asked her.

She shook her head, shrugged. "It's harder on that one note. I just need to get a better F sharp."

He said, "Yes, of course, how interesting. Maybe you can go next door and borrow an F sharp from someone." He watched her face fall. He said, "Support it. Sink into the ground. It's a push and a pull at the same time. Again. Pick up to rehearsal D." She sang the note and he stopped her. "Again," he said. She sang the note and he let her continue to the end of the phrase before stopping her. "It's pressure in your body, not a lungful of air that you need. Again," he said. "You should feel in your lower abdomen like you're about to laugh."

When she did what he wanted he saw it in her face, saw her listening, watched her eyes change, watched her smile. She wouldn't be doing that piece wrong again.

Lauren Clay, fresh from her middle-school chorus — with no sense of her real talent, no sense of the difficulty of the pieces he was asking her to sing — but still weak in her body, slouched at the piano in a black hooded sweatshirt, the liquid silver sound of her voice just beginning to come into vibrato, ringing, and filling the empty echoing church, waking him after a long sober slumber, bringing him home.

Lauren had a soloist's voice and she liked winning, which made it a pleasure to take her every year for juried competition. He sat off to the side and the judges convened before her in their folding metal chairs. She wore the same black linen dress that started out too big and got smaller every year. Her eyes lined with charcoal-gray pencil, a thin blue beaded bracelet on her narrow wrist, her hair tied back. And each year she got a perfect score right down the line. One hundred percent from timbre to sight singing. The day he brought her to Curtis was one of the proudest in his life. He knew what resonated there in her throat, in her mouth, in her chest. The spirit and pleasure and joy and grief that she could bring clear and whole to the sound. He knew what would happen that day, and he had not been wrong.

It was the All State and All Eastern concerts — the yearly trips that her high-school choir teacher drove her to, that Troy credited for her idiotic obsession with choral music, with the crush of harmony and anonymity and with spare, clear sounds. Sleeping in hotels and practicing all day long and coming to love the ease and grace and oceanic power of voices fitting. Caught up in it like watching waves crashing. It was a short step from there to holy music, and that he knew was his own goddamn fault. And from there to the starkness of minimalism, something he hadn't expected. As if she wanted to live only in winter, to be buried in ice, wanted no other sound in her head. He joked about the pieces she chose to practice the last year she was there. He'd rub his hands together. He'd say, "I can see your breath."

But all that was a long time ago. She was back now, and silent. He would love to hear her sing an aria now that she was not a girl. Sing alone with her woman's voice. He tapped her CD against his knuckles absently. He would play it in the car, figure out what she had to do next, call Curtis himself if he had to. The last thing he wanted was for her to start hanging around the church with him. Hanging around and not singing like she was on guard duty. Bored, distracted, and vigilant at the same time.

Troy put on his long tweed coat still damp from the morning rain, locked the clutter behind his office door, and went out the back into the parking lot. A group of men were standing just outside, hunched close to the building beneath the stone archway to stay out of the rain, passing a bottle back and forth.

He stood with them for a minute, waiting for it to let up. They handed the spirit to him and he took a quick convivial sip and passed it back. One of the men pulled a pouch of TOP from the pocket of his spattered sweatshirt and rolled a cigarette; he had damp, shoulder-length gray hair and his hands were wide and rough, the nails bit down to the nub.

They passed the cigarette between their callused fingers, taking in the sound of the rain and running gutters and watching the weight and burst of relentless drops on the cracked black asphalt. They were calm in the failing light and had no particular place to go. Troy remembered when his days were like that too, after he was home, after he'd spent eighteen months doing nothing but watching the soaring fires of the Kuwaiti fields, following the same futile orders every day without exception, spending his evenings trying to scald and scrub the thick viscous black from his skin and listening to conversations that were humiliatingly stupid to even acknowledge. He'd never liked those men. Any of them. Never liked the smell; some evil distillation of every human error collectively rising and burning. But there was a sound to it. A tone, a rushing hiss, a vibration. The power of the world coming undone.

Troy took the cigarette that was offered him and cupped his hands around the lighter, protecting the flame.

TWELVE

Lauren walked along the edge of the road in the gutter, the headlights from the passing cars casting her shadow before her, a backlit rising form that grew and fell over and over. She'd seriously fucked things up with Shane but she wasn't about to let him get close to the thing she brought home that lived inside her skin. And she needed to protect herself, make sure she didn't get soft.

Someday he'd be smart enough to realize she was protecting him too. Keeping him from falling victim to some lie about second chances and homecoming, some fairy tale that was unbecoming of him. She respected him too much for that.

One of the first things she'd learned down range, a revelatory disappointment, was how soldiers loved fairy tales. This shouldn't have been surprising, the superstition, the irrationality and the romance of it all. A war story is as gruesome as it is a sentimental protective lie. The stations of the cross. And with all the rush of risk, the high of novelty and foreignness, how do you not love the people you fight beside? How do you not hate them? Your body does it all for you, it's risk's tidy trick. Almost every soldier she knew was waiting to bleed out their life for the contents of a castle. For the promise they would be loved or be a hero. The false idea that there was something bigger, something more, that there was a reason. But not Shane. He was no soldier.

Shane was a person she chose and could continue to choose, not a body picked for her by fear and proximity. She didn't think she would ever want anyone the way she wanted him. The shape of his forehead at his temple. The slightest indentation, almost a dimple, at the left corner of his mouth, the curve and swell at the edge of his lip. And then his breath, the sweet perfect smell and taste of him. There was always his height and weight and pace that no one could match. And his delicate way. No one was at once so hard and so soft as Shane Murphy, so fast without being rash or incautious. So focused. No one wore his flaws with such clear aggressive confidence the way Shane did.

He was never the kind of boy who would be caught and impaled on a hedge of thorns, waiting while some cursed person murmured in her sleep. No matter what he said to her, no matter how he felt about her, she knew he would not be lingering around for some spell to be broken. The sooner he understood that she was really gone, the better for both of them.

She had things to do. She had people to take care of. That's how it was in the real world. How it had always been.

It was small things at first. Light bulbs burning out and going unreplaced. Narrow, almost translucent slivers of soap, toothpaste tubes flattened paper thin. But they were all fixable, really. Light bulbs can be unscrewed from fixtures at other people's houses, taken from storage closets or reading lamps at the public library; toilet paper can be lifted from the girls' room at school, stowed in a backpack; toothpaste tubes can be cut open and scraped clean with a toothbrush. Or there's baking soda and salt, that works too. Needles and thread can be stolen from the home ec room; packets of ketchup, creamer, sugar, salt and pepper, plastic silverware, piles of napkins can all be lifted from the cafeteria.

The incidentals for an entire household can be obtained through stealth, an underground economy, items paid for in good grades and track medals and All State choir.

Food was a different story though. She could make money babysitting and she could get money from her dad, but she needed to get to a store that wasn't a 7-Eleven.

"Dammit, babygirl," PJ said one evening when he pulled up beside her on the dark road to town. "I told you to call me. I don't want to see you walking five miles two ways this late in the evening."

"I usually run on the way here," she said, then got into the car and set the bag on the floor by her feet. "It's giving me muscles."

"All right, that's true enough though, that's true," he said, and she rolled her eyes because she didn't need him humoring her.

"What you got there? Puffed rice? That's some good stuff. You ever eat that frozen orange juice right out the container with a spoon? It's not bad."

She laughed as he eyed the rest of her groceries. "Oh hell yeah, they musta had that ten-for-two-dollar ramen. You like the shrimp flavor one? That's my favorite."

She nodded. "And you get the frozen broccoli and mixed vegetables."

"Yep." He smiled. They said, "It's *perfect,*" in unison.

"What about meat? You got meat?"

She nodded. "Ground beef, also oatmeal, beans, peanut butter."

"That's all good protein," he said, put out his hand for her to slap. "This girl's got muscles *and* a brain."

She nodded, then cut to the chase. "Peej, can you teach me how to drive?"

"I *can,*" he said, laughing.

"No, but *will* you?"

"I told you, just call me," he said. "I'm happy to take you around." He looked at her for a minute while they were stopped at the light. Then he said, "Next year okay?"

"What if something happens?"

"You have my damn phone number."

She shook her head in frustration. "What if the phone gets cut off?"

"And what? The phone gets cut off, you have an emergency, you get in the car and drive and the pigs — excuse me — the police officer pulls you over and then what? You're not a grownup, little Low. Why d'you think I call you 'babygirl'?"

"Uh . . . 'cause you call everyone who doesn't have a penis 'babygirl'? I heard you call my gramma 'babygirl' like the year before she died."

He looked at her and they started laughing hard. Then she reached into the grocery bag and got out a pack of bubble gum, unwrapped it, and handed him a piece.

"What's this? Hubba Bubba? You go through all that Hubba Bubba I bought you last week?"

She popped the square into her mouth and winced slightly, shaking her head. "New flavor," she explained, chewing. "Sour apple."

PJ put the gum in his mouth and smiled. They drove on quietly together, blowing bubbles.

He came in with her and filled the tea kettle. Danny was sitting in the hammock in the living room, reading *Harriet the Spy,* eating peanut butter out of the jar with a spoon, and listening to one of their father's Charlie Parker albums. Lauren tossed him a piece of gum and he said, "Thanks, Lowey." She went to the kitchen to put groceries away and cooked the beef because its sell-by date was yesterday. She was hungry and had to keep herself from making too much food because of it. It helped to have a wad of gum in her mouth.

When the teapot whistled she turned it off and went into the living room to ask PJ if he wanted milk in it, but there was only

Danny, swinging his feet to "Now's the Time."

"Where's Peej?"

Danny looked up and smiled at her distractedly, his thoughts still in the book; and she felt good because of how cozy he was and because he got to do cool things like sit in the hammock and swing. His homework was laid out on the aquarium table already done, and there was a pile of records nearby, which he had probably already listened to. He was wearing her old track sweatshirt with their last name on it. He was such a cool kid.

"He went upstairs to Dad," Danny said, still smiling.

"Oh shit."

"What?" He looked at her anxiously and she said, "Nothing, I just forgot something." She didn't want Danny to ever feel her worries. Still she bounded up the stairs two and three at a time, hoping to protect her father.

It was too late. When she got to the room the door was open and PJ was standing inside with her dad and she could feel his shock without even looking at him. She did not want anyone to go in there. When anyone else saw Jack, saw his room, it was as if she were forced to see it for the first time through their eyes. It had been a few weeks since Peej had been over and she did not want to feel that dank, trapped feeling of deteriorating things.

"Hi, Daddy," she said, standing in the doorway.

He looked up at her and smiled and tears welled in his eyes. He put out his hand to her.

She came over and kissed him on the head. The room was stuffy, smelled bad. Like laundry, sweat, sheets that had been unwashed for too long. Milk that had been left standing. Breath through tears and a mouth of unbrushed teeth.

"You just wake up?" she asked.

"Mmhm," he said drowsily, and his eyes stopped focusing on her and his expression turned blank with thought, then he took a couple of deep shaky breaths. Tears ran down his face. Another thought surfaced, a memory, something urgent that made him hold her hand tighter.

"Sweetheart, did you get your brother from after-school yet?"

She nodded. It was already seven o'clock. "Sure did."

PJ was sitting on the side of the bed, surveying the room, and she tried not to look at the places his eyes rested. Like on

Jack's robe, which he hadn't taken off in a month.

"I'm just going to get a few more minutes of rest," her father said.

"Okay, Dad. Sleep tight." She wiped the tears from his cheek and gave him another kiss. "It's going to be okay," she said. She could tell it was, actually; this was better than the nights he kept them up crying.

There were good days and bad days and PJ didn't know enough to tell them apart, and it annoyed her that he was sitting there staring around the room, sitting there doing nothing. They were fine. She'd gotten the paperwork for food stamps and filled it out. And as soon as there was another good day she and Jack would go to the DSS and get their benefit cards, and then when he was feeling better he'd go back to work. He told her early on, when his eyes first began to have that glazed look, that he was having a hard time but that it was "situational" and that conditions like this are self-limiting. "They go away," he told her. "One way or another."

Back downstairs she set out plates and silverware and put the beef, ketchup, taco shells, and lettuce on the table with glasses of water for her and Peej and a glass of milk for Danny. Then she called, "Dinner! Hey

156

Dan, put on some dinner music." She heard him hop down from the hammock and the slight scratch of the needle on the album as he took it off. Then the sound of David Bowie's voice. He was such a cool kid.

She piled food on Danny's plate, asked him if he had brought his laundry down to the basement, and then they both held their spoons like microphones and sang *"Smiling and waving and looking so fine!"* along with the music.

"What's this?" PJ asked as he came back into the kitchen. "We got some rock stars come for dinner. What happened to Birdie?"

"Birdie's reading music," Danny said. "Bowie's dinner music."

"Who decided that?" Peej asked.

"I did," Danny said. "Duh."

"Don't say 'duh' to Uncle P," Lauren told him.

"All right then." PJ clapped his hands together, looked at Lauren. "Aw, damn, baby G. I love tacos just like this," he said. "But I ate before I picked you up. I can't eat another bite."

Danny smiled as he said it and reached quickly for another handful of lettuce. She felt relieved and instantly more hungry, tried not to sound it when she said, "Oh, that's too bad."

He patted her on the back. "Okay, I'm unna be over tomorrow, have some stuff for you children. Then you and me gonna take the car out."

She looked up at him and suddenly felt exhausted. Some tension broke enough for her to fall asleep right there. She exhaled and wiped her mouth, nodded.

He bent down and hugged Danny and kissed him on the top of his head. He said, "You listen to sister, my little man."

Then PJ put out his hand for Lauren to slap. "Lock up when I leave," he told her. He looked around the kitchen, nodded to himself, rested his hand on her shoulder for a moment. She could feel he didn't want to go.

"We're good," she told him, nodding. And they *had* been good. Bellies filling up, Bowie on the turntable. After this she'd read some chapters out loud to Danny. "We got it, Peej." She smiled up at him because there was nothing else to do. "You have a good night."

He saw her beneath the fluorescent lights in the checkout line of the Super Duper where he was buying cigarettes after work. She was wet and shivering with an armful of groceries; her nose was running, and she wiped it on the back of her coat sleeve. Her eyes were glassy and her hair a sopping mess. She stood looking out the front window, not noticing that he was there. She looked like she hadn't slept since he'd last seen her.

PJ walked closer and cleared his throat and she still didn't respond.

"It's nice out there, huh?" he asked. Then watched her eyes focus in recognition, saw a moment of calculation before her face broke into a smile, she shook her head.

"It's a winter wonderland," she said.

The girl had always been good at this, doing what was expected, appearing as though everything was fine as long as she knew you were looking at her. And for so long things had been fine. Her grades, her music, her tough sweetness with little Danny. She'd managed. Lauren kept things together. Girl was his champion.

PJ said, "Just this morning in my window box, I swear to god, some crocus buds poking their little heads up, thinking it's spring."

She smiled again as she put her groceries on the counter.

"What's this?" he asked. "You fall in the river? You buying milk and bread, but it looks like you should be buying a damn life raft."

She nodded tiredly. Paid for the food, took

the plastic bag. They walked together toward the door.

"You got things squared away?" he asked her. "I ask because I been seeing a lot of stop-loss action lately, not because I think you can't handle your own affairs." This was partially true. The government had been extending active duty service for soldiers in this war like nobody's business. Five men in his vet group had gotten sent back after being home for just a few months and thinking it was over. He'd never seen anything like it. The way they would keep taking them back until they came home in pieces or not at all.

She shrugged. "I'm not worried about getting sent back."

"Ain't nobody care if you're worried. That's a situation that happens whether you worry about it or not. Point is to know where you stand with your contract so you don't get surprised."

"Nothing's gonna surprise me," she said blankly. Then she shrugged again. When she looked up at him he could feel it all, the weight of bodies and mistakes, invisibly shouldered but pulling her down. "Besides, we're not going to be over there forever," she said. "Eventually there won't be a war to get sent back to."

160

He looked down his face at her, curled his lip in amused disappointment, and said nothing for a minute. "You're wrong there, babygirl. There is *always* going to be a war to send us back to. You know that. C'mon, lemme give you a ride home, groceries are gonna get wet."

She followed him out to the parking lot.

"Troy's been coming to my group over at the Nabe," he said, pulling his jacket out to cover the cigarette he was lighting.

"What for?"

"We're open to everyone who served." He looked over at her. "You been in touch with Curtis since you been home?"

She shook her head.

"That deal still stand or what? Hey, buckle up, I don't wanna get a fine."

She said, "I'm not your daughter."

"Nah," he said. "You're my goddaughter, what's your point?"

"I can take care of things," she said. She stared through the windshield, hunching down whenever they got even an inch closer to the curb; at one point he watched her reflexively slam her foot into the floor. She began to reach for the wheel and stopped herself.

"I know that's true," he said easily, making the car warm with his voice. He could feel her surveying the rainy street, feel her eyes scanning it. He knew what it was to be her right now, the way the street itself was some kind of trap. He remembered being terrified and paranoid of walking through doors even after he got home. The sense that he might trip a wire and end up impaled remained with him long after the war. He still occasionally dreamed that his foot had been caught in a punji trap. He watched her fight against everything her muscles were ready to do so that she would appear normal.

She nodded curtly. "So what's wrong with Troy?"

"Nothing's *wrong* with him." He laughed. "You don't gotta be fucked up to come to my group."

"But it sure helps," she said, finishing his sentence.

PJ looked at her from the corner of his eyes. "You sure you not my daughter?"

At this she turned and looked right at him again. She laughed darkly and he heard the music in her voice. "I'd be interested in seeing any kind of birth certificate at this point," she said. "I'm pretty sure I was manufactured at FOB Garryowen."

When Lauren came along Vietnam already

162

seemed like a lifetime ago. Nam and college and Panthers and the Student Nonviolent Coordinating Committee. All of it over. The war and then the various wars at home trying to make right the things he'd done. Trying to burn away the memories of fire. He dropped out of graduate school after Donna left him, went back to full-time community organizing, and it was still another eight years before he got his temper under control, another two before he cut back on the drinking. The nightmares, though, they weren't going anywhere.

Paul Jefferson of the 82nd Airborne did not imagine he would live to be twenty, or thirty or forty. Never thought that he'd one day call some skinny white boy who wore socks with sandals his brother, or be given the task of holding that skinny white boy's loud pink baby while a priest poured water on her head. But PJ held Lauren Sophia Clay on the day she was named, in a church full of pale, square-faced people half of them with the last name Donovan, who believed that this ritual would absolve the infant of guilt, protect her from punishment and infuse her with God's grace.

PJ knew there was no way the sacrament could protect her. And this strange Irish hippie family was enough to foment guilt in her for the next eighty years, but by the time she had grown into a chatty, dreamy child it was hard not to see her as truly possessing some kind of divine grace. She had an easy kindness and sensitivity, was a slight, delicate kid who sang while she played, who wanted to be carried and was afraid of loud noises, and loved to pretend. She often fell into giggling fits that went on until she was red cheeked and hiccupping, tears streaming down her cheeks. The defining characteristic of baby Lauren was her easy happy laugh.

When he would come over in the evenings to play Scrabble and talk about work with Jack and Meg, Lauren would climb into his lap and help him spell words. She would fall asleep with her head against his chest and Meg would scoop her up and carry her off to bed.

When she was older and Danny was born she painted pictures for his room, took to caring for him from the beginning. Knelt in front of him repeating words she wanted him to learn, and was thrilled when he started repeating bigger words. She once called PJ at his office and put the baby on. "Pancake," Danny's little voice said over the phone. "Pancake." He could hear her laughing in the background. It made his day.

When things got bad for those kids Lauren shut it down hard, created a little household within the one that was coming undone, kept things running. He saw in her then what recruiters saw in her years later when they promised she could be an officer, when they told her about the signing bonuses, and the GI bill and the size of the checks. When they hooked her and reeled her in so the army could give her muscles and fix her posture and pay for all those things she could yet barely understand.

He told her what he thought about the decision, said, *Nah, Nah, babygirl. You know that's not right. It's not worth it. You get yourself set up with Curtis and you just keep going, that's the way to do it.*

Who's planning for Danny? she asked.

Ain't nobody got to plan for him. Danny's like you and me. He tried to keep his voice easy but he wanted to drive over to the recruiter's office and rip his motherfucking lungs out. He breathed slowly, concentrated on what was possible in the moment and tore his thoughts from images twenty years old but all too ready to play themselves out in full color and sound and smell. Ready to play themselves out with her in the uniform.

Danny's gonna make his way in school and come out fine, just like his big sis. You know how we do.

She smiled and looked at him, her eyes dark and shining with pride and resolve.

This is *how you did it,* she said.

THIRTEEN

DISPATCH #53

Dear Sistopher
It's been a few days since you left the country and I checked the difference in time zone and I wonder if you are going to write me an email. I hope you do it soon but I can only get them at school so I wonder before I go to sleep if there will be one when I go to the library tomorrow. I got the package you sent from Fort Lewis. The Zombie Survival Guide should come in handy around here.

The day after you left Mom called and asked how I would feel about moving to Buffalo. I said I didn't think Dad had plans to move and she said, no, move to Buffalo to live with her. And I was like, I just started middle school! She said Dad has a disability and it would be better if

I lived there. I could start middle school there.

Does Dad have a disability? Is it that he thinks he's Obi-Wan Kenobi? (ha-haha) He wears the same brown robe all day long and he's let his beard grow in — he's kind of a long haired Obi-Wan. You should see it, it's pretty funny. Sebastian has those white whiskers now so the two of them make a good team. He's worried about you but I'm not. I know nothing can happen to you. Dad's worried, that is, I don't know about Sebastian, maybe he's worried too but mostly he's into napping and begging.

You probably don't want to hear this kind of bullshit. I don't want to leave here obviously. Mom's house is nice and she has a great garden but what's the point? She said there was really good schools there and she has the Internet at home so we could talk to you all the time. I would rather come and live there with you if you can have families on the base in Iraq. Is Garryowen a big base? PJ says it's not very dangerous like Vietnam was and that you are with the best army the country has ever had, and with the best medical care the country has ever had, and the best transportation so

168

nothing can happen to you. Do they ever let family visit there? Do they have schools on the bases like in the U.S.? If Dad is disabled more than being a Star Wars character then I should probably come and live with you, right?

PJ's been hanging out for a couple of days and he told me that you almost don't have to do any combat either, that it's just really hot. And that you are making more money than Dad and Mom put together so you're going to be rich and tan and pretty when you come home. I wasn't really even crying or anything but he keeps telling me how great it is there in Iraq. He's such a fucking boner sometimes and he talks a lot but I'm glad he's here, it's good for Dad.

The thing is I really don't know what to do now. I don't think anyone takes me seriously like you do or like they act when you are around. So I can't get them to be normal. Or just go away. I can't live with Mom because all my friends are here. And Dad can't live alone. Don't I get to say what I want? If I wait and ignore everyone they'll forget I'm here. I'm pretty sure of that. But just let me know anyway if it's possible to visit or if they have a school there.

Be safe I love you
Danny

When she read the letter in the barracks at Garryowen she felt sick and had to stand up and turn away from the screen. She'd just gotten in from patrol and was still covered with sweat and fine gritty sand, sand in her mouth and inside her nose, and a smell like burning rubber and brake fluid clung to her uniform. She felt she might cry but she didn't deserve to cry. It was her fault. She'd fucked up. Miscalculated. Of course someone had a plan for Danny. But it was too late.

The loud hollow *whump* of helicopter blades beating the sky reverberated above the CHU and she felt it in her gut. Lauren wracked her brain for how she could have done things differently but there was nothing else. There was no money. She'd made the right decision. She couldn't have taken care of him if she'd gone with Curtis. And it looked like no one else was going to either and now this new plan just made no sense, would take him away from the only security he had.

She felt the gulf, the free-falling feeling of being thousands of miles away, completely powerless. She could not order people back home to do things, and that thought enraged her. Why would her mother do this? Why hadn't she even asked Lauren to visit before she left? She felt alone and unwanted, sitting in the shitty barracks, everything perfectly ordered; the neat squared-away life that makes it possible to act in a single second. The neat squared-away life that makes inaction close to physically intolerable. A rush of fear and sadness and something unnameable, the taste of tears at the back of her throat. She tried not to think about the only thing that was coming to mind. A question that was beneath her in every way, but beneath her like the whole surface of the earth was made from it. Why hadn't their mother tried to get custody of both of them a long, long time ago?

She wrote Danny. She told him he could make his own decisions. He didn't have to go anywhere. She told him she'd be home in a year. She told him he was old enough to decide to stay where he was. She told him to call PJ. She told him she'd take him on vacation when she got home. She told him to focus on school and that Dad wasn't his responsibility at all. She told him the smarter he was the sooner he could get away. She told him she loved him and if they ever needed she could be his legal guardian, but that he was a champion, a champion in every single way, and he could rely on himself.

She sent it but she would call him later too. Because really there was no way he could rely on himself. He was just a child. One more way she had fucked up. Doing everything for him, thinking it would be better that way. But now he was at everyone's mercy instead. She sat on her cot facing the dented gray locker, looking at a picture of Danny and Sebastian she had taped there. Danny was laughing, holding something in his hand, and Sebastian was jumping to reach it. Their father's slippers and part of his leg were in the right corner of the photograph. She sat for a while unable to think at all, then shut the computer and dressed to go back out on patrol. They were going house to house for insurgents.

And it was her job to search the women.

Fourteen

After Shane left, Holly filled a bar towel with ice and pressed it to Patrick's mouth, standing close and quiet beside him. He was subdued, eyes narrowed in thought, breathing heavily through his nose. Holly didn't know how many times she'd administered barroom first aid to this man but it was losing its charm.

"He thinks I'm looking for some stage or some pulpit," Patrick said quietly, reasonably. He sounded genuinely puzzled, like he was disappointed in his nephew, couldn't figure out how to reach him. "And he's wrong, of course. I don't give a fuck if anyone knows my inner thoughts, or what I'm reading. That's not what this place is to me. If I cared, why would I live like I live? I wouldn't choose to live in obscurity. I'd live like he does. I'd go to school for the pat on the head, get pedigreed, have my name on papers."

She said nothing, handing him a glass of water to rinse out his mouth, then walked through the back door out onto the deck and lit a cigarette, listened to the rain on the awning. There were only five people in the bar and she was praying it wouldn't be a long night, that they'd wander off and find something else to do. Once she shut down she could go home to Gracie, make plans with Lauren, read the book Patrick had lent her until she fell asleep.

She didn't know what had happened in the parking lot between Lauren and Shane, and she didn't much care. Lauren had looked tired and a little nervous, but she'd also never looked so fit or alert. Holly wished she could walk right out of the bar now and pick her up, drive around in the rain and talk.

It was rare that they could get away even in high school. Most of their time from middle school on was spent playing in Lauren's driveway, doing homework, watching television, calling boys on the phone, and always hanging out with Danny, making up games, pretending with him. When Danny was at a friend's house they'd walk down to the river, or skateboard in the industrial park and build their fires.

By the time they were seniors all of Lauren's time was taken up with rehearsing for recitals or competitions or auditions and all of Holly's was taken up with Grace. The rare times when they got away and could drive out to nowhere were the best. Confirmed their imminent flight. They were like animals that were getting stronger and braver every second, and they surveyed the land from which they'd come with a kind of angry pitying awe, knowing even then the dead town had given them sight, had made them understand things, see the connections people ignore. Had made them ready to fight anything that got in their way and fix anything they wanted to keep.

Holly wished for those feelings now. She watched the rain striking the puddles in the gravel parking lot, smelled the mud and cool air like it was spring, how different it was from the crisp smell of snow and woodsmoke. She thought about Christmas break their last year of high school. That was the year the nurses union went on strike and her mother stayed home the end of December. NYSNA paid part of her wages so Bridget treated it like a preholiday vacation. Making cookies and watching Gracie every day. Just before Christmas she invited Danny over to bake with her. The kitchen was warm and smelled like chocolate and cinnamon.

"Go on now," Bridget said. "You girls go out! We need some time to ourselves, don't we, Dan? Me and these short people got plenty to do before Santa gets here."

"Gracie's not short," Danny said. The baby was a pale blob of soft features with bright, strange and searching eyes. She wore a onesie covered with tiny pink stars and a green sweater. She clutched Danny's finger in her tiny fist and he looked back at them smiling, his lank black hair falling into his eyes. "She can't stand up yet, so she's more flat than short." He turned his attention again to the infant, touched her round cheeks. Gracie stared at Danny, kicked her feet excitedly, and tried to draw his finger to her mouth; she made contented sounds. "Look at how small her nose is," he said. "Look at her fingernails."

"Oh, she's a keeper," Bridget said. "Now wash your hands." She handed Danny an apron and a wooden spoon. "And you," she said to Holly. "Move it before I change my mind."

The air was shockingly cold and still after being in the warm kitchen; large snowflakes came down, dusting their hair and coats. She and Lauren let the car warm up, watching the frost and ice melting and receding across the windshield. Holly pulled the box of Newports out of the glove compartment, punched in the lighter, and turned on the radio.

It had been a long time since they'd made their rounds, the aimless driving and occasional stops at scenic points, 7-Elevens, the thrift store, the playground outside of Lourdes Church, old industrial sites, waterfalls, or boys' houses. Lauren called it "field research." They'd listen to the radio waiting for the ads to end and Dido or Eminem or Outkast to come on so they could sing along, have a soundtrack.

That evening they drove past the neighborhood porches strung with colored Christmas lights. No one was out except for some boys in puffy coats, walking a strong square-faced dog on a leash, passing a cigarette back and forth, their conversation visible as white clouds about their mouths.

They drove by the bare branches and blanketed tennis courts of Thompson Park, watching the swirling snow strike the windshield before them. Then out to the wider, better-maintained streets lined with houses set back from the road, their windows glowing and tall, ornately decorated trees visible, delicate strings of white light wound up the columns that framed their front porches.

They cruised slowly by Asshole's house, looking for his car in the drive. They passed the frozen falls at the Black River, and the vast abandoned brick expanse that once housed some industry or another but was now empty. The place they made their fires was frozen.

Holly said, "Someday, Lowey, all this will be yours."

The sky was at once pale and rich, a glowing violet color as they cruised past the boarded-up shops of downtown out to nowhere, watched the flood-lit, razor-wire fences of the base slide by. The farther they drove the better. It was exhilarating to be out for no reason and away and free. Holly turned up the heat and once it was warm, almost hot, she rolled down the window so they could feel the fresh cold air, and occasional electric sting of ice against skin. She headed along Dutch Settlement Road and then took a narrow turnoff with no shoulder that ended in an unplowed dirt path. She was headed for the quarry.

Lauren took a CD from her pocket and slid it into the player, Joan Sutherland singing "Lucia's Aria." Again. She'd been playing it for a whole month now, but something about the quiet all around them and the weirdly contemplative drive made it sound different. The soprano's voice rose like something so perfect and controlled and enormous it dwarfed the fleeting, darkening landscape and seemed to swallow the car.

Holly pulled over to the edge of nowhere, clicked off the headlights. She remembered how the stars shone bright upon the snow. How Lauren turned up the stereo so they could hear it when they got out of the car, how she stood in her old wool coat with the worn elbows and frayed collar wearing PJ's watchcap, how dark the sky was that far out of town and how still everything seemed with the snow coming down silently all around them. It might have been as far away as they had ever been. And she could feel how happy her friend was, how excited and relaxed.

Lauren smiled and squeezed her hand, her eyes bright with love for the song. Then she walked to the edge of the vast tiered cliff-side in the dark, her boots crunching over the snow and ice. And Holly came and stood beside her. Massive blocks of stone were faintly visible below, silvery black in the starlight. The place felt like a crater. Like standing at the end of the continent. A whole hollow universe of emptiness lay before them. The place echoed like a massive cradle of stone.

"Lucia's Aria" drifted from the car, and now Lauren began to sing along. Sing into the belly of the quarry, her white breath like a spell being cast upon wreckage and emptiness and darkness. The air was filled with nothing but her voice and its reverberation, a haunting echo in the snowy, starry night.

Holly felt it then: how the song and all it contained fought off the world they came from and yet was made of it. She lay across the warm hood of the car and gazed up at the sky until she felt like she was floating, rising.

Never before and never since had she felt that free.

FIFTEEN

Since getting home Lauren had been forced to weather her dreams, so filled with strange detail they made her nearly conscious of her sleeping self, her body, a thing in a trance, eyes speeding along blindly beneath their lids, stories that clutched her heart, made it thump against her breast, made her muscles jerk, but left her lying still and unable to wake. These dreams made her tired and they did not stop. Each one with its own inextricably sinister back story.

They all began with her standing beneath a complicated tower of black metal that could have been a witch's house. Thick white ashes floated down, each jaggedly cut into lace and hearts by small hands using blunt, round-tipped scissors. Sometimes the snow rose in the distance. Sometimes there was a little girl.

The little girl who made the ashes. She was sick and Lauren had to take care of her.

She was sick and there was a camera crew on-site and everyone loved the little girl because she'd been the star of the TV show *Law and Order.* Though she was still only four feet tall and very thin, she'd played a tough cop and everyone took her seriously. But now she was frail and ill.

Lauren was holding her hand and kneeling before her and the girl told her what the doctors said. "I have crumbling lungs," the girl said. "They also call it crumbling crown." She could see then the girl had a tattered paper crown on her head, a thin, ragged, regal thing that trembled and curled at the edges. And her arms were covered from where she had drawn on herself with magic marker. The girl took a shaky breath and then began to sing.

Lauren covered the girl's mouth roughly with her whole hand, picked her up quickly and began walking away, but she was too big and gangly to carry very far. The camera crew followed them and wanted to ask questions about *Law and Order.* Lauren tried to leave but couldn't see through the ashes. Finally she put the girl down and held her close, held her tightly by the shoulders and whispered through her teeth into the child's ear.

"I will do anything, anything, *anything* I

can to make your pain go away," she said. "I will do anything. But you are going to die. That's just how it is. You are going to die if I have to see to it myself."

She would wake feeling heavy and dehydrated, and grateful to be alert again. The significance of the nightmares was not lost on Lauren. The thoughts that repeat themselves suddenly and unexpectedly, the need to be vigilant. Some of these things she took with her to Iraq, did not gain over there, and she was not ignorant of their meanings nor the way they could be used to keep her sharp. It was, in fact, this sharpness she pointed to in conversations with herself that made her an exception now; her discipline, her ability to analyze what she was experiencing, these were the traits that got her home. The skills that had found her on a plane on Christmas Day instead of spending the next several weeks still outprocessing in some shithole base in Washington State, sitting around taking orders that she had no intention to ever do again.

It was all about understanding the narrative. Knowing history and the facts and what you could expect. This allowed you to get what you needed. She would get the new narrative under control. She would stop dreaming these dreams. Just like she'd done before.

The old narrative was a series of truths. A history that had to be rethought to the point of meaninglessness. At best it was a number of random events involving incompatible people and someone who never got a chance to go to college. At worst it was something else. Her father was too weak to make her mother stay, and her mother was worthless to want to leave two kids. The kind of woman who meticulously and continuously pointed out her husband's flaws, made an airtight case for their lives being a living hell, and then saved only herself. Leaving Lauren and Danny with someone who could not get out of bed, who worked with all his might to open a can of soup in the evening without falling apart, who was visibly grateful for the end of "dinner" so he could leave them at the table and retreat to his room.

But that was better than when their mother was still there. An eight-hour screaming argument that postpones lunch and dinner and makes bedtime impossible is not preferable to having two parents.

When Danny was four their father and mother asked him what he wanted for Christmas, and he was practical enough to ask for food. A bag of groceries to keep in his room. A week later he knocked on her door, wearing shorts, snowboots, mittens, and a tiger mask and asked her if she wanted to come over to Africa and eat a giraffe. He was holding two pieces of wheat bread from his personal stash and he pushed them toward her. She picked him up and slid the mask on to the top of his head and kissed him on the cheek. Something slammed in their parents' room and the word "you" popped and burst into the air around them. She watched his shoulders hunch and eyes widen reflexively.

She tore a piece of bread and put it in her mouth.

"This giraffe meat is good," she said. "But you're not dangerous, are you?"

"Not to other tigers," he explained matter-of-factly, waving his hand.

"Oh, right," she said. She sat him on her bed and then went to her desk and took out her eyeliner, leaned in toward the mirror to draw whiskers on her cheeks. "There."

She looked in her drawers for something else befitting a tiger, found a black and white long-sleeved T-shirt and put it on. Danny nodded solemnly at her, his mouth full, clutching the remaining crust of giraffe in his mitten.

She sat on the floor beside the bed and growled and he growled too and offered her another bite.

A whole sentence Lauren did not want to hear or understand rang clearly through the wall. Followed by several more.

"It's a loud jungle tonight," Danny said.

She looked at him, the big boots hanging off the edge of the bed and his little bare knees. It was a loud jungle every night. And they needed it to be quiet. She picked Danny up again and carried him across the narrow hallway, knocked on their parents' door. She would ask nicely for them to stop and they would see how cute Danny was in his tiger costume and they would stop.

"Butt out!" her mother yelled at her without opening the door. Lauren knocked again. "Butt *out!*" her mother screamed, throwing the door open. "*What* are you doing? Why would you bring your little brother in here? What a manipulator! Look at this. Get out! Take him out of here!"

Her father stood to the side in the dim room, still wearing his work clothes, his arms folded across his chest looking at the floor; they'd been at this since four.

"Stop yelling!" Lauren shouted at her mother, her eyes narrowed, her face almost comical with the eyeliner whiskers, much shorter than both of her parents as she glared up into their faces, holding Danny on her hip. She'd wanted to ask politely, to talk quietly. But as soon as she saw them just standing there doing nothing, not even caring that they said the same things over and over and over, while Danny had to pretend they were animal noises, she felt sad and weak. And if she didn't yell at them she'd be crying, and that would be just more bad noise, more confusion for Danny. "Both of you. Shut up!" she snapped. "This isn't good for us."

Danny pulled his mask down over his face and held on to her hair and his bread with one mitten. He patted her back gently with the other. "Lowen," he whispered into her ear. "Let's be tigers."

"Oh, for god's sake," her mother screamed. "Listen to this. Guess what? People fight. You're not a fragile little thing. That's the way it is. It's not going to kill you." Her eyes were red and she raised her chin defiantly at Lauren, smirking at her. "Now you'll have something to talk about. Now you'll have an interesting life!"

"Meg." Her father reached for her mother's arm, but she shook it off.

Her mother looked angry and exhausted, and Lauren wanted her to stop and hold her arms out to her children. The whole thing could stop if her mother would just hold them, or turn and smile at her father. Lauren loved her. Loved the turtleneck sweaters she wore. Loved the shape of her face and the way she smelled and her thin gold hoop earrings. She even loved it when her mother was sarcastic or mean or wanted to be alone, because it meant she was really thinking about things, like she always said, not some little housewife. Maybe if they stood there long enough their mother would say something funny. She would see the absurdity of yelling at two children dressed as tigers and she would laugh and hold them. Forgive them whatever it was. Lauren stood mutely holding Danny, and Meg took a deep breath and then made a low, frustrated sound in her throat. In one second she could change everything. She could make everything right.

"All of you!" her mother shouted, a tight fury in her throat, damning them with something more that remained unspoken.

Sixteen

"Where's Dad?"

He looked confused for a minute like he hadn't heard her and then said, "At work."

Where? She stood in his doorway with her head to the side, toweling off her long hair. Her sopping clothes were in the dryer; the scratch and click of the buttons hitting the sides as they spun was audible from the vent in Danny's room. She'd changed into sweats and her olive army T-shirt.

"Work," he said loudly. "It's Monday. He's got a couple clients Monday and Wednesday."

"It's the day after Christmas."

He shrugged. "People are poor and crazy all year long," he said. "They don't get holidays off."

Something about that information was disorienting and she felt she was about to lose her temper, what little of it she still had hold of. While she'd been wandering around town in the rain her father had gone to work and just left Danny in front of his computer. She sat down on the floor and rested her back against his bed and listened to the ping of instant messages and concentrated on her breathing the way they tell you to. But concentrating on a thing you can do that your friends can't anymore is some pretty fucking bad advice.

He laughed to himself periodically and typed rapidly. "Who are you IM-ing?" she asked.

He didn't answer right away but laughed again and then shouted, "Scott accidentally texted his mom this picture he took last week of us peeing on this last little pile of snow over by the 7-Eleven on Hoard Street!" Lauren realized he was wearing earbud headphones. "She's so pissed. Oh!" He shook his head, laughed at what he'd just said. "Why would anyone be mad about that? It's so insignificant."

"What are you listening to?"

He took the headphones out. "David Bowie."

"Put it on speaker."

"I don't have speakers for the computer — just these."

"We should put the album on downstairs."

"The turntable's broken."

190

"Really?"

"Yeah, like for almost a year. The belt or something."

He sat on the floor next to her and put one of the buds in her ear and one in his, rested his shoulder against hers.

"I'm going to get a tattoo too," he told her.

She grinned. "Oh yeah, what?"

"Sebastian eating some underwear. And I'll be all like — *What?* That's right, bring it! You gonna fuck with me?? Here's a dog eating some underwear! How fucking bad-ass must I be if I got this fucking tattoo of a little dog eating some tighty whities? People will be, like, terrified." He broke into his goofy laugh.

"He has to have the face," she said.

Danny did the face of Bad Sebastian, evil mixed with guilt and confusion.

She laughed so hard her sides hurt, and she lay on the floor and covered her mouth.

"Yeah!" Danny shouted again, "What now? Imma motherfucking schipperke, motherfucker! Imma save you from the Nazis and lead your horse down the Erie Canal, and balance on a beach ball! But first I gotta eat some underwear. Bring it!"

He giggled to himself, then said, "Oh wait, I got to show you . . ." He stood up and went to the computer. She'd forgotten about his wired way, had made him softer in her mind while she was gone.

"Here's the YouTube thing of that ice shelf," he said. He made it full screen and sat back down next to her. She was still laughing a little — then he pointed to the image: the glacier crumbling, a flood of white water rushing into a black sea. They were quiet and stunned and then Danny pointed at it and made the Bad Sebastian face again and they started laughing, ashamed that it was so funny, which made them laugh harder. He lay down on the ground and just wheezed out the last of his mirth. Every time she looked at him she started again. Her face hurt from smiling and she was out of breath.

"God, you're fucked up," she told him tremulously.

"Yeah. I'm going to get a tattoo of Sebastian stranded on an iceberg like a polar bear, not funny, right?" He nodded vigorously. "Because that shit's really happening, that's why it will be so badass. A little underwear-eating American housedog stranded on a iceberg. Oh my god what does that even *mean,* it's so fucking brilliant!? Then like, 'Thug Life' or 'Everyday I'm Hustling' written under it in calligraphy."

"Both those phrases would be completely appropriate," she said.

"I know! Not as captions for him, though — but for me. Especially if I get some kind of corporate job. If I was a banker with, like, stranded Sebastian drawn on me, eating underwear.

"Thug Life," he said and laughed again. "But if it was a caption for *him* it would have to be just 'help!' " Then he broke into his officious NPR voice: "Scientists have not yet uncovered the mystery of where these dogs came from, or to where they might be floating. But Lauren Clay, deployed with the Tenth Armored Infantry Division, has come here for answers." He made a *shhhh*ing noise like a waterfall and then held an invisible microphone out to his sister. "And she won't leave until she gets them."

"Thank you, Carl," she said in an exaggerated southern drawl. "We've been tracking these motherfucking canine ice monkeys now, for, oh . . . more'n a month and I think we're close to smoking 'em out. You see, you haveta understan' these creatures don't see the world like you and me do, no sir. They'll give up five, six — hell, ten *thousand* possibly *ten million* of their kind for every one of us. They'll give up their whole genus and species, essentially, is what we've found."

"Why do you think that is?" Carl from NPR asked southern radio Lauren.

"Well, 'cause really, they don't have any weapons and they can't read or write or strategize. These knuckleheads just sit around all day long like a bunch of fucking faggots in a dick tree . . . so . . . our jobs are pretty straightforward. We've got a clear mission to remove this insurgency by heating up the whole goddamn world so ah . . . so their little snow ships melt."

After a while the giddiness subsided and they stared at the computer again. The ice and the force of the waterfall in the video, the tinny sound of David Bowie still singing quietly from the headphones on the floor. She felt so good from laughing, loose and tired like after a long run.

"I got a good friend who lives close to some glaciers," she told him.

"Really?" His tone changed to real interest, back to his sweet nerdy self.

"Yeah, I do. A buddy a mine from Amarah. We could go visit him."

"Does he live in Greenland?"

"No," she said. "His wife's from Canada, and they're back there now."

When the phone rang she thought it might

be her dad — something might have gone wrong and he'd need her to pick him up or run some errand. She ran downstairs, grabbed the receiver, and froze when she heard Eileen Klein's voice.

"Hi, Lauren, this is Dr. Klein, I'm glad I was able to reach you. I've been looking over this 15-6 and some other paperwork that I just received from Captain Nash and I realized that during your PDHA we didn't have an opportunity to talk about some things. I want to make sure we're compliant with the terms under which you are ending your enlistment."

Lauren's blood turned to ice. "I went over everything with you to the best of my knowledge, ma'am, and as far as I understand I'm on terminal leave. Unless I get arrested for something, or get unlucky with stop-loss, I'm all squared away."

"I'd like to talk to you about Daryl Green. I understand the two of you made a lot of plans for when you got back to the north country."

"Yes ma'am, we did, but I believe if I had anything else to say about Specialist Green's performance I said it to Captain Nash during the 15-6."

Dr. Klein said, "Soldier, I've scheduled an appointment for you with a colleague of mine at Fort Drum for 1:30 P.M. on December twenty-ninth. I suggest you make that appointment or be in contact with them twenty-four hours in advance to reschedule it. Otherwise you risk breaching the conditions of your terminal leave."

Lauren said, yes ma'am, thank you for your call. Because there was nothing else to say.

She went back upstairs and stood in Danny's doorway. Now he was laughing at a YouTube video, stop-motion animation of Santa talking to some toy-making elves. When he saw her in the doorway he handed her the headphones so she could hear. The audio was from *Full Metal Jacket,* the drill sergeant yelling at new recruits. She laughed but it annoyed her that he found it funny. He had no right to find it funny.

He wasn't himself. He was still quick but he was different. She'd left him in the care of these people and now he didn't read books anymore, didn't paint or study or make collages with music playing in the whole house — just sat silently with his head stuffed full of sounds no one else could hear.

The sooner they left the better.

SEVENTEEN

He put Bowie back on when she left the room, found more footage of glaciers, texted Scott and riffled through his closet for a rain jacket even though he had no plans to go outside. On the floor near a pile of sneakers that no longer fit he came across a stash of beef jerky with an expiration date that was fast approaching, so he opened it and ate it while watching videos of the ice shelf melting, the frozen world turning to water and vapor. Then he looked up the Union of Concerned Scientists' Website and followed links that eventually led to an article about oil-eating bacteria. It had been developed by a guy named Ananda Chakrabarty in the 1970s, and the scientific name for the stuff was *multiplasmid hydrocarbon-degrading pseudomonas.* He said it out loud a few times to make sure he had it right, then read about another bacteria that eats plastic, thinking about how little things can take enormous things apart, or can grow to immense proportions. Seeds and cells, objects and organisms measured in nanometers. The component parts of the world lose their power when separated. He thought about how literally everything could be magnified until it seemed like a universe. A drop of water a whole ecosystem.

Then for the first time since he was very small he remembered *The Snow Queen,* a book Lauren used to read to him. A story in which a speck of glass — a speck of broken mirror — causes all the trouble.

That was definitely the story that made him want to see the North Pole. All these things seemed so tightly and minutely connected. It made him laugh out loud for a moment.

He remembered he and Lauren built a cave of pillows and blankets and climbed inside. The book had a black cover with a photograph of dollhouse dolls — a little boy and girl — on the front. They were posed next to a miniature window box planted with red roses that looked like paper, had hair that looked like embroidery thread, and bright blue painted eyes. Drawings of snowflakes were superimposed over the photograph.

There were devils in the story who made

a distorted mirror that turned everything hideous and wrong, and it slipped from their hands and smashed into millions of pieces — nanoparticles, Danny thought now, excited that the book could be about something else, bacteria or viruses.

The little boy and girl in the story were good friends. They played together in their garden and they watched the frost form on their windows when it got cold. He didn't know how they did the ice in the photographs; maybe it was Styrofoam. He loved the ice and also how the dollhouse children looked three dimensional — not illustrations. It made you feel like you could walk around in their world. Talk to a crow or a reindeer.

One day the little boy in the story felt something strike his eye; it was a piece of the broken mirror, and suddenly everything he saw was ugly.

Then the Snow Queen came for him in her white sled and they left the little girl behind.

The little girl goes looking everywhere and finally finds him in a frozen place drawing on ice with another shard of ice. He remembered the little dollhouse boy kneeling in the snow, and thinking how amazing it was that he could have survived all that cold, everything still, all life around him camouflaged in the absence of color. The boy didn't even feel it. He didn't even recognize his friend, but then she rushed to him and cried and her tears fell into his eyes and washed out the fragment of the devils' mirror. And they went home and played in their garden again. He loved that book. It was the beginning of all his reading about the arctic, about animals like white rabbits and narwhals, foxes with snowy fur, tiny lemmings that make tunnels in the ice and nests out of other animals' fur. But somehow it seemed he'd been interested in living in the arctic even before that. Those things had just reminded him of who he really was.

Later, when he learned about expeditions to the North Pole, he thought they were some of the bravest people in the world. Until he read more, and then he thought they were also some of the stupidest. The first arctic explorers brought things with them like whole sets of silver and china, weighing themselves down, lumbering along with some imaginary tea party in mind at the end of the road. He liked to read to Lauren about all the failed expeditions, became obsessed with them because they were so strange and, in a sick way, funny. Like Salomon August Andrée, who tried to get to the North Pole in a hydrogen balloon and died from eating infected polar-bear meat.

But other expeditions he really did admire and want to recreate. He wanted to be like Knud Rasmussen, who crossed the Northwest Passage on a dogsled, who grew up in Greenland hanging out with Inuit hunters, speaking their language. Danny had become obsessed with the idea of surviving in the cold. Treating hypothermia, frostbite. By the time he was seven he wanted to live at the North Pole. When he learned that people really do live in Antarctica as researchers it seemed too good to be true.

He didn't know what happened to his expedition plans. The desire to see the North Pole was still strong, but he didn't imagine how to get there anymore, didn't dream of dogsleds or talking with the Inuit or tireless, courageous wind-burned hikes over mountains of ice.

Smaller things seemed more important now, a microscopic world beneath this one, beneath all worlds, inside your own body. There was no real way for a person to be alone, he thought. Every single person is a vast crowd of other living things, a universe.

It was the grain of mirror that really mattered in the Snow Queen, and the drop of salt water that washed it away.

- - - -

EIGHTEEN

"Why doesn't Danny know how to drive a car?"

Jack Clay tried not to look startled. She was sitting at the kitchen table directly in front of the door, her hands folded in front of her. He set his ratty briefcase down and kicked his shoes off, tossed the mail onto the counter, and slid into the threadbare slippers that lived by the back door.

"Your brother's only thirteen, Renny."

"So?" She raised her head defiantly. The last time he'd seen her like this was just before Meg left. Angry with him, disappointed, officious. If he hadn't gotten sick he'd have been able to help her.

He shook his head and smiled. "You're my girl, you know that?" He lifted a thick manila envelope from the pile of mail and handed it to her. "You got something here from Philadelphia."

She frowned, and then he watched as a

brief flash of excitement and relief played across her face. She took the package from him and began to open it, but her shoulders stiffened and she dropped it back down on the table without glancing at what was inside. "What does that have to do with Danny not playing sports and not being able to drive a car?"

"Nothing," he said with an amused smile. "I think it has to do with your studies."

She winced.

Jack said, "Look, your brother is a different person than you. He has a different temperament. He's a little more sensitive about things, not in a big hurry like you were."

Her eyes welled up with tears. She leaned her head back and took a breath, and he felt a knot in his stomach. When she finally spoke it was with such jarring menace and vehemence he barely recognized her voice.

"I couldn't afford to be fucking sensitive. I had to get things done."

He took a step closer, brushed her hair away from her face, and looked into her eyes. They were heavy lidded, bloodshot, focused on something in the middle distance.

She looked like Peej had in '69. He came back hating and it took months for them to really talk again. All he could do was be there and try not to say something stupid, make sure bad evenings didn't become worse. Jack was there when PJ broke every piece of furniture in his apartment, talked out on the front stoop to the cops who'd been called about a disturbance of the peace. Jack had stood between Peej and people who "looked at him funny" or "were thinking bad things" on more than one occasion. Stood in front of oblivious strangers who were "asking for a beatdown." It took months. But Peej finally made it home, understood how he'd been screwed, had been a victim of the war. Jack and Meg went with him to Washington when he threw his medals back. The day he really became a soldier.

He held his daughter's chin and looked into her eyes. Lauren was taking everything on herself like she always did. But he was well now, he told himself again. He'd seen this kind of thing before and he could help her.

"Ah, sweetheart, it's true you had to get things done. I'm sorry you had so much to do for all of us. But it's really very different now."

She looked straight through him and he saw something else in her expression.

Hunger, he realized, feeling a deep well of shame in his stomach. She's hungry. At this he caught his breath and his eyes stung with tears and she turned her head away from him. He should have stayed home today and made sure she had three meals. This was her first day back and he'd left her all alone. He hadn't fed his child. He wiped his face quickly and straightened up, filled the tea kettle and put it on the stove, and put two bags of Red Rose into the chipped yellow teapot. "I plan on teaching Danny to drive pretty soon," he said casually, then asked, "What have you eaten today?"

She took a deep breath, her expression unchanged. "A Guinness, a Jameson's, and a piece of cake."

He opened the cupboard and put a box of crackers on the table, went to the refrigerator and got out cheese and peanut butter and an apple, and began making her the kind of snack she used to eat when she was four. He sliced the apple up and put it on a small blue plate and then made her some cheese and crackers, handed them to her one by one, and she ate them.

"You need a snack, Ren."

"I guess I do."

The kettle whistled and Jack poured the boiling water into the teapot and set it in the middle of the table. He was happy to see that it was just after four o'clock when they sat down. They'd had four o'clock tea since she was a baby. Her mother had even given it to her in a bottle, sweet and milky and a little bitter. It was one tradition that had survived the breakup.

"Are you going to open that package from Curtis?" he asked gently, trying to bring her back to the present for a moment.

"No. I am not."

He watched her take a long gulp of strong sweet tea. He had faith the taste would help restore some true and gentle way of being.

"Everyone feels out of sorts after a long trip," he said.

"What the fuck are you *talking* about?" she asked him incredulously, the restrained rage returning to her voice. "I didn't go on a long trip like some vacation to Costa Rica or something."

"No, you didn't. But it's important to remember your body is adjusting to the time zone and a different schedule and you're getting used to not having to do the kind of work you were doing."

She laughed though her teeth. "*Work?* Are you fucking crazy?"

"No," he said carefully, "I'm sorry. I don't know what to call it. We haven't really talked

207

about it."

She shook her head at him and he handed her a peanut-butter cracker, then a slice of apple. She ate them automatically and her expression didn't change.

"You don't know what to call it? What did PJ do?" she asked sarcastically. "Was he working hard out there in the jungle?"

Jack sat down at the table beside her. "I know Uncle P was really unhappy when he got home, like I told you yesterday. Maybe you'd like to talk to him, go over to the Nabe."

At this she laughed out loud. Looked right at him, her eyes clear and focused. "I'm not PJ. Understand? I didn't get drafted. I wasn't some sitting-target chump with eight weeks of basic. I enlisted. I was educated. I had people under my command. And just like you . . . JUST like YOU I am a beneficiary of this war. You get it? Don't think for a second I'm going to go sit at the Nabe with a group of fucking dipshits who think they're the ones who suffered. We got paid. YOU got paid. Motherfucking Freddie Mac and Chase got paid. If you never make another dime I've still saved enough to put Danny through state school and pay his rent until he graduates. I'm alive and there's not a scratch on my body. Does that sound like anything Uncle P went through?"

Jack poured more tea into her mug and she paused in her revilement to drink it. Color was starting to come back into her face, and even as she was admonishing him she looked more herself.

"Yeah, kinda," Jack said easily. "He came home without a scratch too, you know."

She looked at him blankly, spooned more sugar into her tea, cooled it with some milk, then drank the whole mug in a few gulps and set it on the table.

"I'm sorry I yelled," she said, the look of tired resignation returning to her face. Something in her had given up again, her moods shifting before he could adjust, before he could really respond to anything she'd said, but they were talking now and it was going to be all right.

He said, "It's okay, Low, there's a lot to yell about."

She just needed a snack and to be heard. He'd make dinner tonight and they would all be together. She was smart and strong and she was going to be fine. She was right, she'd been in a better position than Peej, he knew she would work through this. He was well and could see what was going on and he could help her now.

"Where did you get this thing?" she said,

finally picking up the manila envelope and tearing it all the way open. She glanced over the glossy cover page of the booklet and then let it fall back on the table.

"Someone jammed it in the mailbox," he said simply. "Looks like Curtis knows you're home. You been over to talk with your teacher?"

She looked at him with an expression somewhere between contempt and pity. Then got up abruptly and left the kitchen.

In her room Lauren thought about Meg. How Meg would get it about benefitting from war about making sacrifices about leaving people behind. She remembered how thcy would go for walks together after dinner in the neighborhood beneath the yellow streetlamps surrounded by fluttering night insects and they'd step over cracks in the sidewalk, arm in arm talking about things, about books like *Stuart Little* or *Cricket in Times Square.* They looked into the lighted windows of their neighbors' houses as they passed. Sometimes they'd walk far out to the blast wall. No. That wasn't right. There were no blast walls. Blast walls are in places at risk for shelling. Blast walls surround the FOB. And the perimeter of the rig. Why had she pictured it there at the outskirt of the neighborhood where it wasn't, where it would never be? They would walk far out until they could see the old paper mill. And they would skip back home, shoes scuffing on the sidewalk, singing songs that they played all the time on the radio. Her mother smelled like perfume from the drug store. She would talk about how she wanted to go to college and the boyfriends she had in high school. She was exciting to be around. Her mother was like someone young. Like a girl. Someone who needed a friend.

Lauren went into the bathroom to brush her teeth. When the dog came in she shut her eyes so she could pretend he wasn't there, leaned over and drank mouthfuls of cool water from the tap, and found herself wishing something that would have been inconceivable just days ago: wishing she had guard duty tonight. Wishing with all her might that she was back at Garryowen.

NINETEEN

Daryl Green was familiar to Lauren from the minute she met him on base. Green was not a complainer. He was a quiet, respectful and very funny man. The two of them were late to the party, he and Lauren. They'd each spent time Stateside taking courses and they occasionally got shit about it, her more than Daryl. But they weren't rich kids, weren't from the Citadel, nobody had pulled any strings for them; that's just the way it worked because of timing and training and for Lauren twice getting placed with a unit that was rotating back.

It was also about skill. You had a particular aptitude, you got sent to a particular school. She was glad for it. Lauren was an NCO at twenty-one, a fine shot, on track for career if she wanted it, making significantly more money than when she enlisted. And Green could speak Arabic and Farsi.

He was good and sharp and reading every

second of downtime he had. By the time she met him he was on his second tour, had subscriptions to *Dissent, The Nation, Counterpunch, Foreign Affairs,* and was talking about moving to Canada to live with his wife's family, getting a good job up north and then applying to law school when he got out. He was a far cry from the good old boy his parents had raised, but the accent and the love of guns remained.

It was the surge that changed things for Daryl. And it was the surge that he talked about, sometimes all he could talk about during their long nights on the FOB. Listening to him break things down was refreshing. She had no arguments with his ideas and kept the things he said to herself. He was glad to be there at Garryowen. Creeping the streets of someone else's destroyed city was not a thing he wanted to do. Getting out and going after the people who came up with that strategy was. Daryl was a warrior. And as far as justice and protecting his fellow soldiers was concerned, he had long-term plans.

"You fucking Green?" Godwin had asked her one evening when she got back from guard duty.

"Daryl's married," she said simply.

"Not my question," Godwin said. "That

213

boy is so fine. You don't want beauty like that to go to waste, do you?"

She hadn't thought about it. He was short, broad shouldered, all his features like straight lines. Thin lips, square jaw, eyebrows flat above his almond-shaped eyes. A roman nose. Everything about him even and level.

Lauren shrugged.

"You guys got some secret," Godwin said. "Everyone can see it."

TWENTY

The smell of coffee and the thick smoky overlay of bacon grease greeted Lauren as she stepped into Holly's house. Grace was sitting on the living-room floor in front of the television, cutting pieces of leftover wrapping paper into strips and taping them to the table legs. She was wearing pink footie pajamas. Holly's mother, Bridget, was so happy to see Lauren she got up and squeezed her tight, rocking her back and forth in her arms. Lauren smiled and put her arms around Bridget, rested her head on her bony shoulder.

"Is your daughter home?" Lauren asked.

"Now wait a minute," Bridget said. "Let me look at you." Her voice was raw and low, and she spoke at an almost comic clip, like a character in an old crime movie. She stepped back and regarded Lauren, holding her firmly by the shoulders. "I almost don't believe it. Let me just set eyes on you a little more."

"I'm glad to be back," Lauren said.

"I *bet* you are. Holly," she called. "Get down here!" She turned to Lauren again. "She's been sleeping. Closed the bar around three last night, poor girl. She's gotta get up anyways because my shift starts in a few hours and I know you two want girl time."

Gracie came running into the kitchen, and Bridget handed her a piece of bacon. "Hey, li'l gal, you know who this is?"

Grace shook her head.

"This is Lauren. You remember Lauren? She knew you when you were just a baby."

Grace shook her head again and took a bite of bacon.

Lauren said, "Pleased to meet you," and held out her hand for Grace to shake.

The girl looked like Holly. Shrewd, a tiny strategist.

"Pleased to meet you," the girl repeated.

At the end of tenth grade Grace's father still had a name, one that you could hear shouted from the bleachers surrounding the basketball court. Back then the tall languid boy in Hilfiger polos who would soon become Asshole was all about Holly: how funny she was, how street, how cool, such a bad girl, so smart, such a fast runner, how hot, how tough, how sweet, such an angel in her black miniskirt and neon tights, talking all wrong like his parents hated and getting the grades they wished he could get. She was a dangerous new species, not seen on the Southside. He had discovered her.

Asshole had house parties at his parents' big place for the whole team. He drove a black VW Golf with a Guinness bumper sticker because that was his brand and he drank nothing else. He was a dumb boy who would go to a good enough college because there was money for it and he loved Holly with the kind of desperation that made it clear he wished he was one of them. Longed for their shitty lives as though living in their neighborhood was a trip to Disneyland. He was delighted and awed by Shane's stark kitchen and the pictures of his tattooed uncles. You could tell he wished he was missing a mother or father, or better yet that someone had actually died so that he could look damaged and brave and wistful about it.

Lauren had never liked Asshole very much, and when Holly brought the two-pack pregnancy test over to her house in the afternoon, giddy and scared and laughing at how fucked up it was, Lauren pulled her into the bathroom immediately and shut the door so they wouldn't disturb Danny.

She waited while her friend peed on the stick and they set it on the side of the tub and waited some more.

"That's got to be wrong," Lauren said.

"Right?" Holly agreed.

"Open the other one," Lauren told her, filling a glass with water and handing it over for her to drink.

A couple hours later the other one said the same thing, and they sat together in Lauren's yellow room hostage to a kind of stunned dreadful excitement.

"This isn't going to stop me from doing anything," Holly said. "We're still going to get out."

Lauren held Holly's head in her lap while she cried.

Later the boy would comfort her, would tell her how they were both going to go to school and have a life and raise a baby, but by the time she was showing he'd seen enough.

Asshole's fantasy of running with a tough crowd made him a daddy at eighteen, but he lived somewhere else now. His mother babysat sometimes as a favor.

Holly ran down the carpeted stairs wearing a light windbreaker open to reveal a black shirt emblazoned with a pink skull and crossbones. Her hair up in a ponytail, five small silver hoops dangling along the edge of her ear. She picked up Grace and kissed her several times on the cheeks, then put her down and grabbed the car keys off the hook by the back door. Holly kissed Bridget and quietly said thank you.

"I want to go too!" Grace cried.

"Sorry, sweet stuff," Bridget said. "Grammy needs your help with something special."

"Please!" she shouted, as the back door slammed shut and Holly grabbed Lauren's hand and skipped down the stairs and out to her mother's dented turquoise Kia.

The car's interior smelled like candy and ashes and Handi Wipes.

"It's fucking sixty degrees out!" Holly shouted, as Lauren squeezed in and made room for her feet amidst the crushed and empty juice boxes that littered the floor of the passenger side.

"She likes to toss them up over the front seat when she's done," Holly explained, throwing some of the boxes into the back, laughing. "You sure you ready for the Salmon Run Mall?"

Lauren said, "Affirmative, girly-girl, I am a warrior. I am ready for anything. Except for this shit, what *is* this shit?"

"Nirvana," Holly said. "It's all my mom had in her car. I think we played musical chairs to this album at one of my birthday parties, right?"

"What's that guy's fucking problem?" Lauren asked, leaning forward to eject the CD, and then stopping herself because she knew Holly liked it. "He can't be serious," she said.

Holly pulled out into traffic and then flipped the visor down and a pack of Newports fell into her lap. She punched in the lighter and offered the pack to Lauren, who took two and lit them. The seamlessness, the autonomic actions were a comfort. Life was made up of millions of small repetitive motions and words, and the repetition alone built a human being; loading a magazine, slipping the ceramic plate into your vest, over your chest, routine, reflexive, comforting.

It was a pleasure to smoke, a bad-kid thing she could rarely do in high school because of training. Lauren leaned back and listened to the end of Kurt Cobain's mordant whining, then clicked over to WJNY where strings were playing. Warm undertones like a human voice, a precision and competence that made her feel more relaxed, like someone knew what the hell they were doing. Holly laughed, shook her head, tapped her cigarette against the ashtray. "I was thinking about what a freak you were about music just yesterday," she said. "Freak!" she screamed, like she used to in fourth grade. "Oh my god, you're really HOME!" Holly took her hands off the wheel and waved them around and they both screamed out the windows.

"Oh my god, dude, I'm sorry, but this crap isn't any better than Nirvana," Holly said. She pulled onto the freeway and Lauren broke into a sweat, leaned away from the door. She felt naked without a radio and her gear, and visibility was bad in the light fog. They were goners. She wished she were drunk or believed in God. Some benevolent God that had created her in his image; had spared her so she could buy shit at the mall and get in fights. She thought of Troy singing *My soul doth magnify the Lord* and felt she understood the words for the first time. All year she'd been magnifying the Lord, reflecting back something that didn't exist, becoming stronger and richer and emptier. Troy was wrong: They were powerful words. A true prayer.

Holly gave her a funny look. "I know this road," she said. "It's safe. Hey, check it out."

She put the cigarette in the corner of her mouth and began talking; this was how she made fun of her stepdad, Dave, who would hold a butt in the side of his mouth until it was practically all ash.

"So," Holly said in muffled stoic tone. "You got them parts ordered over from Nichols?"

"Yep. Yep," Lauren said, less tense, laughing a little. "S'posed to was they'd be here 'bout Wednesday."

" 'Fraid I can't do much 'til then, then," Holly said, making the cigarette bob comically as she spoke. "You want me you know where to find me. Ain't had much work in what, oh, six, seven, maybe thirty-seven weeks . . ."

"Nope. Not much," Lauren said, then she broke into her own voice again. "Man, that's so fucking weird that your mom ever married him," she said. "Isn't it?"

Holly nodded. "You know he was in the same unit as Troy?"

"That can't be right," Lauren said. "Troy is like a fucking genius."

Holly said, "*Troy* is a genius? Oh, wait. Are you joking?"

"No. Troy is a genius."

Holly raised her eyebrows and said slowly, "Dave was in the same unit with Troy in

Kuwait, and he said Troy is a retard."

"That doesn't even make sense," Lauren said.

"You *know* he is."

Lauren shook her head.

"Well, whatever," Holly said, "him and Dave go way back and Dave said he was retarded."

"Right." Lauren nodded slowly. *"Dave* said."

"What do you think of Patrick?" Holly asked, changing the subject.

"Which one?"

"Patrick," Holly said, laughing out a cloud of smoke.

Lauren did not like the sound of this question. "I think he's a forty-five-year-old alcoholic who still gets in fistfights, lives in a rooming house, pretends he reads books by reading their introductions, spends all his money the day he gets it, and eats and does laundry at his sister's house."

"But he's still good-looking, right? Strong from lifting all those bundles all day," she said hopefully. "The ladies want to get with him."

"But they don't want to stay with him. Have you ever seen the inside of his place? It's horrifying, smells like mold, stacks of papers everywhere, always a few dozen empty bottles on the floor. And all this incredibly pretentious shit hanging all over the walls, framed photos of guys playing chess, pictures of philosophers he ripped off the backs of books and thumbtacked up around his bed, it's fucking bizarre."

She could see by the embarrassed, knowing resignation on Holly's face that her friend had indeed seen the inside of Patrick's room.

Lauren opened her mouth to say something and then just shrugged.

"Ahh!" Holly shouted, pointing at her and laughing so Lauren could see the vein sticking out in her forehead. "I'm just fucking with you," Holly said. "Seriously, oh my god, your face!" She tossed her cigarette out the window. "Anyway. Speaking of Troy," she said. "My mom ran into your dad at the Tops and he told her you were prolly going to be going to music school."

"He's fucking delusional," Lauren said. "Danny's got five more years of school left here."

"No, he said *you* were going to music school."

"I heard what you said," Lauren told her.

The Salmon Run Mall comprised vacant cavernous spaces, weird half-empty shops that sold only seasonal stuff, and three different dollar stores. It seemed to have shrunk while she was away. But what hadn't changed was the soldiers walking around; plain faces and tight bodies in jeans and their army T-shirts, some of them wearing camo. Sitting at tables in the food court, standing in the arcade, like high-school kids, which is what they were maybe just months ago. Soldiers were a familiar feature of growing up in Watertown, and she'd always thought of them as older, rugged, dedicated people. Now they looked hopelessly green, vacant and restless and bland like physical manifestations of the mall itself. She stood and watched them as Holly waited in line for coffee and thought about the FOB. About all the cheaply constructed structures that were built to warehouse people like her all over the world. Places to store them like meat and send them out like butchers; neat, efficient, working-class folks who served the demands of a hungry population and over time would get used to the smell of blood.

Holly came back with their coffees and they sat on a bench outside the bookstore.

"It's great your dad's back at work, huh? You can prolly spend a lot more money."

"Yeah, I dunno how much he's actually bringing in. But there's groceries at least."

"He must be making a lot of money being a therapist."

Lauren laughed.

"They make a lot of money, right? It costs so much to go to them," Holly said.

"He's at a clinic with a sliding scale so you can pay like five bucks if you need to."

"No shit?"

"Yeah. You've never gone to counseling?"

"Why would I do that?" Holly asked, looking at Lauren with a perfectly blank expression. She waited until Lauren was about to say something and then burst out laughing again, the sound echoing in the empty hollow space.

They headed to Claire's Boutique, where everything was pink and sparkling and easy for middle-school girls to pocket. Lauren bought a pile of barrettes and hair clips and bracelets for Gracie, and whatever else Holly said she liked, even if Holly said, Don't get it. They went to the sporting goods store where Lauren bought things for Danny. Sweats and sneakers and shirts and more cold-weather gear.

They went to Bon-Ton and tried on dresses. Calling to one another from behind the flimsy white doors of the fitting rooms.

Holly chatted with the women who worked there, she moved easily about the store, browsing through the racks. She bought a pair of red corduroy overalls for Grace.

Lauren thought about how everyone was something else back home and she needed to slip back into another skin to walk among them. She thought about Sue Godwin and Danielle Apelt, the soldiers she lived with in Amarah. She thought about how Danielle re-upped after her husband was laid off. How when they were not out on patrol or searches, or at the checkpoint, they just hung in the containerized housing unit and everything was pullups and Skype and shitty movies. She'd heard so much about Danielle's kids she felt like she'd yelled at their teachers and taken them to visit Gettysburg herself, grounded them for smoking pot, bought them soccer cleats halfway through the year because their feet kept getting so goddamn big. They heard one another talking to their moms and dads and kids and boyfriends and sisters and brothers and husbands, and they heard each other never once mentioning the details of the day. She remembered Sue Godwin pale and still shaken from an IED that didn't miss the truck in front of her, nodding as she listened to her aunt talk about getting a new grill for the deck and how they were going to make pork bellies when she got home. She thought about what they might be doing now. Sue was back in Beal City, Michigan. Danielle had another year. Daryl was home.

He'd described the place so well she felt like she knew it. Said when he was done in Iraq they were going to Canada, to Camille's parents, build a house nearby with his combat pay, and he would work on a rig or logging just long enough to make real money. Lauren listened to the way he talked about Camille and their boy. She seemed like such a good mother. Exactly the kind of mother you'd want. And she'd put up with Daryl, living in the States and down south too — and now they were finally going to get to be where she wanted — where they both wanted, up north where things are beautiful and untouched and still a little wild. He'd grinned as he described it, popping the last of a Thank U Berry Munch Girl Scout cookie into his mouth.

"These Girl Scouts are some bloodthirsty, supporting-the-troops motherfuckers, aren't they?" he said earnestly, offering her one. "We run outta chow here we'll prolly still have the energy to keep on killing 'cause of Peanut Butter Patties and Savannah

Smiles."

"Speaking of killing, you pick up that lanyard for your pistol yet? As I may have mentioned every single fucking day for the last three and a half weeks, that weapon needs to be attached."

"Oh, we've become very attached."

She said, "Do it, motherfucker. I'm not the one getting shit if that thing goes missing."

"You dressing me down, Sar'n?" He looked into her eyes long enough for them to feel it. These looks could feed you for a week.

"Ah. Anyway," Daryl said, his voice suddenly hoarse, quieter, "what was I saying? Oh yeah, oil's the big employer up north too, which is good. I don't know if by the time I get through here I'll want to work on those rigs, or blow them sky high."

Lauren smiled. "You'll be well prepared to do either," she said.

He nodded, his face sweet and earnest. "That's right, Sar'n Clay, it's all about options."

There was a pop and sirens. Then flares went up over the CHU and the dark outside was suddenly brighter than day.

She said, "Move, soldier." And followed him out and down.

■ ■ ■ ■

After-Christmas shoppers were walking
through the mall with bored vacant faces,
carrying bags of things they were returning
or hurrying to buy even more, compelled
by postholiday sales, pushed to spend by
boredom. Lauren recognized the military
wives from Fort Drum too. Some of them
with their guys and some alone. The mall
was like an ethereal plane between war and
commerce and real life where they could
take shelter. They were shadows of themselves, meandering the food court, the
hungry left-behind wives accumulating
some comforting pounds, trying to put flesh
on a feeling of not being there at all.

Holly stood and talked to a pregnant
woman for a few minutes, laughing and
nodding knowingly. She touched the woman's stomach and Lauren felt herself recoil,
nearly gag. She looked away. Her friend
could do all the simple stuff that didn't
seem so simple anymore.

When Holly came into the dressing room
to see what Lauren was trying on, she
seemed shocked, said, "I didn't know you
had those tattoos."

Lauren had gone with Sue Godwin to get

the second and third one. Godwin got the badge of their unit and an Irish harp. She missed Godwin. She remembered dressing to go out, the way they sealed one another into their armor, how she snapped the neck protector on to Godwin's vest. Even under seventy pounds of gear there were gaps at the sides and at their armpits, at their waists. There were places small as a grace note from which they could be dispatched.

Lauren looked down at her arms quickly, then shrugged. "Yeah," she told Holly. "I got these about a month ago."

"They're kinda ugly," Holly said. She pulled a Twizzlers out of her jacket pocket and handed it to Lauren, saying, "Eat this," then she stuck one in her own mouth.

As they walked with their bags down the wide tiled thoroughfare of shops and abandoned spaces headed for the parking lot, they heard the first chords of the carolers.

Holly grabbed Lauren around the waist and squeezed her excitedly at the sound. "It's you!" she said.

They followed the music, and there outside the Payless shoe store a group of high schoolers in red blazers stood bright and square shouldered, holding black choir folders. Lauren and Holly stopped walking and stood before them, two in an audience of eight, four of whom had crew cuts and tight shirts. Holly chewed absently on her strawberry licorice, but Lauren was transfixed.

They were singing "O Holy Night" a cappella and she felt her heart race, remembering the solo. Their attentive faces and round mouths were beautiful. Their voices were filled with a kind of airy richness and innocence. Their voices were sweet and resonant and wholly, sloppily distinguishable from one another, like little sheep stumbling and running side by side. Here and there an individual voice cut distinctly through to lead a section, then dropped back and blended in an attempt to unify the sound.

The flaws in phrasing and missed entrances and wrong notes were actually lovely. Exciting and funny and interesting, like hearing someone learning how to speak, like watching Danny in the bouncy castle. The harmonies perfect and the disharmonies perfect. Their breathing in unison as if they were one and the real joy on their faces.

"Fall on your knees!" they commanded in crescendo. *"O hear the angel voices!"*

Lauren closed her eyes and inhaled sharply a beat before the solo. A tiny chubby girl with a short bob haircut and bright pink lip gloss sang from where she stood amidst the choir. Her voice full and high and honeyed. Her voice like a golden bell that called Lauren away, out of this place, out of her skin, and far from the fear and waiting. Far from the dust rising in the distance.

"That's you," Holly whispered again beside her.

TWENTY-ONE

The house phone was ringing when she walked in the door with her packages and she was too distracted to remember not to pick it up.

"I'm so glad to hear your voice!" her mother said, and the only word Lauren could think to respond with was, "Really?"

"Really." Meg Clay laughed. "Oh, Sweetie. And I would *really* love it if you and Danny could come here for a few days. I'm on semester break and we could do some fun things."

"Yeah? What kind of fun things are there to do in Buffalo?"

"Oh, I don't know. We could go to the philharmonic or we could go to the Allen Street Dress Shop."

"I'm sure Dan would love that."

"Honey, I thought maybe *you* would like that."

"You put a lot of thought into what I

might like."

Her mother was quiet and it seemed they were both waiting for Lauren to say the next part of the sentence. So she did: "You must have thought I'd like raising the son you left behind."

She listened to her mother exhale but could already tell she wasn't really upset at all. "Lauren," she said clearly, with no shame, no hint of unhappiness, "I am very sorry that you were hurt when I moved away." It was as if Meg was a prisoner who had to periodically restate her crime in public. Lauren hated that she was the one who made her do it, but she couldn't stop.

"In the middle of the night," Lauren finished the sentence. "And stayed away without calling for a year and never checked on us. How long does it take to go to fucking college? Don't professors make money they can send to their children? And now you think that I am going to talk to you on the phone and go to your house and let you be an influence on my brother."

There was a pause and Lauren could picture her mother nodding, again. Could picture the curve of her face and her lipstick, her thin frame, even the word "Meg," the cute curt name seemed filled with indifference. Lauren knew it did take time to go to college and that Meg had only been an adjunct professor for years, that she had student loans to pay and worked part time at a diner, but still she couldn't stop herself from saying those things. She hated that Meg was impervious to her words.

"I love you," Meg said firmly. "I have always loved you and Danny. But sometimes leaving makes the most sense, does the least damage. Sometimes it's the better option."

Lauren said nothing.

When Meg asked, "Are you still singing?" Lauren hung up the phone.

Danny woke up at noon and she was standing in his doorway with sweats and sneakers. She'd packed the cold-weather camping supplies, a case of water and water-purifying tablets, thermal underwear, and the best insulated boots she could find for both of them in the trunk of the car. She tossed the running gear on his bed. "Merry Christmas again," she said, and he smiled sleepily at her, his hair wild looking and face lined from the rumpled sheet.

She clapped her hands together. "Let's go, kid."

He rolled over and groaned, so she went and sat next to him on the bed.

"Danny. C'mon, man, for real, let's go.

Time to go for a run."

"It's raining again," he said sleepily. This was the thing she couldn't stand. The not listening, not doing what she said when she said it. Lauren had become very used to instant obedience and she liked it. She knew it was different back home, but she didn't care. It was safer if everyone listened to her.

"That's all right, c'mon, we'll go down by the river. I was just out, it's not bad."

He sat up and leaned against the head-board looking dazed. She knew he'd been awake until three, transfixed in front of the Internet. She wondered if he ever went out or had friends over. He seemed to be in constant contact with them but it was entirely online. Did they do anything out-side? Did they tramp through the neighbor-hood like she did when she was a kid?

He rubbed his eyes and got out of bed and she high-fived him. "Good man," she said. "There's no snow on the ground, we can bring Sebastian."

He laughed, and then she remembered the dog was dead and made herself laugh too.

She waited for him in the living room, stretching on the floor in front of the Christmas tree, and when he came down she handed him a cup of coffee.

"After this we'll go out driving."

"Really?"

"Hell yeah, you learn how to drive now and you'll be ahead of everyone."

He looked genuinely excited, and she felt it too, excited and relieved. They headed out the back door and cut through the lots that led to the river. It was barely raining, just a light mist on their faces. She felt amazing moving her body through the cool back streets.

She could tell as soon as she'd gotten home that Danny was out of shape. He was a strong kid but easily winded, not used to physical exertion. He kept up with her pace but, after just ten blocks, stopped and started walking. He looked exhausted and was shivering from the cold rain. He drew his hands inside his sweatshirt and she became silently furious with her father. With his school. With PJ. With Exxon, Mobil, Shell, Halliburton. And then finally furious with herself, where the feeling found its home and she knew this was entirely her fault. She should have gotten him swimming lessons at the very least. Should have made sure he was playing on a team, found a way to take him to real places, should have taught him how to do things instead of just reading all the time. He'd never been out of the state. He'd never seen the ocean.

She jogged back and forth beside him while he walked.

"You're doing great, man!" She stopped and put her arm around his shoulder. "Let's just get down by the river and then we'll go a little slower, okay?"

He nodded and then stretched up and took a deep breath and began running beside her again. She made sure he could see her smile. Made sure he'd keep running to make her proud. After this they would spend one more day here and then head north to meet Daryl. She'd keep it a surprise, otherwise he'd start looking things up online and then nothing they did would be new. There would be pictures and stupid Web articles and satellite maps and reviews and recommendations and he'd have no reason to use his brain or have the slightest feeling of being on his own. Thrust into a new experience with all its promise and excitement and danger, he'd be able to become himself. He'd be free.

Twenty-Two

That night Lauren woke from the sound of something heavy scraping past the outside sill of her window.

She was completely alert and silent, took her gun out from beneath the pillow and stood quickly, pressing her back against the wall, waiting. Another thump against the side of the house. She looked to see if Sebastian was there, which would mean she was dreaming and didn't have to take this so seriously; otherwise she would have to make sure the house and nearby buildings were clear. Sebastian wasn't in the room.

Something hit the window with a click. Someone whistled a signal, or part of a song. She lifted the edge of the curtain and could see a figure outside standing in the driveway, looking up.

She left her room and ducked into the hall, checked Danny's room, made sure it was clear, shut his door, went downstairs where the lights of the Christmas tree were glowing brightly in the dark, reflecting off the ceiling and bookshelves all around. She cleared the downstairs, the basement laundry room. Near the back door of the kitchen she silently pushed her bare feet into her combat boots. With no sound at all she turned the lock and slipped into the yard. She was fast and light in her boots and sweats, but twice as careful without her Kevlar vest. She wished she had her night-vision gear, willed herself to see in the dark, crept along the driveway, and stood in the shadow of her father's car. Then she raised her gun and waited. The figure threw what looked like a shoe at her window.

She aimed at its head, exhaled the air from her lungs, then it turned, revealing Shane's face. Startled, its hands moved in jerky reflexive motions, lanky arms and elbows raised to protect itself from something that would rip right through it. Dispatch it from one minute to a definitive next, with a flat pop.

She lowered the gun quickly and jammed it back into her sweatshirt pocket. "You are the stupidest motherfucking human being on the planet," she said, then took a deep breath and turned away from him, sickened at the idea of his life ending below her

241

window.

When she looked at him again he was clearly still shaken. He came over and was about to put his arms around her but didn't. "I'm sorry," he said, his breath thick with alcohol. "I thought I'd do like old times."

She forced herself to keep her hands at her sides because she wanted to grab him. Her muscles ached to make contact. To shove him, to take him down, force him to the ground, get her knee in his back.

"I thought you'd be up," he said, and he looked pale and disheveled in the moonlight.

Lauren nodded. He was right about that. She didn't experience anything close to sleep anymore. The driveway shone in the glow of the streetlamps, puddles holding the reflection of the pale globes and telephone wires. It wasn't cold at all.

"What do you want?" she asked him. And really, what the fuck could he possibly want from her that she could actually give?

"Just to hang out," he said, reaching for her hand. "Come on."

They cut through the backyard and climbed over the chainlink fence at the dead-end street that ran perpendicular to Arsenal. People's houses were dark and their yards looked silver when the clouds separated enough to let moonlight reach them.

He brought a small bottle of whiskey out from his jacket pocket, took a sip, and handed it to her.

"I didn't get to say welcome home," he said as she drank, filled her mouth with the warm burn of cheap alcohol.

"Are you kidding?" she asked, and let herself smile. "You were my one-man welcome home party."

The grass was wet and soaked their shoes as they set out on their regular route, backyards they'd run through in high school, rarely buzzed but often giddy with being together. Something about being the good kids in their class made night adventures so gratifying. They were anthropologists in the land of rotting porches and construction refuse, scientists of the black pinpricked blanket of sky they strode beneath.

Other kids in their classes came from the Southside and lived in big houses, their dads worked at the hospital or had some important job on base. But she and Shane were different. Back then they were kept safe under the reputation of the Patricks, were determined to do the right thing and be nothing like their burnout neighbors, nothing like their stuck-up classmates. Despite their efforts it hadn't quite worked out.

Small differences could have made up for so much, she thought. Shane should have been raised by her gentle dad, who'd have been proud of where he went to school. She should have been raised by his mom because that lady was so practical, had a whole family surviving on what she made as a secretary and part time at the phone bank.

But they were there now walking along the sidewalk and she was as alert as any animal or soldier could be, holding his hand, and inside her pocket holding her gun. She could clear the whole town tonight if she had to. Make sure it was safe.

Down at the edge of the Black River they threw rocks and chunks of concrete in the water. Shane picked up plastic bottles and bits of garbage and sticks and made two little boats out of them, poking them out into the current with a long piece of wire he'd found on the ground. She watched as they bobbed along in the rippling water, then took out her gun and sank them with one clean shot and then another.

When they got home she told him to come inside, and they sat on the low couch in the pretty glow of the Christmas tree and she stretched out and put her head in his lap like she used to. They would read that way sometimes on the weekends. Him sitting up and her lying down, quiet all day. She knew he always got more out of reading than she did. He and Danny were alike that way. She was good at math and music and track but had an awful memory. Shane was good at thinking. Eventually he'd stretch out beside her and they would kiss and touch and sleep.

He put his hands on her hair and looked into her face, then he took off his glasses and set them on the coffee table. He looked exhausted and confused and sad. She realized she hadn't even thought about what he'd been doing or studying.

"How's school?" she asked.

"Good," he said, smiling softly, and she could see just mentioning it made him feel better. "I still love it. I never want to come home." He said nothing for a while and she could see him thinking, laughing a little to himself. "Do you ever notice how we talk? We have an accent."

"Aw shit, you should hear some of the folks coming out of Benning," she said. "It's ridiculous. We don't have one, maybe I talk funny now, but you don't have one at all."

"No." He said, "I do, believe me. And I can finally hear it. Not as bad as my uncles but it's there, all the 'a's are flat. I use expressions other people never heard before. I don't think I realized the word 'pro-bab-ly' had three syllables and two 'b's in it. We might be champions here, babe, but we're not even well read out there."

"Out fucking *where*?" she asked, her voice low and filled with disappointment and exhaustion. "Who the fuck cares what some rich kids read before you did? Or how they talk? They don't even know how to fucking think. They read about someone getting stabbed in Shakespeare or killed in a war or arrested or something, it's nothing to them. They can't feel it so they don't really understand it. How can you care at all what people like that think? They don't know a thing."

He stroked her hair calmly and looked into her eyes, studying her even as he was taking pleasure in touching her. "It's not about them," he said easily. "It's about us and what we can do. They always do the same thing out of callousness or ignorance, I get that, I see it — but we have to do something different, right? You gotta watch the way you think about this stuff, Low. I just heard something pretty similar coming out of Patrick's mouth earlier."

"Aw fuck you, Shane." Being compared to his uncles was the lowest insult, and he'd never said anything like it before.

"No, baby," he said, his voice heavy and languid, "I punched Patrick in the fucking mouth last night for a decision he made thirty years ago that's still a weight around my mother's neck. And I was glad I hit him." He laughed to himself. "Glad. But then I started thinking how I'd never known what he was like before he got back from the Gulf, and all that shit they say about depleted uranium or traumatic stress. I thought maybe he really was going to go back to school but couldn't make himself do it. I never saw it as clearly as I do now."

She was not surprised to hear he'd hit Patrick. That man was decades overdue for a beatdown from his nephew. "That's probably the nicest thought you've ever had about him," Lauren said. "But let me assure you that guy was cut out to be an asshole. Troy was over there twenty years ago and he's one of the best educated people I know. It's Patrick, not the war. Even before he had to go hand out lice combs to POWs or play checkers or whatever the hell they had those fuckers doing back in 1990, he was messed up."

Shane said, "Right, no, I know Patrick is a fuckup but just listen to me for a minute, okay? You got the same kind of decision to make. Same as Patrick and same as my mother both. It's no wonder you're all I can think about. I must be crazy. School is where we belong. I know this and you don't yet. For some reason you don't or won't get that through your goddamn head. Baby, the worst day there is better than the best day here."

She nodded but wanted him to leave. The privilege of talking about good and bad days disgusted her. She didn't think he knew much about bad days. And she was not about to describe one to him.

She'd come home to a world of fragile baby animals. Soft inarticulate wide-eyed morons with know-nothing epiphanies and none of them — not one of them — did what she said, which was beginning to grate on her, cut to the heart of how wrong things were. Still, she could accept that these people didn't know how to lead or follow, but they could at least shut up. If anyone owed her anything for serving in Iraq it was to shut the fuck up.

Shane's gentleness was wasted on her, was incommensurate to the task of holding the person she had become: a thief who was greedily breathing and walking and seeing and fucking and eating, greedily laughing at her brother's jokes, greedily washing the dishes, or strolling through the mall with her friend. It was all for her, and none for them, the folks that don't come home. None for them ever again.

He stroked her arm, his face against her neck. She struggled not to give in to his languid way. He said very quietly into her ear, "I don't claim to understand what it's like," and she breathed in the warm sweet scent of him and absently laced her fingers through his while he kissed her softly on the neck, put his lips so lightly against hers. She felt her throat close, thought again of the people who came back and the people who didn't, and how she had no right to cry. Beneath the colored lights of the Christmas tree in the dim, musty, book-lined living room she held sweet Shane Murphy's hand for what she hoped would be the very last time.

TWENTY-THREE

December 28th, 4 a.m.
The Bag of Nails

It was hard to believe a place could hold an entire life. A town. A building. Everything you'd done or said or wanted or tried was somehow contained in that space, spread out, every surface imperceptibly covered with what's been lost.

People shouldn't be so attached to the material world. You think your long habit of living; your words, your breath, your dreams are contained in the places you've been or the objects you've touched, you think some evidence of you has grown like lichen, crystallized like frost, accumulating over the wide plank boards and the tables and floors, the barstools and glasses and windows and taps, until your transparent presence becomes the place itself. And the place resonates with this charged silence of everything you'd left unsaid or undone. A madrigal from an invisible choir.

But none of that is true. Nothing can contain you. And this is easy to prove. Easy to show. You don't *need* anything, the very suggestion . . . the very fucking suggestion after all this time, that you need anything from anyone. And this place. You need it least of all.

They don't see how it is after everything is gone. How you sit and watch and move and think and dream and all the while you are burning; an eternal flame; everyone else's symbol, your pain.

And at some point it becomes obvious that there's no other option but to light the way. To show them the fate of every cell; show them what awaits each vulgar object infused with spurious grace.

And there in the rising heat and rush and pop of whole towns delicately changing into white and orange petals thin as a ghost's tattered shawl, they might at last understand what that vow you took really means.

What it means to be a guardian of freedom.

To deploy, engage, and destroy.

TWENTY-FOUR

Deana answered Shane's call on the first ring as the late-morning sun was coming through the window of his boyhood room. She said, "Hi baby, how's break going?" and he smiled when he heard her voice and lay back on the narrow, spent bed, dehydrated but the aspirin was starting to kick in. He'd left Lauren's around three and barely slept after that because of sirens in the neighborhood. He'd been waiting for a reasonable hour to call her.

He said, "Tell me about yours, because it's probably way more fun."

She laughed. "It's good. Good. Good. Sooo happy not to have any papers to write, my god. I think I forgot what it's like to just talk to normal people. I can gladly report I've not heard anyone mention poststructuralism, originary censorship, or the discursive limits of sex in over a week."

He smiled. "Neither have I."

"My mom says she's sorry you couldn't be here," Deana said. "It's so pretty. We're going cross-country skiing later. Oh my god, you should see this: I'm standing at the back door and my nephews are outside building this giant snow thing, they jammed the carrot in too low I swear — it looks like a snowman with a carrot penis." She started laughing. "Hold on . . ." Her voice got muffled and he heard her calling to her mother, then a chorus of laughs. "Okay, I'm back. I have to get a picture of this. I'll send it to you in a second. Oh my god . . . so funny. How are things going there?"

"Well . . ." he said, half laughing, "there's no snow here. It's been raining all week. Um, I got in kind of a bar fight with one of my uncles, I've been drunk for about twenty-four hours, and, uh, Lauren is home from Iraq."

She paused. "Oh my god, baby," she said. Then: "Wait. Really?

"Really."

"Are you okay?"

"I . . . yeah. I guess. I mean, this is how it is here."

She said nothing for a moment, then finally, compassionately, "You must be so relieved, at least about Lauren. How is she?"

"Not quite herself. She almost shot me

accidentally last night, and then we walked around getting drunk."

She laughed nervously. "Wait, you're making all this up. C'mon, Shane, stop kidding."

He said, "I'm not," and immediately regretted telling her anything because he could hear the tension in her voice now.

"Jesus," she said. "Are you okay? Why don't you come here?"

"I'd love to but I need to deal with this stuff."

"Shane, what stuff? It's been almost a year since you even talked. For god's sake, you've both been seeing other people for four years now. We've been 'us' for almost a year."

He blinked. The only person he was seeing when he closed his eyes was Lauren Clay, and that hadn't changed. He loved Deana. She was quick and funny and driven. Gracious in the way of people who have been well cared for but not entitled. Not arrogant. He could talk to her for hours, and she was smarter than any person he'd met. When he thought about it he knew he would be with her. There was no question. She was better suited to him. They had the same plans, same goals.

But he could not want her the way he wanted Lauren. That way where there was no need to talk at all. Some preverbal love.

A loyalty that had nothing to do with sex that he couldn't shake if he tried. They were tied.

"It's not just Lauren," he said, and his voice broke and his chest ached when he said it. For whatever reason she was no longer the girl he knew, and the thing that bound them was some black Irish nonsense neither of them had yet managed to escape. "I have to be here this week for my mother," he said, and he was suddenly, horrifyingly aware she was the only thing that stood between him and the path Lauren Clay had taken. His own abilities and his intelligence had barely meant a thing. He knew that he loved Lauren because she had been like his mother, doting on a boy who would soon be too spoiled to realize what she'd done for him. Spoiled and neglected in that way that breeds contempt. Putting her voice aside so she could pay the bills. Keeping her head down, keeping everyone safe. No one had ever suspected there was something wrong with her because she seemed to have it all together, and what could they have done for her anyway? He would not be that boy that carried contempt for another minute.

He said, "I love you, D." Then he hung up

and called his mother at work to tell her the same.

That's when he found out what had caused last night's sirens.

"She's stable," his mother said. "I think they're letting visitors in."

TWENTY-FIVE

December 28

Lauren was tired and rattled and hadn't slept but she still made it out the door for a run before her father and Danny woke. She'd meant to go for only a few miles, but once she got out there was no real reason to stop. Maybe she would never stop, never be able to get it out of her system. Last night hadn't helped.

She ran along the river toward the industrial park at a light jog. Entered into the rhythm of her body, her breathing, her heart. Felt light and fast and slightly nervous running without a gun, without a vest, without gear and other sets of eyes nearby.

It was disorienting, not the wide flat enclosed space of the FOB, sand and dust getting into everything, every tiny corner. In winter when it rained the stuff became like wet clay, a heavy mess, weighing them down even more. She thought about the vastness of the space and low fortified concrete buildings. The cold comfort of the bunker and blast walls and looking out beyond the high fence at the expanses of nothing — paranoid when any man or animal wandered into range. The way fear and boredom could become one, could become anger, could become some kind of holy distance. Fear and boredom in the tents and containerized housing units, fear and boredom beneath the floodlights and satellite dishes. And all around them the expanses of gravel and dust-colored, dust-covered vehicles. The towering rigs in the distance. The landscape spread flat around them, here and there a date palm rising out of the distant sand like a solitary element from paradise set down in the middle of hell's staging ground. She could feel it all as she ran. That sense that they were baking in some slow fire. The smell of diesel fuel and shit and things burning, and inside the CHUs the smell of sweat and soap and Pine-Sol and coffee and the ubiquitous motherfucking never-ending supply of Girl Scout cookies.

She thought about Daryl and Walker.

She thought about how the whole thing had taken less than ten minutes, but now every single detail seemed to have its own lifetime. A fifteen-minute loop for Walker adjusting his glasses. An hour for opening a car door. A whole day for blood. A single sentence spoken thirty days ago that never came to an end.

Dust rose from a road in the distance, a long beige cloud being towed by a short smoke-colored car. It seemed to hover above the ground, its tires invisible. She heard the sound of her own voice shouting "Vehicle." Looked up at Daryl and Walker. Daryl was on it. Walker had just gotten there a week ago, replaced someone's kid who'd had his arms and face burned off. Walker was a dumbass fuck and belonged back in Granite Shoals, working at the Cracker Barrel grocery. He raised his rifle but there was no way in hell she was going to let him fire it. That order was not his.

"Haji's in a very big hurry," Daryl said to her.

He called out in Arabic over the megaphone, "Stop or you will be shot," and she raised her rifle. The air rippled in front of her and she kept her eye on the approach, fired the warning that should have halted the car. But nothing.

Walker watched, and she could hear his breathing change in excitement. The high tone of his voice when he spoke made her feel pity and disgust. He said, "Aw, my fucking god, what is this stupid motherfucking piece of shit doing?"

"This guy wants his virgins," Daryl said calmly. "Sar'n Clay gonna ruin his day if he don't slow down though, isn't that right?"

She nodded. "Roger that." She had a steady bead on the windshield above the steering wheel but couldn't yet see him. She felt the determination of the driver. He wanted something that was different from what she'd felt before. Daryl's voice rang out again with the promise the driver would be shot. And the vehicle seemed to pick up speed, as if the warnings were calls to hurry. She ignored the sounds of terror-stricken exuberance coming from Walker.

Adjusted her aim, emptied her lungs. A second took a year to pass and then she fired. A loud pop and tick and the windshield blew out at about the same time as the driver's-side window. The car sped up, swerved. They hit the ground, bracing for explosives, but the car just smashed against the barricade, scraped and ground against a low concrete reinforcement, the horn blaring. She looked up at her men, felt a manic burst of laughter leave her mouth, then stood again. The car's wheels were spinning. It was not on fire, but she and Daryl knew that didn't mean a thing.

■ ■ ■ ■

When she passed the sign for the Jefferson County Highway Department she realized she'd gone too far and had no memory of getting there. No memory of the road or cars that had passed. No memory of the Black River. She was maybe seven miles from home, the sky was getting light, and she was headed to Burrville in the cold morning air. She felt like she could run another hundred miles but turned back. Cut into the neighborhood at North Massey Street.

When she got home she was soaked with rain and sweat. She ignored the dog because he was dead and then went to stand in the hot shower for a long time, letting it scald her skin so that she could make the call.

Even exhausted and repentant she almost hung up when Meg answered. But she made herself say hello, say she was sorry. She lay across her father's bed looking up at the stucco ceiling while her mother talked, while her mother said she understood, and that she was sorry too.

"Sorry for what?" Lauren asked.

"Sorry you're not feeling well."

Lauren shut her eyes and knew the call was a mistake, but she would get through it for Danny's sake.

Her mother said, "Honey, you should think about taking a break and going somewhere nice."

"Like where?"

"Somewhere where you can relax, where you can read and think and see beautiful things."

Lauren laughed at the thought. It would have been really funny if someone who knew her said this, but hearing it from Meg just made her sad. "Where would that be?" she said simply. "You want me to leave my family now that I'm finally home?"

"I want you to do what you want," Meg said. "What you actually want. Not something for anybody else."

"You said you missed me before, but from *when*?" Lauren demanded, changing the subject. "From ten years ago? How could you even miss me because I was in Amarah, when you hadn't seen me for years before that!" It hurt her throat to say it. She closed her eyes tightly. How could a stranger make her feel like this? Someone who was there before she wore a bra. Someone who had never seen her win a race, who just sent a card when she graduated high school.

"I miss you now," her mother said. "I do." Her voice trembled, a distant sound from some place of self-exile, the refrain of one who returns to be unforgiven. She should have known to begin with there is no such thing as a prodigal mother.

"I miss you," Meg said again. "And I'd like you and Danny to visit."

"Okay," Lauren told her, though it was not part of her plan and was never going to be. "Okay," she said. "All right."

Twenty-Six

Lauren had gone to the car the night before when she couldn't sleep, put all of the MREs in the trunk in case they ran out of food. She stowed her gun beneath the front seat. She brought two cold-weather sleeping bags, the poncho liners, thermal underwear, wool socks, a new pair of insulated snow boots, size ten for Danny's big feet, a case of Clif bars, and a ten-pack of BIC lighters.

At nine o'clock she put on the Christmas compass bracelet Danny had given her, woke him, and then went to her father's room. Jack Clay was ironing his work shirts and listening to NPR. She had a fleeting but overwhelming urge to order him to stand up straight. He wore a ragged pair of slippers, boxer shorts, and a frayed T-shirt he'd had since she was a toddler, the word ORGANIZE and a crumbling and faded image of a big fish about to be eaten by many little fish across the front. The clean smell of steam and starch hung comfortingly in the air. But the sight of him up and pressing laundry was almost ridiculous, out of any context she could recall, as if she'd opened a door into an alternate universe. If she wandered around the house maybe she'd find herself practicing solos, maybe she was home on break from conservatory, some diva who sang alone. Maybe her mother was downstairs making breakfast.

The phone rang; she could hear Bridget's voice before she got the receiver to her ear, then nothing but sobbing.

"What is it?" Lauren asked. "Bridget, what's happened?"

When she said the word "Holly" Lauren felt for a moment like she couldn't breathe, like she was about to vomit.

"What?" she asked again hoarsely.

"The whole building. It's barely nothing but ashes," Bridget said. "My baby . . ." Then she broke down again and Lauren's heart raced as she waited for her to go on. ". . . My baby was in the basement, trapped down in the basement restocking, and all that liquor upstairs, it practically exploded. She's okay," Bridget added quickly, calming herself by saying it. "She's alive, she's got . . . she inhaled smoke and she got burned. Her clothes burned, some of her clothes burned to her skin. But she's all right."

Her father looked up from his ironing, concerned, attentive.

Lauren did not have to imagine what clothing and skin looked like when they had melted together. She pressed the phone to her ear and shook her head slowly as she listened, as though she were refuting the details. Finally she said, "It's going to be okay, I'll be over. I'll come over now. Soon."

She hung up and looked at her father. "There was a fire at The Bag of Nails early this morning, Holly's at Samaritan."

"Jesus!" her father said. "Was she hurt?"

Lauren looked away, shook her head. "Smoke inhalation." Her voice shook and she made it stop. "Some burns. Bridget says she'll be out in a couple of days. I'm going to go over."

He looked suddenly angry. "That damn place is a firetrap and with everyone hanging out in the back there, that big pile of recycling . . . God *damn* it, that kid doesn't need one more thing." She wished she could feel what he did.

Lauren said, "I can't believe she was there that late. She shouldn't have been there." She sat on the edge of his bed and let her focus soften and blur, stared into some middle nowhere, wallpaper, the closet door, the edge of the ironing board, like there was no more subject to the shot, someone had set the camera down while it was still running. She was suddenly very, very tired.

Jack came over and put his arm around her. "Holly's resilient, babe, she's going to be just fine."

Lauren had seen burn victims, some of them were just fine and some weren't. She wanted to focus her gaze again, she wanted to stand, wanted to leave immediately, take Danny and leave, but her body wasn't letting her; it needed just another minute, just a rest, and then she could make it do what she wanted again. Now more than ever she needed to get out of there.

"Mom called," she told him. She noticed that she was holding his hand tightly and let go, straightened her shoulders and looked at his face.

"Did you get a chance to talk?" Jack asked.

"Yeah, I guess. It was fine, whatever," Lauren said. "When's the last time you talked to her?"

"Your mother? A long time ago. She still calls the house phone for Danny, but we don't really talk much. Why, does she sound okay?"

"Yeah. I mean she's fine, she's herself. She

267

always sounds okay." Lauren shrugged. "Anyway, she wants me and Danny to come for a few days and I thought we could drive there today if you're good with giving me the car. I could see Holly on the way too. Get out of this rain for a while, get a couple of quality days with Danny."

"Today?" He thought about it for a minute and shrugged. "You know what? I don't see why not. You know, in fact, I think that is a very good idea. Your mom's really going to be happy to see you. And if you take the car you'll have some freedom to come and go if it gets uncomfortable. I'll ask Peej for a ride this week."

Lauren nodded and he smiled and then he looked searchingly at her. "I don't want your brother driving, okay? I'm serious. He hasn't had any experience at all and it's winter and in Buffalo it's really winter right now, so I'm telling you don't do it. Okay?"

"Okay," she said, raised her eyebrows. A civilian guy with a part-time desk job giving her orders.

He nodded and then looked at her like he had any idea at all who she was. "Well, this is great. I'll get you guys some breakfast while you pack."

"We're already packed," she said. "We'll get breakfast on the way."

■ ■ ■ ■

Lauren waited in the car for Danny, turned the key in the ignition when she saw him hop down the back steps. She was eager to get to the hospital and lay eyes on Holly, make sure she really was okay.

"Wait," Jack called. "You got everything?"

"Oh shit, that's right," Danny said almost to himself, then ran down the driveway. As he disappeared into the garage Jack anxiously told Lauren again not to let him drive.

"I got it," she said. "I got it."

"And give Holly my love, tell her I'll be by to see her after work."

Lauren felt the cool prickling of shame. She had not protected her friend.

When Danny emerged from the garage with a beat-up red plastic sled, she popped the trunk so he could jam it on top of the rest of their gear before running up the steps to give their father another kiss.

"Okay, *now* you got everything?" Jack asked.

"Oh wait, wait!" Danny crouched down, patted his leg. "Here boy." He made kissing sounds. "Here boy, that's right . . ." He held the car door open and then patted his leg again, paused for a moment, said, "Good

269

boy." And then he shut the door.

Their father shook his head. "Dan, that's awful," he said. "That's not funny." He laughed at them. "You guys take good care of each other. And call me sometime this week."

"Love you," they sang to him, and Lauren backed the old gray Nissan out of the wet weedy driveway. Her father didn't even notice the new tires she'd had put on.

As they pulled away she looked up at Jack Clay one more time. He had the same tired wistful smile he'd always had, but his eyes were different. Looked like they had when she was a little girl. Like there was nothing in the way now, like he was wide awake and could see his children driving away from him. Hesitation caught her somewhere around the shoulders, a hunch that she was doing the wrong thing. For one brief second she thought of staying, turning the key the other way and unpacking the car. Instead she waved again and headed out and down Arsenal Street with the wipers on.

"What happened to Dad?" she asked Danny.

"He went to crying class with PJ."

She laughed. "Really?"

"That and some low dose of Effexor."

Something in her froze and she drove

silently for a moment, watching the narrow road, the potholes filled with gray water. She was happy with the new wiper blades. She went through a mental checklist of what she'd done to make the car safe for winter. Things her father hadn't done, of course. He hadn't gotten snow tires. No tuneup, there was no blanket in the trunk or flashlight, and the spare kit was rusted beyond practical use. It looked like all he did with maintaining the car was forget to put the anti-freeze away and kill their dog.

She fought against the halting tension that seized her when they approached cross streets. A precariously tilting pile of garbage bags crowned with a tinseled Christmas tree made her brake abruptly.

Danny looked up. "Was it a squirrel?"

"What?"

"In the road?" he said.

"Oh." She nodded. "Yeah."

Finally she asked lightly, "When did he start taking that stuff?"

"I don't know, a few months after Mom pulled that bullshit about me moving," he said. "You must have noticed when we were Skyping."

She shook her head. "I thought he was acting that way because he didn't want to upset me. Why didn't he start taking it

271

sooner?"

"He didn't know he was depressed," Danny said, and looked at her for a minute deadpan before raising his eyebrows and giving her an exaggerated crazy-eyed grin.

She exhaled tensely through her teeth. "He's a psychologist," she said, almost to herself.

"That's why it's funny," Danny said. "Also, he doesn't take it now, he just needed it for like six months."

The words hung dully in the air between them. She resisted saying what she thought because that would cast everything dark between them. But it was as present as her own body. She'd spent nine years. Nine years of her life as head of household for what amounted to the common cold. When their mother woke up enough from her back-to-school party to think she needed a kid, their father suddenly figured out he had one and should take care of him. Nine years for a thing that could have been solved in a matter of weeks.

She was too angry to speak. She looked straight ahead and felt Danny thinking. Turned to catch his eyes but his head was down, his face drawn. Then he glanced up at her, his cheeks flushed, whatever heavy thought he'd had already gone. He shook his head and laughed his goofy laugh.

"That's the funniest part," he said. As if he could read her mind.

They drove through the grid of narrow side streets that comprised their neighborhood.

"I have to stop at the hospital first to see Holly," she told him. "Then we'll get going."

"How is she?" he asked. Then before she could answer he said, "I saw footage of that fire on the *Daily Times* website, it was huge. The fire looked much bigger than the building — like taller than the building, there was a tree on fire next to it. She's a badass to get herself out of there, huh?"

"She is," Lauren said, proud of him for being concerned about Holly, glad she was taking him the hell out of Watertown, where it clearly wasn't safe for anyone.

She held out her palm to him and he slapped it, then turned his hand over for her. She slapped his hand and then held it, felt how big he was now. Felt his soft smooth palm and long delicate fingers.

"My kid," she said, quietly.

When the bus dropped her off at the corner she would walk home and let herself in, take food out of the freezer, and check on her dad. Then she would walk over to the after-school program to pick up Danny. She would usually get there around snack time, when he was eating half an apple with peanut butter on it and drinking grape juice. He was short and round and his eyes always looked so dark in contrast to his pale skin. She would sign him out, take his backpack from his cubby, and they would walk home together.

He'd walk beside her carrying the art project he'd made that day. Some special thing he'd concocted from the weird generic "crafts" supplies. A construction-paper tree or a cotton-ball polar bear, elaborate antlers made from pipe cleaner and pieces of egg carton glued to a paper ring he placed around his head; a mass of glitter and glue covering a cardboard box that was really a time machine. And he'd always say, "This is for you."

"I love it," she'd say. "Let's give it to Daddy too."

"Okay."

Sometimes if it was cold or he was tired she still picked him up and carried him. Or if she'd had a bad day, she'd pick him up and hold him close while she walked and sing whatever she'd been practicing with Troy. Sing the whole way home.

She'd bring him up to their dad's room first thing to deliver the work of art, and their father's smile would be the best of all.

"Look at this," he would say. "We have an artist in the family."

She would make dinner while Danny sat upstairs with their father on the edge of the bed, telling him stories from school.

After dinner Danny would sit in the hammock and swing and read while she did homework. And then later in his room they would look at the places they would go. Places she would take them. She remembered she'd found him a snow globe that someone in the neighborhood had left in a free box by the side of the road. Inside was a plastic gingerbread house, and the snow was made from white plastic chips and silver glitter.

Sometimes before he fell asleep he'd lie on his back looking at it, fall asleep with it still in his hands.

"That's the Snow Queen's house," he told her once, holding the globe just above his face.

"She lives in a gingerbread house, not a castle?" Lauren asked absently, sitting on the floor, her homework in her lap.

"She doesn't live in a castle anymore," he said drowsily, giving the globe a shake and holding it up to his eye as if he were trying to see inside the little house. "Maybe she just takes away people who want to leave. I think I see a fireplace inside one of the rooms," he said.

"Maybe it's the little boy and girl's house instead," Lauren said.

"Yeah, I think you're right," he said. "They got it from the Snow Queen when she moved away. She left them this nice house even though everything in it is frozen. She made it so they can't feel cold and they can go anywhere."

Lauren took the globe from his hand and put it on his nightstand, then she pulled the covers up, kissed him on the forehead.

"They can," she said, shutting off the light. "They can go anywhere they want."

TWENTY-SEVEN

Holly was asleep when Lauren went in. She had tubes in her nose, her left arm was completely bandaged, and the hair on the left side of her head was short, singed, and brittle, but her face was miraculously fine. A wave of relief washed over Lauren. If there was any more damage it was hidden beneath the sheet.

She sat beside the bed and touched Holly's hand lightly. The last time she'd visited her in the hospital was when Grace was born. Amazing Grace, seven pounds and ready to go, holding up her tiny fists, eyes an undetermined alien blue.

Lauren stayed with Holly all day. They spent it looking at the baby, holding the baby, smelling the baby, making phone calls and working on their social studies homework when the baby was asleep. They were captivated by her terrifying fragility, barely touched their fingers to the soft spot on her skull, which pulsed rhythmically with the beat of her heart.

If she'd never started working at The Bag of Nails she'd be fine now. There every day with the Patricks, actually thinking *Patrick* was anyone she should spend time with, anyone who could make a decent mate. Thinking of her friend's desperation made her sadder than thinking of the fire. Holly hanging on there after everyone had left, looking for one smart person to talk to who hadn't already judged her. Of course she was lured by the thin charm of the Murphys. Saw something of herself in bookish thugs, in failures. It hurt her to think of Holly seeing Patrick as someone who had drive and freedom, as some rogue intellectual who just needed a little caretaking so he could finally bloom. Someone with whom she could make a life.

She pulled her wallet and an envelope from her little daypack and wrote a check for eight thousand dollars, sealed it in the envelope, wrote Holly's name across it, and propped it against a plastic pitcher of water on the bedside table. That ought to get the girl somewhere. Her own place at the very least.

Lauren stepped out into the hallway, saw Shane approaching, and fought the twin urges to walk past him without talking, to run and hold him. She made herself stand still in front of the room.

He looked hung over and slightly sick. Walked up close and put his arms around her. She felt the cool wall of the corridor against her back and rested her head against his shoulder.

"How is she?" he asked.

Lauren pulled away and held his hands. "She's asleep. I couldn't see much, she looks okay." The fact was she looked completely fine to Lauren. She'd been in a fire. But she had not been inside something made of metal filled with flammable fuel and fortified with artillery while it had exploded. Holly had run from a burning building. It was bad that she didn't have a job now, bad she'd have scars and be in pain for a while. Lauren did not want her to be in pain. But she was fine.

She watched him studying her the way he had outside The Bag of Nails and suddenly felt a wave of exhaustion. She didn't have the heart for it, to stand and be scrutinized. She knew she'd failed to look sufficiently upset. But their friend was alive. The Bag of Nails was gone.

Things were going to be okay for Holly, but not for her and Shane. He was so used to a good life now he could see surviving a catastrophic fire as bad news. She squeezed his hand and headed through the building filled with people sick with slow diseases, nearly well after accidents. It barely seemed like a hospital at all.

TWENTY-EIGHT

Lauren told Danny to wait in the car, which was fine. He wanted Holly to be all right but there was no way he wanted to see what she looked like after spending the night in a burning building. He also did not want to see other sick people and he was glad Lauren understood.

He texted Scott and told him he was going to his mom's for the week, then opened the glove compartment and went through the junk that was in there. Pens, napkins, receipts, the car manual.

The footage of The Bag of Nails was beautiful but not if you knew Holly was inside. It was a tall fire and he wondered how it had started. Maybe Holly had started it with a cigarette. The place really was an oversized rickety shack. It should have been called the Bag of Bones, not The Bag of Nails, because it looked like some kind of sway-backed living thing. It had a narrow wooden staircase that went up the back from the restaurant to an apartment. Maybe the guy who lived in the apartment had set it on fire. Maybe he was an alcoholic and couldn't pay his bills and his electricity got cut off and he fell asleep reading by candlelight and the candle got knocked over and so did his whiskey, then his book caught on fire and took the whole building with it. But the guy got out and was now a hobo because he lost everything. One drunken spark between him and the road for life.

He thought about how fire is like rust. Using oxygen to swallow up the world. Just one hundred thousand years ago people were learning how to use it, how to cook or scare off animals or something, and before that they didn't even know how to make it, so for them it didn't exist. He thought about Sebastian being converted from fur and flesh into gray ashes and chunks of bone. How he once had a personality and now he was fertilizing the roots of the pine trees. Sebastian never really got much farther than the yard. Even in death. Should have dumped his ashes in the river so he would be carried away. He loved to lie beneath the pine tree, but that's only because he didn't have much to compare it to. Danny thought about the remains of dinosaurs, their bodies in the ground turning into oil to be set on fire. The ancient past isn't gone at all. Dinosaurs are more dangerous now as oil than they ever were when they were flesh and feathers.

A loud rap at the car window made Danny jerk and scream involuntarily.

Shane's uncle Patrick was bent down staring at him — his face close and ugly behind the glass. He tapped again very lightly with one of his knuckles, and Danny rolled the window down.

Patrick smelled like cigarettes and paper and sweat and fried food. He hadn't shaved in some time. He was wearing sooty or ink-stained jeans and a grubby red wool jacket. His skin was ruddy, seemed loose and leathery. He looked sad and mean at the same time.

"Where's your fucking sister?"

The snarling anger with which he said it was another shock. But it was also ridiculous that he was asking when they were both there in the hospital parking lot.

"Visiting Holly," Danny said, glancing down quickly to make sure his door was locked.

Patrick wiped a dirty hand over his forehead, rubbed his eyes. He looked dazed. Stood and turned his back to the car, squinting up toward the windows of the hospital as if he were trying to figure out what room she was in.

Danny didn't know what else to say, so he began rolling up the window. It was halfway up when Patrick turned back around, stopped it with his hand, looked directly into Danny's eyes without seeming to see him. As if he were calculating something and needed a place to fix his gaze.

"She's dangerous," he said.

"Who?"

"Your sister. People like that coming back with more than just stupid ideas in their heads. You send a person to hell you should keep them there, know what I mean? Would you keep a police dog? Would you keep a pit dog as a pet?"

"Pit bull?" Danny asked. "I —"

"Two worlds got to be kept separate," Patrick interrupted. "You do your reading, you'll see. The one shouldn't even exist at all, am I right? You know what the Demiurge is?"

Danny wasn't sure Patrick was using real words anymore. He felt the hair on the back of his neck stand up. He shook his head and felt for his phone in his pocket in case he needed to call 911. He understood Shane's uncle was upset about Holly or about the

284

fact that the place where he spent his entire life had burned down, but he sounded crazier than someone who was just upset.

Patrick rubbed his face again. He had tears in his eyes and he looked very old and tired.

He would not tell Lauren about this when she got back in the car, she'd be pissed the guy had even talked to him or that he'd rolled down the window. She'd had enough bullshit. He knew because she said just this morning when he was slow to wake up that she'd had enough bullshit. He didn't want anything to upset her.

Patrick put his hand firmly on Danny's shoulder.

He said, "Better be careful, little man."

TWENTY-NINE

Lauren walked out through the sliding doors and down the ramp past cars waiting near the emergency exit. She saw Shamus and Gerry sitting on the curb smoking and wondered if Shane had given them a ride over to visit. Just what Holly needed, barflies flocking to her aid. She raised a hand and nodded quickly at them as she got out her keys and sprinted across the parking lot.

Danny was hunched down in his seat texting, and she slammed the door and quickly got back out on the highway.

"Well?" he asked.

"She looks great," Lauren said. "They have her on oxygen and she has some burns but otherwise seems fine. Shane's with her now. I guess Bridget was with her all night."

"What did she say about the fire?"

"Not much," Lauren told him.

He put his phone away and messed with the radio a little.

"How did you learn how to drive?" he asked her. He had really wished he could drive when Patrick had shown up.

"PJ."

"Really? When did he teach you?"

"Don't you remember? When we were kids."

"I guess I do. Really?"

"Really. Dad wouldn't teach me so I asked PJ and he did. Over on Sullivan Street.

"Did you tell Dad?"

"Yeah. He was pissed. But what if something happened and *we* needed to go to the hospital or something happened to him and we were alone?"

"Nothing like that ever happened," Danny said.

"But it could have, and then we'd've been screwed."

They passed along the Black River and saw how swollen it had become from the rain, flowing fast along the muddy, weedy embankment.

"Let's take the scenic route. Let's take the bridge and go up and across Canada, stop at my buddy Daryl Green's and then go down to Mom's."

"For real?"

"Hell yeah, kid. We have plenty of time, we can do whatever we want."

He smiled broadly. "Okay," he said. "Yeah, let's do it!"

Waiting to cross the Thousand Islands Bridge into Canada she thought of leaving Holly there alone, thought of what she was about to do and lost her resolve for a moment. Then put it all out of her mind and focused on the road.

Just over the Canadian border the weather began to change rapidly. Thick wet clumps of snow hit the windshield. They got on to Highway 1 and drove along in steady snowfall. Something about it calmed her, made the road seem safer, the idea of IEDs more absurd. She hadn't felt so calm driving in a year and she smiled, looking out at the dense wet blanket of white that clung to tree branches and hung from the eaves of buildings and tops of billboards. As they got farther on the snowflakes became smaller, swirled and swarmed like white bees toward them, and the bright sun pierced the pale gray clouds, revealing a wide swath of high blue sky. She put on her aviator glasses.

In his sleep Danny looked like his baby self: his head back and lolling to the side, his skin still soft and cheeks round. He'd put the radio on some shitty hip-hop station, and she turned it off. She reached over and put her hand on his chest. Felt him breathing. Then she reached into the pocket of his cargo pants, gently pulled out his phone, rolled down the top of the window, and tossed it out onto the highway. She had to do it. Otherwise she wouldn't be able to take them out of this world.

■ ■ ■ ■

PART TWO

■ ■ ■ ■

THIRTY

When he woke up a thick snow was falling and he watched it absently through the windshield for a moment before realizing the car was parked. There were tall pine trees visible all around in the distance, and the sky was bright and the afternoon sun was warm coming through the glass. There was a long low wooden building, a truck stop maybe or a diner. But his sister was not there. Then he heard the trunk slam and her boots crunching along in the snow next to the car. She opened the passenger-side door, handed him a large square box that said DANNER CANADIAN on it, and said, "Merry Christmas. Again."

Inside was a pair of dark brown boots with thick wide black soles. They were solid and would last and he was sure they'd keep his feet warm. Even the laces seemed constructed of something indestructible. He'd never had anything like them. He didn't know what to say.

"Those are one hundred percent water-proof," Lauren said. "They have six hundred grams of Thinsulate in the lining. You could prolly wear them with bare feet and still be warm."

He leaned over to lace them. Then he got out of the car and jumped up and down in the sturdy boots. They were so simple and so fancy at the same time. He ran across the parking lot and then back to the car.

"We found winter!" he shouted. She laughed, happy, relieved. She opened the trunk again and got out one of the silver emergency blankets and put it in the back seat in case they needed it on the road, but he leaned in and took it, tied it around his neck like a cape.

"Aw hell yeah, son! We're on vacation!" He hugged her tight. "Thank you for the boots, Sistopher!"

She waved it away. "They're gonna keep you warm."

"Oh you bet, I'm going to be so fucking warm. I'm going to have to change my name to Toasty. I'm going to change my name to Adorable Little Bunny. Oh, you know what? I don't remember why this was, but I was actually thinking about what would be a good name for a pet bunny. And I came up with Furious."

Danny loved it when people laughed but especially Lauren, because her voice was pretty and she always jerked her head back a little like she was startled. One time he made her laugh so hard tea came out her nose.

He went on: "I'd be like, 'Here's my pet Furious. He looks real mellow but he's going to tear your fucking face off.' I'd be like, 'I'm serious, why do you think I fucking named him that? You *should* be scared. He's a fucking killer!' And then the rabbit would just be hopping around, nibbling on grass or lying there sleeping. OH I know! I would get him a whole outfit of baby clothes! With a little hat that pushes his ears down on the sides of his head! And then I'd shave his body and get him covered in jailhouse tattoos, so under the baby suit he'd be a terrifying badass." Danny started giggling and she looked at him, incredulous and weirdly proud.

"And then you feed him with a baby bottle," she said.

"I'd feed him *grain* alcohol in the baby bottle."

"Then get some woman to bring him to The New Bag of Nails and pretend he's the love child of one of the Patricks," she said, and then lost it again, shook her head picturing the stupid shithole burned to the ground and the Patricks, gathered around like an Irish wake, staring at the wreckage.

Danny said in a tearful falsetto: "Don't you remember your own flesh and blood?"

"And the family resemblance would be so great he couldn't deny it," she said.

"And he'd be so dumb he'd have to keep paying child support for a shaved rabbit. No, you know what I'd really do, though?" Danny said, suddenly serious. "If I had a bunny I would just hold him a lot because they're really soft."

She nodded in agreement. "Let's get some chow, kid, what do you say?"

A car pulled into the parking lot. A middle-aged couple looked at them and then sat gazing out their windshield, saying things Lauren and Danny couldn't hear, which also made them laugh.

"You look nuts in that cape," Lauren said to him.

"I'm going to save their lives," he said. "I'm going to go over and knock on the window and be like . . ."

Danny stopped talking as the couple got out of the car, still looking at them. They smiled. The woman said, "I was just telling my husband I haven't seen two people having such a good time in years."

"Look at my new boots!" Danny said to her, holding one foot up.

"Not bad," the man said.

They were friendly and tender looking and short. The man was wearing a green Carhartt coat, and the woman was wearing a puffy down vest and a white knit hat.

"We're on vacation," Lauren said.

"With our dog," Danny said, and he started cracking up again. The couple looked around for a dog, then he said, "That's not true, he died last month, but he'd always wanted his ashes scattered in the Great Lakes."

"Oh," the woman said, looking confused.

The man started laughing. He said, "I think we got ourselves a couple of comedians here, Bobbi."

The diner was big and the dark wooden tables were covered with red-and-white checked table cloths, the real kind made of linen. He loved it. Nearly every inch of wall space was hung with photographs of animals: moose, owls, wolves, bears, and otters, and with rectangular wooden signs sporting some of the stupidest stuff he'd ever read. Phrases like "Got beer?" And "Sometimes I wake up grumpy, other times

I let him sleep." "If it has tits or tires it's gonna cost you money." And also "Can I get a caller ID for the voices in my head?"

The dessert case was flanked by a counter that held a wide variety of souvenirs. You could buy flags and pennants and little snow globes and bells and spoons, unidentifiable cartoon figurines and T-shirts that all said WAWEIG on them. Waweig! What did that even mean? It was ridiculous but also cool and foreign and remote. Like a planet in an Ursula Le Guin novel. They'd been gone just a few hours and already they had docked in Waweig.

"I've got to take a picture of this," he said to Lauren, reaching into his pocket for his phone. He experienced a moment of disorientation and anxiety when he couldn't find it, looked on the floor beneath the table.

She sat across from him — leaning back in her chair and reading the menu, sipping her coffee. She didn't look worried about it, in fact she looked more relaxed than she had since she'd gotten home.

"You must have left it in the car," she said, glancing up absently. "Think maybe you should take the cape off now?"

He had the urge to go find his phone right away but knew he should stay there. The tension was finally gone from her face and he didn't want to bring it back by taking pictures and texting, which he knew bothered her but he didn't know why. He honestly didn't feel that much like doing it anyway — which was weird, but still the boots and the diner and all the snow needed to be documented so he could post it online.

She said, "It's okay, buddy, we're going to get on the road soon, you can look in the car." Then added, "They have milkshakes."

He picked up the menu. Remembered another story he wanted to tell her. Knocked his boots together under the table. He felt happy.

"If you go to music school can I visit you there?" he asked. He could imagine driving around Philadelphia and seeing a big city and going to visit Shane with her. He'd have a place to be other than home. Shane said there were libraries at his school that had any book you'd ever want, and they showed good movies there all week long.

She looked up, shocked. "Why would you think I'm going to go to music school?"

He said, "Duh, what else are you going to do? Hey, have you ever heard of a Reeves's muntjac? It's a real animal. It's like a deer but really small."

The muntjac was really interesting, and the history of how it got to the west from

China was too. He also wanted to remember to tell her about how birds' eyes make it possible for them to see in colors that are invisible to humans and other animals. He'd watched a lecture about it online because his biology teacher was kind of a tool when it came to explaining things. He'd show Lauren the site where you can watch all those lectures and also the video of crows placing nuts at a crosswalk so cars would run them over and crack them. And when they got to their mom's they could also watch *South Park* because she had cable.

He looked up and realized that from almost every window in the diner you could see snow-covered pine trees. This was the farthest from home he had ever been, and it felt amazing, like they could just keep going. They had broken free from some gravitational pull and could keep going forever. They could be weightless.

THIRTY-ONE

In a spotlessly clean, efficiently sized office with two beautiful leather chairs and a wide cherry desk, Dr. Eileen Klein told Captain Nash exactly what she wasn't going to do. Which was nothing.

She liked Nash, he was a good man and stable, and it wasn't his fault some jackass screwed up the paper on his unit. He shook his head at her. Clamped his lips shut and breathed in through his nose. He was not happy with what she was saying and she knew she was making more work for him, but she was entirely fucking done with it.

They'd lost one hundred and forty last week. Stateside. Here at fucking home. Most with firearms, then drowning, over-doses which couldn't really be categorized accurately. And then the one gaining ever more popularity: suicide by cop. For enlisted overseas they were looking at one a day.

"You can make this a problem for Clay or

you can let it go," Nash said. "You gonna start tracking everybody who's got an inconsistency on their debrief, Eileen?"

"Not everyone, no. But this one for sure."

"This shit's above your pay grade," he said, using a cliché she was getting very tired of hearing, an excuse worthy of Eichmann.

"Next you'll be telling me a funeral is cheaper than medical treatment."

He shook his head. "I'm not interested in calling this person AWOL no matter what she filled out or told you, even if she misses the thing on the twenty-ninth. This soldier is home and not our problem."

"She told me she and her family are going to be staying with Daryl Green," Klein said.

Nash took a deep breath and exhaled through his nose.

"I'm sorry, Eileen. Even if I back you on this one you know it's going to be a fucking shitshow."

She nodded. Took her glasses off and put them on her desk, then rested her head in her hands for a moment.

"Clay's a good NCO," Nash said. "She presided over an accident, everything's been signed and put away, really. It's that simple. She's not going to do anything. And even if she does, what the hell can we do about it?"

THIRTY-TWO

It was a full twelve hours of driving after they left the diner. After dark she pulled over somewhere on route ON-137 to rest her eyes, tucked the silver emergency blankets around herself and Danny, and ended up sleeping for hours. It was December 29. The windows were frosted over when she woke, and a bright morning light shone into the car. She ate a Clif bar and got back on the road.

Danny was fitful and not quite awake when they passed a sign for Hebron and then another sign giving their proximity to the Jeanne d'Arc Basin. It was thrilling to see the name and know she was finally closing in on her plan. Would be able to show Danny this place, this hollow edge of land like a scar from where the continent was torn apart. To stand with him in a place where the earth had changed.

She turned off the highway and drove on

a smaller sloping road for another few hours. It had been plowed but there was no traffic. The roads down into the valley were impassable in the little Nissan, even with the snow tires. She drove as far as she could, then parked on an overlook, a good vantage point to see the white-topped mountain ranges as they cut into the blue sky and to look down into the hollow landscape below. The world was a bleached pearly frozen blue, filled with pines and maples.

Out there off the coast, beneath the ocean, out of sight was the White Rose oil field. A place Daryl had talked about incessantly the last weeks of his tour. The region was filled with offshore rigs, but you couldn't tell from the majestic emptiness of the landscape. If they could get work there, Daryl strategized, offshore, they could make what they were making in combat, maybe double it, sock it away so his kid Roy and Danny didn't have to go through what they went through. Otherwise it was temping or carpentry and ten dollars an hour and back to nowhere fast. Once they'd made enough money they could do what they wanted. Once they knew the rigs their options changed considerably. She looked again at the pristine landscape. It was as if she'd walked out of Amarah last week and into a parallel universe. Sand and high blazing sun transformed to snow and the thick shelter of forest.

No footprints or tire tracks marked the snow, but there were deer, or maybe caribou tracks, and she noticed, close to where she'd parked, paw prints from some small animal.

The air was bitter as she got out of the car, a startling, awakening kind of cold. Lauren looked down the edge of the slope, in the late-afternoon light. Below them a cluster of low, crumbling stone and shingled houses, some with caved-in roofs, leaned in a semicircle around a pile of bricks and cobblestones. She got out her binoculars and surveyed the buildings more closely. They appeared abandoned, looked at least a century old. An old hunting camp maybe, or the remaining houses from some remote village left behind by progress. From where she stood she could see no tracks around the buildings, apart from a single narrow deer trail. The place looked still and placid, and she wondered how close they were to the coast. It could have been a fishing and trapping outpost. Woods and thick stands of trees had been common sights on the trip, but this place below them looked more open and flat, absent of visitors and inhospitable to significant vegetation. She took a few more moments with the binoculars while Danny woke up, and began searching again for his phone.

"Hey buddy, check this out." She walked over and handed him the binoculars, and it distracted him as she'd hoped. "Don't worry about the phone — we probably don't have reception out here anyway. Just stop a minute, see where we are."

He took the binoculars from her and looked down at the ring of houses.

"I thought we were stopping at Daryl's," he said. "Where are we?"

"We're almost there. I think that over there is the John Dark Basin," she said.

"The what?" He looked dazed and cold, and she reflexively pulled his hood up and tied it tightly at his chin.

"The Jeanne d'Arc Basin. The edge of the earth and the ice around here. Remember we were talking about maps? All this stuff around here broke apart, it used to be Pangaea, right? Now there are these faults and rifts and ocean and continents."

The sky was already turning violet over the rounded tree-lined hillsides in the west. The place was more beautiful and distant than she'd hoped it would be, colder than it had felt in her dreams. As if sacred music had become a place, found a material form.

She felt her heart pound with something other than the instinctual chemical flood of being a hunted, hunting animal, the grounded yet soaring feeling that comes from using your body to sing. She smiled and filled her lungs with the cold clean air. The things that take your breath, she thought, don't have to take your life.

Danny stood beside her, transfixed. "It's fucking amazing. It's amazing!" he said, and her heart soared to hear him, so pleased with his reaction, so happy she'd taken him away. "Let's go check it out down there."

She got the sled out of the car and set it at the edge of the slope. Danny sat in the front and she sat behind him, rested her head on his back. She listened to his heart-beat. She resisted the urge to put her fingers on his wrist and feel his pulse.

"Wait," he said, his eyes sparkling darkly. "Get Sebastian."

"Oh," she said, "here." She leaned over and handed him a block of air. "Hold him in the front. Hold him tight or he'll jump."

Then she pushed them over the edge of the crest and down the slope.

The flimsy plastic sled flew and she leaned out over Danny's shoulder so the icy snow would sting and whip her face. She held him tightly around the waist and they screamed together, racing down into the beautiful vespertine ruin.

They drifted to a stop near a circle of wood and stone houses and the scattered rubble of what had clearly been outbuildings or smaller bungalows. The doors were blown wide open, hanging on hinges. Roofs caved in or partially caved in. A whole building leaned precariously, frozen in mid-collapse, a drunk in the midst of a slow-motion tumble. The structures looked empty but she needed to make sure no one else was down there. The sky was turning a deeper smoky purple in the west and the horizon glowed orange.

"You want to stay with the sled or clear these buildings with me?"

"Clear them from what?" Danny asked. "Dust?"

She squinted at him in annoyance, then went into the largest of the houses. The place was gutted. And also very familiar, a dreamlike slip in time into someone's wrecked and vacant home, the landscape of soldiering, but frozen and free from the guilty terror of patrol. The remains of broken furniture piled in the stone fireplace. The floor was made of wide weathered planks that sloped toward the hearth as if the weight of the chimney was sinking the house. She walked briskly and quietly through the one-story building. The roof had caved in over the kitchen, and the room was filled with drifting snow that clung to long-disconnected light fixtures and switches. Perfect piles of luminous snow that had been shaped by wind, and curved like ripples in sand, or the subtle rise and hollow of a man's chest, crested over the floors. In a small room off the kitchen a pile of ragged blankets and wooden crates lay strewn across the floor. An old gas refrigerator and a basin with a single faucet stood untouched beneath slanting and partially rotted cabinetry, the doors open, revealing faded shelf paper patterned with cherries and lemons. The house was a ruined palace of ice at once exhilarating and calming.

After walking through the first house, she made Danny come with her so she could show him the proper way to walk safely and with authority through a stranger's broken home.

The rest of the houses were in a similar state, though one was littered with beer cans and the burnt-out remains of a fire in the center of the main room. The place was too remote to have become a hobo outpost, she thought, and probably served as a good resting spot for hunters or some variety of hermetic adventure seeker. December was not high season for this resort.

"I wish I had my phone to take pictures of this," he said.

"You'll just have to remember it."

"We should come back here in the summer," he said, "if we could ever find it again."

"We can just stay until summer," she said, opening the door of a pantry filled with dust and cobweb-covered Mason jars.

He picked up a brittle mold-darkened newspaper from a stack beside a collapsed fireplace, the print illegible, the headlines written in French.

She chose the building with the straightest chimney, its roof and walls still intact, and she brought the broken wood from the larger house and set it inside the hearth.

"We can stay here tonight," she said.

Danny laughed because he thought she was joking and she laughed because she wasn't, and it would be funny when he figured that out. But when he looked at her with sudden panic, it hurt to know she'd caused his fear.

"I thought we were going to visit your friend," he said.

"We are," Lauren told him. "But not tonight. We better hike up and get the ponchos and MREs before it gets dark — oh, and the sleeping bags, and we'll bring that pile of papers from the other house."

He looked shocked.

"I got two subzero sleeping bags in case we'd need them," she told him.

"Why would we need subzero sleeping bags at Mom's?" he asked.

She said, "I dunno, bud. Sometimes you need stuff. It's always better to be prepared. It's a good thing I brought them, otherwise we wouldn't be able to stay here. The bags are high tech but the poncho liner would be good even if we were in Siberia."

He stared at her, his eyes narrowing in confusion, a flicker of the kind of tantrum a younger kid might throw.

She turned away from him, held the sled on top of her head, began walking up the hillside, and he followed her. There was nothing else he could do. The temperature was falling and they were lucky there wasn't much wind. She'd bring down as much gear as they could carry. Make sure they stayed warm.

It was silent and the snow beneath their boots was deep, a crisp powder over several layers of freeze. They crunched along and she felt elevated. Relieved to be away, where it was desolate. But no risk of insurgents, no IEDs, no heat, no sand, no dust, and the air so cold and clean. The white slope played tricks of perspective with their eyes, an Escher drawing headed up or headed down. Looking straight on you could see it either way.

Danny helped her pile their supplies on the sled, and then they walked down holding it between them, sturdy and efficient on the slope in new boots. Above the sky was a vast, deepening blue. Snow stretched out around them flat and white, and behind them to the west lay a tall pine woods, with snow-covered trees. She was sure they were near the coast. She would take him out there, to the pristine and rocky edge of the continent. And show him what he needed to see.

The house she chose for setting up camp was made of cobblestone and was at the center of the ring of crumbling buildings. She built a fire, then collected snow, melted it in a small aluminum pot, boiled it and put in two tea bags. Lauren poured the tea into the mugs she'd brought and they sat close together on the floor in front of the fire, warming their mittened hands and sipping it, bundled side by side in hooded sweatshirts and coats, wrapped in sleeping bags and silver poncho liners that reflected the glow of the flames. She thought for one brief moment about The Bag of Nails, pleased to imagine it swallowed up, gone.

"Snow tea," Danny said, his voice a tentative tremulous noise between excited and afraid. She was happy to give him something completely new. Bring him to a place where he'd have to be brave. Have to learn to be on his own. He walked cautiously around the building, looked out the windows at the dimming sky.

"Are we going to freeze to death?" he asked, suddenly entirely scared again.

"No way, dude. Are you kidding? We got a nice fire going and we have the right gear and know how to use it. We are not even going to be cold."

It was cold, though. It was freezing.

"I don't know how to use any of it," he said.

"Yes you do, bud, you read about it, and you're smart. You're gonna pick this stuff up in a hurry. Besides, you're the arctic expert. Right, Shackleton?"

He looked at her blankly. She wondered if his fingers were numb inside his gloves, took out two gel handwarmers, popped them to activate the chemicals, and slipped them inside the top of his Swedish mittens.

"People are stronger than you think," she told him. "We'll look for a motel tomorrow if we need to. But I'm sure we can do this. Maybe we'll like it a lot. We're probably so badass we don't need a motel."

He shivered and brought his mittens up to his face and held them there. She moved closer and put her arm around him, sipped her tea. "There are dozens of handwarmers in the trunk," she said. "If you were in danger of freezing — which you will not be, because we also have dozens of lighters and a place to make a fire, but if you were . . ."

"I know what to do for hypothermia," Danny said, impatiently. "The problem is, when hypothermia starts you don't know what to do anymore because it affects your brain."

He shook his head. "I can't believe we're here." He sounded truly astonished. He had the tense and tentative look of a boy trying not to show fear and discomfort that she had seen so often. She respected this. There was strength there and strength to be gained in watching a person cope. Getting used to something real when all there had been before was the dream of it — the imaginary you in the imaginary place. Here they were, alone and far away at night in the snow, with just the things they brought. So many feelings rush in to fill the silences in times like these, bump up against the desire for old habits and diversions.

She remembered the sensation well. The fact of your animal being is exposed when you are solitary, unsure, terrified. It's almost a cellular desire, a surge in every aspect of your being to live no matter what that living was going to be like. She wanted to regain that feeling, the instinct to stay alive at all costs.

He was quiet in the firelight, the world they knew receding.

"We should really call Dad," he said.

"We'll get ahold of him tomorrow," she assured him.

"You think there are animals out there?" he asked.

"I think there probably are."

"Stuff like bears and shit?" He said it really fast, as if getting the words out of his mouth would get the thought out of his head. He sounded pained, embarrassed at needing to be reassured.

"I don't think we gotta worry too much," she said. "Unless some wolves come and try to steal you so they can raise you as one of their own."

"That already happened," he said. Then he gave a little nervous howl, it boomed and echoed in the empty room, and he took a deep breath and then coughed from the shock of the cold air. She watched him closely, his confidence growing and receding. Making noise to feel brave, to occupy the place. "That already happened," he said again. "I was raised by Sebastian."

As uncomfortable as Danny would be this one night, he would be twice as confident in the morning and he'd understand. The place relaxed her, the long-standing emptiness of it. She was happy to get Danny away from staring at a screen, filling his ears with noise. Living through his fucking phone. He'd be afraid to begin with and then he would be better than ever.

She was already better. No cars, no familiar faces, no dust rising, and with any luck no dreams.

It was as though what happened in Amarah shattered all the terror that existed and sent it out into the world in particles and fragments. A mirror bursting into sand and dust, the fear traveled and imbedded itself, hid in everyday objects, blinded people, muffled or enhanced sounds. She was either never or always afraid after that last time. And she knew now the difference between never and always was small. Never and always are separated by a wasp's waist, a small sliver of safety glass, one bead of sweat; separated by the seven seconds it takes to exhale the air from your lungs, to make your body as still as the corpse you are about to create.

THIRTY-THREE

Lauren didn't dream the first night they slept in the hollow of abandoned houses. But Danny did for her. More alert than he'd ever felt, he watched his breath rising, a white cloud above his cold face. He was warm, zipped into the sleeping bag and poncho liner, but still frightened of freezing, of animals or people, or, god knows, some combination of the two; a fur-covered thing, invincibly smart, stalking around beneath the stars, upright and able to look in on them. He knew a lot about animals and he was embarrassed to be so afraid of them.

He watched Lauren, bundled and awake and tending the fire. There was always something about how she moved — like her body had an authority, an ability that made it possible for her not to worry. You didn't worry if you could run twenty miles, if you were coordinated, if you knew how to fight

— you weren't concerned about things in the same way other people were. She had a kind of physical alertness that he knew he didn't have. Maybe he missed it genetically and all his agility, all his speed was in his mind. He thought the body must have its own kind of intelligence, one he missed when he missed Little League and swim lessons and soccer and everything else people did instead of go to after-school and go home and then read next to the record player or in his room.

Danny knew his sister's steadiness well. The sources of his own steadiness were at his desk and in his head, and it was already dark and now was the first time he realized that the stuff he liked to do was very flat. On a screen or on paper and they didn't technically exist in the real world at all — or they did but you didn't; you were watching or reading about them. The real world was his sister melting snow and boiling water for them and the smell of woodsmoke and the sound of wind. It was the rough wool of the Swedish mittens she'd bought him, keeping his hands warm. And the boots. The real world was crisp and metallic with cold, and silent in a way that brought songs or images to his mind and played them in disturbing repetitive loops.

In his head Lady Gaga's voice would not stop singing that stupid radio song p-p-p-p-poker face p-p-pokerface. The stuttered "p"s like chattering teeth. A song he had no interest in, hated, and now it wouldn't leave, the same few words over and over, giving him some stupid obvious message. Maybe she brought him out here to empty him of this noise. Maybe it was all pouring out of him now into the emptiness.

And where was his phone? If he could just talk to another person or get online or check the news or chat. He could update his status to Arctic or Firestarter. And he could tell people where they were.

He lay on his side and watched her with his hat pulled down over his ears, clutching the crank flashlight she'd given him for Christmas "in case he needed it." Then he shone it on Lauren, and the shadows of strange objects in the room appeared behind her. She looked bulky from the coat and the layers of thermal underwear but somehow still agile. He studied her for the things that were familiar because there were new things about her, new behaviors, and he didn't know if these things were permanent.

"Can you sing something?" he asked. It was so quiet. And the building so empty. It had good acoustics. She would like that.

She used to sing in the bathroom because of the acoustics. She used to sing in church with Troy. She'd brought him there and he played with LEGOs in the choir loft while she practiced.

She squinted in the glare of his flashlight and put her hand in front of her face. "Like what?"

"Anything."

She shook her head a little and looked away. Maybe this was how she was different.

"I can't sing right now," she said. "Turn that flashlight off."

"Um, okay." He turned it off and waited a second, then clicked it back on. "How about now?"

"C'mon, Furious." She sounded tired.

"Or . . ." he said, turning it off, waiting again, looking up at the ceiling, then turning it back on. "Now?"

She was still quiet. The sound of the fire hissing and popping made it seem even more silent.

"Sing 'Winter Wind,' " he told her. The fire had made him very warm and sleepy and he could suddenly recall the arias and solos she used to practice. "The Black Swan," "Fair Robin I Loved," "Lucia's Aria," "Ave Maria," "To This We've Come."

He remembered her voice sounded like chimes when she first started singing and that later it was different, fuller. And then later she only sang choir songs. He thought about colors while she sang, silver and orange, and it changed the air in the room. On very high notes he could feel the sound buzzing against the windows in the choir loft or in their living room. He could feel it in his chest as if he were singing too, an enormous vibrant ringing; a thing so present and invisible at the same time. At home when she was doing chores she would sing phrases from the same songs very quietly but it still sounded clear like chimes.

He turned the flashlight off again because he knew it irritated her.

She looked at him and the corner of her mouth twitched, her face lit only by the fire. She took a breath and then coughed into the cold air, shook her head, and took another slower breath, then closed her eyes as if she were going back to sleep.

He said, "Please, Low." And then thought for a moment something must have really happened to her. Maybe she'd been injured and it ruined her voice and she hadn't told them. Maybe that was why she'd been acting so strange. Lauren had never said no before when he asked her to sing, when anyone asked. It was a free and pretty thing. She sang him to sleep when he was small, and she sang to their father sometimes when she had practiced a song for a long time. She would teach Danny a tune on the way home from school and they would sing it together. She sang alone in her room. Her voice was the sound of their home.

She shook her head.

"I don't remember how it goes," he lied, and clicked the flashlight back on so that he could see her face. She took another deep breath and closed her eyes.

She began quietly, but soon her voice rose, light and clear, filling the frozen empty space with sound, high and agile and graceful the way he remembered it.

Blow, blow, thou winter wind.
Thou art not so unkind
As man's ingratitude.

Thy tooth is not so keen,
Because thou art not seen,
Although thy breath be rude.

Heigh-ho, sing heigh-ho, unto the green
    holly.
Most friendship is feigning, most loving
    mere folly.

Then heigh-ho, the holly.
This life is most jolly.

Freeze, freeze, thou bitter sky,
That dost not bite so nigh
As benefits forgot.

Though thou the waters warp,
Thy sting is not so sharp
As friend remembered not.

Heigh-ho, sing heigh-ho, unto the green
    holly.
Most friendship is feigning, most loving
    mere folly.
Then heigh-ho, the holly.
This life is most jolly.

When she was done he felt calm, relieved, his body warm and heavy. His mind was done racing and he slept and dreamt.

Outside the window of the building a woman dressed in white looked in at them, her face covered with a wax mask. Behind her was a shabby white sled made of chipped particle board, tied to a team of little black dogs with curly tails.

The woman looked through the mask, into the window at him, trying to distract him from seeing his sister getting in the sled. Then she turned and stood — she had only been crouching to look in at him. She was very tall, tall as the building, with long thin legs. In two strides she was back in the sled, and she folded herself up into a crouching position, her back curved and sinister. Lauren sat beside her wearing fatigues and her army shirt, not cold at all, her face blank. He ran out to them but the woman yelled something to the dogs and they began running. The sled heaved and he watched Lauren's body flop as if she was unconscious. He ran out to help her, to get her off the sled, but the woman pushed her upright in the seat and they raced away silently into the snow.

Lauren watched him sleep, brushed his hair away from his forehead, grateful that he had made her do it; here in the middle of nowhere with Danny at least it was possible, if nowhere else. She checked the fire. She knew they couldn't really live there long without more wood and kindling. But there was plenty of furniture in the other houses and there was the woods to hike through and gather more fuel. She fed the fire, then pulled her hat down around her ears and pulled her hood up to keep her head warm.

She lay down close to Danny, put her arms around him, and felt his chest rise and fall. Sebastian came and curled up to the sleeping bag, tucking himself behind her legs.

She felt a chill in the core of her stomach for a second as the dog's body huddled beside them, and she knew someone would have to pay for what she'd done. It seemed unreasonable that it should be any other way. She simply had to make sure it wouldn't be him. It wouldn't be Danny who paid, with his black hair and dark eyes and his lanky, barely muscled form.

THIRTY-FOUR

December 30

"Hello, is Lauren there?"

Jack recognized the voice, it was the doctor who'd called earlier in the week.

"No, I'm sorry, she's gone to visit her mother."

"To whom am I speaking?" the voice inquired.

"This is Jack Clay, I'm Lauren's father."

"Mr. Clay, your daughter has missed an important appointment which is part of her PDHA, and there is a small but significant chance she could be considered AWOL, which obviously would jeopardize the conditions of her terminal leave and discharge."

"I see," he said calmly, though his heart was suddenly pounding. "Well, she should be back in a few days, I'm sure we could reschedule something. She just got home, you know, she's been settling in."

"Sir, I need to speak frankly with you,"

Eileen Klein said. "I don't normally pursue these matters so rigorously, but I spoke with Lauren the day before she left for home and there are some very problematic discrepancies between her PDHA and military records I was unfortunately not privy to at the time."

"Listen," Jack said, "can she make another appointment or not?"

"Mr. Clay, your daughter gave some orders that were recently under investigation. She is not in trouble, yet. But based on my evaluation with her and subsequent conversations with those in her unit I believe she is at high risk for recapitulating a violent scenario. Do you know where she is? Is she by herself?"

Jack said nothing.

"Mr. Clay, this is important. Do you know where she is?"

THIRTY-FIVE

DISPATCH #1

Dear Sistopher,
I got a calendar today at the bank while I was running errands with PJ. There are pages and pages until you come home. How is it going at 'learn to boss people around school'? Are you good at it?

I saw a movie yesterday called *The Endurance* which you would love. It's about Ernest Shackleton. (Which is a great name for a rich prisoner.) It's about his expedition on his boat called the *Endurance.* You probably don't remember this at all but he was an Irish polar explorer and then he decided to explore the Antarctic. He spent his whole life traveling around by ship and on foot in the frozen parts of the world. Anyway the *Endurance* got trapped in the ice and so the toughest guys set out on foot for help. His crew was trapped in the frozen ship for TWO YEARS. TWO!!! YEARS!!! and they lived. He went back for them and got everyone out alive.

Another time his ship went down and he and his crew had to camp out on an ice floe. They were at sea on this big hunk of ice for a week! Camping! I want to do that so bad, Lowey. That's what I'm going to do when I graduate high school.

I just thought you would want to know that. I miss you but I'm glad you're in Washington State bossing people around. PJ says you're going to be good at your job because you're a natural and you always watch out for everyone. I miss you, Sistopher. Be safe, I love you,

— Sir Ernest Henry Shackleton

Things looked very different in the bright daylight. She awoke before him and got the fire going strong, took out packs of granola and two burrito MREs. She put several bottles of water near the fire so they would thaw, and set a pot of snow by the fire to boil it, then put tea bags directly in the pot to make a dark bitter tea. Give them energy for the day.

She went outside and climbed back up to the car and surveyed the landscape with her binoculars. They were near the coast, she was sure of it. It was overcast and she didn't have the visibility she wanted, but she could see there was a steady slope to what she thought was the ocean. And a wider, well-plowed road in the distance.

She looked over into the pine woods and then back toward where they'd come from. Then pulled a map from beneath the driver's seat and studied it for some time. Satisfied, she ran back down the slope and woke Danny, and they sat before the fire eating the ready-made military food. His face was blank but he looked well rested.

"Why did you pick singing instead of some other instrument?" he asked her before even saying good morning.

"It was free," she said.

"Isn't it weird that you were singing all this classical stuff and then you went into the army?" he asked, almost to himself.

"Why is that weird?"

"They're so different."

She raised her eyebrows. "They're not different at all."

"You know what I mean."

"I wasn't like you," she said. "I didn't do good at anything you could make money at.

Not like I was going to have a career running track or singing, you know?"

"Why not?"

She thought about how Troy had taught her to hear properly. Without him she would have been listening to her parents' records forever or whatever crap was on the radio, iTunes, the boring songs people sing in school chorus. Troy played the music for her that first let her escape, let her leave home and the neighborhood and the town and the world.

And when the sounds of artillery and mortars and diesel engines, bad southern rock and hip hop, calls to prayer from the mosque, and dogs and officers barking took up space in her head she had the power to hear these things differently. Amidst the hot and dirty noise of war and waiting she had the promise of Arvo Pärt, cold and white and unreachable.

"Time for pushups," she said, clapping him on the shoulder.

He rolled his eyes and she felt the familiar flash of anger. He was so resistant to anything that required the slightest physical discomfort. And he was poor at taking orders.

"Seriously, Daniel, you gotta get strong."

"What the fuck are we doing?" he said.

She ignored him, got down and did ten and then stopped, did ten more, then ten more. She knew he was competitive enough to at least try. "C'mon, bud. Drop. Don't be a fucking wimp."

He got down next to her and did four, then stopped, struggled to do two more. It was beyond pathetic that a boy his age couldn't do a full set of pushups. But she knew people could be made to do pushups. Just like they could be made to cook meals and pick children up from school or live in a filthy dust cloud and dismantle other families' homes.

"Keep going," she told him. "It's early, dude. You can definitely do fifty by the end of the day." She browbeat him into fifteen and watched the look of genuine pride on his face when he finished. She knew his body must feel good too. Building strength is its own addiction. She high-fived him and then gave his hand a squeeze. Told him she was proud. Situps weren't a problem and she made him do eighty. Then jumping jacks. Then stretching. It was important to establish a routine. Boys are made for growing muscles, and she would make sure by New Year's he was doing what he should, would keep going with it. He could have everything she didn't. He could be smart and strong and free of all the stupid ideas that tie you down, family and nation and god. He could save a life.

She put out the fire with snow and gathered their gear together in one of the little rooms off the living room. Sebastian shuffled around behind her, sniffing in the corners of the house and sneezing, and she remembered again that he was dead and ignored him.

"Now we're going to run," she said.

Danny didn't look at her like she was joking this time.

"Low, this is stupid," he said. "Dad's prolly freaking the fuck out. And I thought we were going to your friend's house."

"I'm sure he thinks we're in Buffalo and we're fine. And we are fine, so we don't need to contact him. You don't have to be in constant contact with people. You can trust that they are doing well. You can write them letters. You want to write him a letter? He's getting a week to hang out alone, big deal. When's the last time that guy had some time to himself?"

He said nothing. She could tell he liked camping and was overwhelmed by the surroundings. When she got him out into the woods she knew he would understand. He would see the things she saw.

THIRTY-SIX

Jack's voice was tight with panic when he said Lauren's name, and PJ shut his office door, pressing the phone to his ear, a welling sense of dread forming in his gut. PJ did not want to hear the information he'd been anticipating for the last two days. She'd been popped for The Bag of Nails, he was sure; they'd arrest her in Buffalo. She'd broken the conditions of her terminal leave and now she would be back in the army, back in an army jail, then court martialed. He gripped the phone and rested his head in his hand, closed his eyes.

Jack said, "She's not at Meg's! I don't know where they are. Meg didn't even make specific plans with them. Just knew they were going to arrive sometime this week."

"All right," PJ said, genuinely relieved she had not been arrested. "All right now. Maybe they did some sightseeing and they're still on their way."

Jack told him what Dr. Klein had said, and PJ's heart began to pound again and now he was sweating as well. He went through it. She would not do something to Danny — this he knew. Or thought he knew. She looked rough when he saw her, like she was still in it. Jesus fucking Christ, how did those motherfuckers at Lewis-McChord let her off base? He blamed himself for not staying with her the other day, but those straight legs at Lewis . . . Nineteen suicides last year, and that boy that came home and put his girlfriend's head in a box was from Lewis, and that fucker who waterboarded his three-year-old . . .

PJ took a deep breath and reminded himself that this was Lauren, not some hillbilly on crank. She may have simply decided it was time to get away from family and have a break. It could be that simple. But he thought again of the last time he saw her. He knew what it was like to go from humping through shit and blood one day and then stand on the sidewalk of your hometown the next — and still he didn't do a fucking thing, he just dropped her home. He saw the pain and determination in her eyes and like a fool he dropped her home.

"I'm going to call the police," Jack said.

"No! Ain't nobody calling the police just

now." Jack clearly had no sense that his daughter might have done more than lie about where she was going, had no sense what it would mean if she was arrested for arson and kidnapping.

"Well then, what?" Jack demanded. "What?"

PJ told him she was far more capable of survival than any of them. What he didn't say was that she was also far more capable of fucking some shit up than any of them; motivated, efficient, and familiar with sacrifice. He didn't say that sometimes people take the folks they're protecting with them when they decide to check out.

"Gimme an hour," he said. "I'll be over in an hour. You and me got this, gonna be okay. We'll figure out where they got to, we'll get ahold of them and fly there, turn it into a nice vacation for the whole family."

PJ called Holly and Shane, who were no help and raised his fears considerably. She'd fought with Shane and left an eight-thousand-dollar check in Holly's hospital room, and neither of them would say more about it.

Other than Shane's "She's not herself."

PJ said, "Thank you, professor, I think we got that part figured out. Now, she say something to you? Anything? You know I'm "not out to get her in trouble, so you tell me."

"She, uh . . ." Shane's voice broke. "She attacked me."

PJ nodded impatiently, felt like that boy was going to endure something worse in about a minute unless he started telling him what was going on. He enunciated clearly: "Did she say to you she wanted to go anywhere?"

"No," Shane said. "I don't know. She said she hates it here."

Holly told him that Lauren was fine but seemed a little distracted and had several black bands tattooed on her arms. And that's when PJ started jamming things in his briefcase and grabbed his coat.

He ran into Troy in the hallway coming from group and called him discreetly back into his office for a moment. The man showed no surprise or concern at all that Lauren was gone, just squinted and rubbed his eyes distractedly, as if he were bored. PJ fought the urge to grab him by the shoulders, his terror rising in relation to every one of Troy's thoughtful pauses.

"She didn't mention any plans," Troy said, his voice crisp and just too slow, too articulate. "But . . . and I know everyone probably already realizes this — she never went anywhere without that little boy when she

338

was at home, did she? It seems like her normal behavior. She would take him anywhere. That's obvious."

"Lauren did not look well when I saw her," PJ said.

"Why didn't you do something then?" Troy asked, and there was no accusation, no anger or malice, just pure, eager curiosity. Like the man was studying him.

"Damnit, you *know* how it is," PJ told him impatiently. Thinking if anyone could understand it would be a man who'd blown his entire career and every penny he'd made, all his recognition as a musician, all his prospects by drinking himself from the Upper East Side into a Bowery rooming house and then, several smoldering bridges and hospitalizations later, down into a church basement in his hometown.

Troy shook his head. "I don't," he said simply. "Well anyway, when she comes back you can tell her I've talked to Curtis. You can tell her she needs to have things ready by August."

PJ nodded, stunned by the man's indifference, his confident detachment. Then he shut off the lights.

Everyone had failed Lauren Clay, he thought as he was running across the slick asphalt to his car, even him. But no one, not even MIA Meg, had failed to love her, and you could see it, the way she rose to care for Danny, the gentle way she carried her family.

But Iraq had changed all that.

She'd finally learned enough of hate to fail herself.

Troy turned himself in at the end of the workday. There wasn't time to waste when Lauren came home, so he would do this now. He watched the officers' faces when he confessed. They all but smacked their foreheads and said "of course." He smiled at them. It had been a long time since he'd been around men like this, and they were very interesting. He knew their ways. They liked tight things and padding and gadgets, they liked shiny things and hiding, hard sounds, consonants, knowing looks, pretend subtlety. They liked lies and also being close to lies, and they liked everything that caused pain, as though it was a monster they could actually fight with their magic blue suits and caps. He sometimes felt very bad for these kinds of men, but he loved the poor theater of their body language.

Things didn't go so well when they wanted to talk to him though. Things never went well when people wanted to talk. He told them he was too drunk to remember exactly how he had set the fire.

When they asked more questions about it he found himself describing Operation Desert Storm and the day he was drenched in oil, and how his unit cleared land mines from around the burning wells. There were ten months of fire. Troy realized he wasn't talking about The Bag of Nails at all and he chuckled to himself.

"You almost killed a girl, you think that's funny?"

Troy cocked his head to the side and looked at the officer again. He was young and nervous. Troy hadn't "almost" killed anyone. He'd helped to kill thousands and thousands, no "almost" about it. He was part of a meticulously planned campaign to kill, and he'd been working for the same company as these men at the time. What he was actually doing here today was saving a girl. Saving a thing that the girl embodied. Her bone structure, her weight, her ribs, the suppleness and strength of her form and the bellows of her belly. Her breath and the gleaming warmth of her voice big enough to cut an orchestra on its own. He was there to save something that lived in Lauren Clay, and he did not care at all if it lived curled right next to the thing that set that fire.

He shrugged.

"You *are* a fucking retard, you know that," said the other officer. "A fucking retard." Troy smiled at the man. He had pale skin and very dark hair on his arms, his slight paunch stuck out above his belt and he smelled slightly spicy, like nice shaving soap. It was delightful seeing him clearly all at once. He was someone's husband. He was someone's soft TV-watching husband. He probably grilled things on his porch and had a nice fluffy dog to pet and liked to snuggle with his wife and feel her smooth body and look at her pretty dresses. Someone made him dinners every night and bought his favorite lunch meats as though he were a child.

Troy smirked at the men. "Isn't one of you supposed to pretend to be bad or tough or something? You're both acting the same."

The first cop slapped Troy hard in the face.

He straightened his head and looked directly into the man's face.

"There you go," he said.

Thirty-Seven

The pine woods were dense and the trunks of the trees were dark and thick with branches, with knots and bowls made from hardened sap. Their height was staggering, disorienting. And the understory was a soft pine bed lightly dusted with snow, protected by the canopy. It smelled fresh and cold, and the sun flickered through the branches as they walked.

"You fall in line behind me," she said. "We'll have to go kinda slow to maneuver around in here, we're just going to hop through — you know, bob and weave between the trees and try to keep up a good pace."

"What about animals?" he asked.

"What about them?"

"What if they're in here?"

"They are in here," she said.

He looked like he might cry, like he was tired and trying to control his face. He stood still and surveyed the trees.

"Danny," she said. "Hup to it, buddy. C'mon, we gotta get fast and strong so the animals don't get us." She made a small amused sound in her throat, then coughed.

He stood still, his hands thrust deep in the pockets of his coat, and then he reached out and touched the branch of a tree, let the long needles slide through his red-mittened hand. Then he took his mittens off and felt them with his fingers. Pulled the pine bough to his face. His breath was visible, rising from his nostrils, and his cheeks were flushed. His eyes were lost in thought and black and flat with fear. Back home his whole room was papered in photographs of nature, of ancient trees and strange animals and glaciers. But just standing still in the woods had caught and hobbled whatever courage, whatever small sense of adventure he might have had.

"Dan. You can do it, buddy. It's a forest. You're not walking to the fucking electric chair." She was disappointed and tried not to get angry. "We're just going for a little run, man. That's all. Turn around and look, you can see the open space from here."

He put his mittens back on and then turned toward their little camp. She looked at her watch. They would run fifteen minutes in and fifteen minutes back. And tomorrow she'd up it to twenty-five.

"Why can't we run on the road we came in on?"

"Because we've run on roads before. We haven't run through the trees."

"Shouldn't we have some bread crumbs or pebbles or something to leave behind and mark our trail?"

"Daniel," she said gravely. "What the fuck is wrong with you?"

"Why can't we walk along the edge and check it out first?"

She said, "Nope," and began to jog in the narrow spaces between the trunks.

He didn't back out, he ran with her, kept pace either because of anxiety or because it was slow going. In the thickness of the trees she couldn't look back to see how he was doing, but she could hear his boots on the crisp snow and brittle brush of the forest floor. Soon she heard him laughing behind her.

Fifteen minutes in she stopped. They were warm, surrounded entirely by the weight of the forest and the snow, and Danny was sweating. He took off his hat. His face was red from the cold and exertion.

The forest was so still and enclosed and slow. The height of the trees were generations of human lives, and it was a comfort.

She watched him as he let his head fall back and gazed straight up into the towering canopy of green and black branches. Inside the tall woods they were at last the right size. Small and insignificant, moving unseen by anyone.

Danny said, almost to himself, "I don't know how to get back from here."

When they emerged from the woods the sun was blinding on the bright sloping expanse of snow, and they covered their eyes.

Back in the unrelieved empty cold of the house, she let Danny start the fire. Knelt beside him and showed him how to stack the wood in a pyramid, placing the lighter, drier kindling in the center. When the fire caught with a little roaring *whoosh,* he jumped back quickly and gave a little shout of delight. She suspected he'd be a natural at these kinds of things, and it was a good fire.

They would need to change out of their sweaty clothes before they became chilled.

"What time is it?" he asked.

She said, "Ten after ten," then smiled at the look of surprise on his face.

"How long will it take us to get to Mom's from here?"

"More than a day. More like two or three."

"Fuck! You're fucking kidding!"

"I'm not."

"When are we going to go?"

"I think we should get out to the coast first and see if we can see any glaciers melting. I want to check things out around here, see if it might be a good place to live." She was refreshed, animated after the run. "There's certainly a lot of stuff for you to study, right, William Parry? After we meet up with Daryl, I'll have a better idea of what kind of work there is for me out here."

He looked confused. "I don't think there's anything melting in this cold," he said. Then he asked her again: "When are we going to go to Mom's?"

She ignored him, stood in front of the fire and took off her sweaty thermal underwear, set the pieces down on the floor by the hearth to dry. The tattoos made her look like some kind of strange warrior from a different time. He looked at the black bands, wide blank rings of ink encircling either arm just below her shoulders. Her back was turned, and he could see the ripple of muscles. It was then that he realized they were black armbands. Permanent mourning, a part of her skin. There were three of them.

She didn't even shiver as she stood in her bare feet on the plank floor, then she put on a dry pair of socks, took another pair of dry wool socks out of her pack and threw them in his direction and put her other layers back on.

He went out and collected snow in the pot and set it beside the fire to melt, and then he stood staring into the fire for several minutes with his arms folded across his chest. He thought of the footage of The Bag of Nails engulfed in those tall flames, the tree beside the building. He looked at her, watched her organizing her gear. She had closed herself off to him, now when he needed to see her, needed to know her most of all.

"If you don't take your long underwear off and dry it, you'll catch a chill," she told him.

"I'll catch a chill because we're in the middle of fucking arctic nowhere," he said.

"Right," she said. "That's why if you don't get out of your sweaty clothes you'll get even colder."

She was glad he was angry instead of scared. Something about it, maybe the familiarity, made her feel relaxed. Anger is the active part of fear, not its opposite. Anger and fear were two sides of the same counterfeit coin that was the currency of war. But anger is what gets things done.

"Low, if Dad isn't worried by now I'm sure Mom is."

"I doubt she's worried," she said.

"I doubt she isn't!"

"Why would you care if she's worried?"

"What? That's such a stupid question," he said, genuinely disgusted.

He shivered, and she could tell the wet clothes were bringing his body temperature down.

She said, "Take your fucking sweaty socks and long johns off, dogbody."

"Don't tell me what to do! I'm not a soldier and you're not even in the army anymore."

"You're not going to last long out here if you get cold," she said simply.

"I don't want to last long out here," he said. "I want to go to Buffalo."

"Buffalo is a shithole."

"Yeah. So what? I don't think people are supposed to camp in the middle of winter in an abandoned building with only army rations and sleeping bags, burying their shit in the snow." He shivered again, and she was proud of his stubbornness.

"Suck it up," she told him.

"No! This is fucking stupid, Low. There's

349

something wrong. You think Mom and Dad are like they were before. They're not. Nobody's the same. You're not the same at all," he said, his voice breaking. "There's something wrong."

She dropped him quickly with a kick to the back of his knee and then grabbed his hand and turned it down hard, pressing his fingers toward the inside of his wrist and holding his elbow in place. He winced in pain and shock. Then she let go, shoving him away hard as she did.

He stood up angry, his eyes watering. "Where's my phone?" he demanded.

She laughed and effortlessly dropped him again with a sharp kick to the back of his other leg. "Not a video game, is it?" she said.

He stood up and she dropped him again. She could do that all day if she needed to.

He stood up and tried to block her but she dropped him again. He looked bewildered for a moment and then suddenly fascinated. And she raised her eyebrows and nodded at him. She could count on Danny to be himself, to be the boy she raised.

He stood up and she didn't do anything. "Take off your wet clothes," she said.

When he said no, she dropped him back down to the ground, and this time he laughed.

She folded her arms and looked down at him.

"Show me how to do that," he said.

By late afternoon he could awkwardly execute several moves from combatives, knew how to protect his neck and how to kill someone with a rolled-up piece of cardboard. They sparred by the firelight. When they finally stopped, exhausted, she made them dinner and then fell asleep before him making fitful noises, startling him horribly by yelling the word "Fuck!" and "Stand down, stand down!" even as she lay motionless, zipped in her sleeping bag.

Danny's heart was racing from the sound of her shouting. He lay bundled near the fire, sobered by sadness at the things she must have seen or done. Sleep didn't want him so he puttered in the cold, got up and put more broken furniture on the fire, moved closer to her and then pulled the poncho liner over both of their bags. Her face was calm now and she was breathing steadily.

Images of their house and his room flickered through his thoughts, the pictures of strange animals and nature and landscapes, his computer, the narrow dingy hallway. The tone his computer made when he turned it on bloomed almost audibly around him, and then another stupid song was beginning to replay in his head. He didn't want to wake her up and ask her to sing, which might make her mad, and she needed her sleep so they could drive to Buffalo tomorrow.

He'd miscalculated. Driving away with Lauren was not a good idea. He saw how she was really looking at something these last few days when they talked about the dog. And she had never hit him before, not even joking around. The ease with which she had knocked him over was astonishing, actually frightening. He needed to get to a phone. Their father was better now but he was still totally capable of spacing out and not realizing how long they'd been gone. Maybe he could get her to drive back into one of the towns they'd passed on their way here. If he could only get a map. It seemed like she knew where they were, but maybe she didn't. Maybe she was making it up as she went, didn't want to be in any known place at all.

This time the song in his head was Madonna's "Borderline": *Borderline feels like I'm going to lose my mind. You just keep on pushing my love over the borderline.* It was because of the silence, he thought. Silence like this can mess you up. There was just the hiss and occasional pop of the fire and now Madonna. He caught himself whispering the words "keep pushing me, keep pushing me." He hated pop music. He was afraid the next song would be something by Queen, which would probably prove he was gay or that he had lost his mind or had the onset of hypothermia.

He couldn't sleep even though he was tired and his body was sore from working out and running and getting knocked down. He'd never done those things and he had to admit he liked them. A lot. They kept him warm and occupied instead of freaking out, and it was amazing the kind of stuff Lauren knew how to do.

This whole thing was crazy. But he did feel more alert in general and strong, and the land was beautiful, beyond joking kind of beautiful. Lauren was undeniably a bad-ass, and no one he knew had done anything close to what they'd been doing for the last few days. It was kind of amazing for a vacation. If she had some problems from the war this was a good way to deal with it; training him to be strong, going to places they were interested in instead of watching them on the Internet. Making fires. She was right that people are tougher than they know. If he came back to school able to survive in the wilderness and having seen real animals — hopefully not up too close but close enough — he would be a badass too. The desire to leave and the desire to be alone with her, to learn, to make her happy, to keep going frustrated him to the point of tears. He wanted so badly to see her smile, to have her know that he was good — those were the things that pushed away the loneliness before he got his computer: her room across the hall, her laugh, her listening to his stories, being a part of her plans, being her helper.

But the whole time he was writing to her in Iraq she'd never written back telling him what she was doing or what was going on and he never asked. She wrote about his life, asked him questions, talked about books he should read or joked around. That was how they were. She'd slipped away from him more than a year ago and he hadn't noticed. Her world, the things she thought about herself and their family, had always been only her own. Unopened, unexpressed, waiting. He knew her life as it pertained to him and nothing more. He knew she loved him. He knew who she was when she left. And he realized now with a hollow terror that he did not know this person sleeping near the fire.

He did not know this person who returned at all.

THIRTY-EIGHT

Holly's short hair became her. The scar was something she'd have to grow used to. Numb and raw and ugly, it was still seeping beneath the bandages. When she delicately peeled them back to clean the wound, it looked like her flesh had melted; thank god Bridget was a nurse. The skin was thin, dark purple, and brick red, and it hurt when exposed to the air, when she touched anything. She wore long sleeves but her left hand looked like it belonged to some kind of devil.

Grace and she had just settled on the couch in their pajamas to watch cartoons when Shane came over. The room hummed with the air purifier and humidifier, and Holly's inhaler and prescription bottles sat on the coffee table within reach. She couldn't stay long in the hospital because she wasn't on Bridget's insurance anymore, but it didn't matter because she was happy to be home.

Holly saw him through the top window of the door and waved him in. He slid his shoes off, leaving them on the plastic mat by Grace's green rain boots. Then he came over to the couch, leaned down to kiss Holly on the cheek, and picked up Gracie, hoisting her onto his shoulders.

"You having a TV party with Mom?" he asked her.

Grace stuck her thumb in her mouth and hunched over his head, still looking at the screen. He swayed back and forth, and she held on to him by wrapping one arm around his forehead. She giggled but still didn't speak.

"What's on?"

Grace pointed to the television. He took her off his shoulders and held her on his hip, looking into her face

"What happened to Gracie's big loud voice?" he asked.

"She rediscovered her little tasty thumb," Holly said.

Grace's eyes twinkled as Holly said it; she raised her eyebrows and gave Shane a sly look. He sat down on the couch still holding her, but she climbed off his lap and scooted over to a pile of LEGOs beneath the dining-room table.

He and Holly watched her organizing the plastic bricks into different colored piles. Holly rolled her eyes. "Everything with this girl," she said. "It's all got to be just so."

He slumped down in the couch and leaned against her, taking her good hand and holding it. "They found who did it," he said quietly.

She looked up at him expectantly, felt she might throw up.

"Troy confessed."

"Troy?" she asked hoarsely.

"I heard it on the radio."

"Do you . . ."

"No, of course not," he said, lowering his voice even further so as not to disturb Grace. "The first thing they said is the suspect is military: There were boot prints all over the mud, and tracks between the bar and the riverbank. You know what I think."

"Yeah, but you're wrong." She shook the inhaler, exhaled, then put it in her mouth and breathed in deeply. "And anyway, you were with her all night."

"Not all night," Shane said. "She's changed."

Holly's mouth tightened; she took a deep breath and shook her head at him, her face telegraphing complete disappointment, a blank, angry, well-practiced tolerance for stupidity.

"Why would Troy say he did it then?" she asked.

"I don't think anyone knows why he does anything. But if he knew who did it, or if he thought it was Lauren or that Lauren might be in trouble he'd —"

"Shut up," Holly said, tiredly. "Shut up, I've had enough of it."

"Has she been in touch with you?"

"No, but I've had enough of it. You know what Troy did in the war?"

"I had no idea he was in the war."

"The first one, the other one," she said quietly, her voice still rough. "He stood around looking at fires that couldn't be put out, just like Dave. If it's him, it's him. I don't care. I'm not mad. Anyway, it doesn't matter. Half the town — more than half the town because of Drum is military or ex-military. Jesus, you know that. It could be some kid from Drum, prolly is. Patrick served, Peej served, everybody fucking served except you and me and a bunch of stuck-up pricks." Her voice had fallen to a whisper and it faltered. He went to the kitchen and got her a glass of water and then sat back down, his thigh touching hers.

She leaned against him and he put his arm

gently around her. "I know you don't think she's different now, but honestly —"

"Different?" Holly interrupted him again. "She's not different. She's always been disciplined. Think about it. She's been protecting every single one of us without relief since we were fifteen. She's been raising that boy since she was ten on her own, without anyone telling her how to do it. She's been taking care of weak people her whole life. There's nothing at all different about her becoming a soldier."

"But those aren't things soldiers do," Shane said. "Not one of them. She didn't enlist because it was part of her character, she enlisted because they paid a twenty-thousand-dollar signing bonus. Don't forget that. Taking care of weak people is not what goes on over there, Holly. She may have done it so she could be the breadwinner at home. But don't be confused about how that money got made."

Holly looked away from him and he laced his fingers through hers more tightly, squeezed her hand, insistent that she listen. He couldn't be the only one who saw what had happened to Lauren, and he was exhausted to the point of tears by the blank-faced denial her homecoming seemed to elicit. He'd held Lauren and looked into her eyes, had felt the strength of her will to hurt him, seen the rage and frustration when people didn't do what she said. Holly had to have seen those things too. He knew PJ had, he knew it when they talked.

But they were supposed to pretend, even now when they had no idea where she was or what she could be doing, even as they lived in the shadow of the base, and heard reports from places like Fallujah, or read about disastrous brutal homecomings, they were supposed to pretend that what she did was some angel's work in hell.

Holly looked back at him, defeated and overwhelmed, and there were tears on her face. He kissed her cheek and she rested her head on his shoulder.

"I know what you're saying." She spoke quietly, her mouth close to his ear, her breath ragged. "I hear it. But it's not her."

By the time Shane got there the police or someone had already been through the apartment and the door was wide open. Troy's living room was a cascade of manuscript pages and sheet music, a tumble of white and black that sloped from an old wooden cabinet down along the floor into the tiny kitchen. It was a small place, an efficiency in a remote part of town not far from base. The painted wooden floor was covered by a threadbare Persian rug.

The room looked like it housed the remains of a bigger, grander life. Walls were hung with gold-framed iconography. Shane recognized Saint Sebastian pierced by arrows; an illustration of the French Gnostic philosopher Amalric of Bena, whose followers were burned before the gates of Paris; a photograph of David Wojnarowicz standing in the street with a cutout mask of Rimbaud's face over his own. He was fascinated and embarrassed by seeing a very private man's possessions.

Shane began to wonder if the police had done this or if it was someone else. If someone had done it in anger, maybe Troy himself.

There were no photographs of family or friends or regular people. Troy's desk had also been sufficiently trashed, but his bookcase was left untouched. Shelves and shelves of books on music theory, psychoacoustics, history, art history, theology. Shane began reading the titles, he pored over the books until the light in the room began to fade. Then he saw it, lying there unframed, a five-by-seven photograph of Lauren, thin and pale in a sleeveless black dress, her posture perfect, holding a black folder. She was looking straight into the camera, her hair slightly tangled where it fell about her shoulders. She was wearing PJ's watchcap, smiling.

Shane turned the picture over. Neatly printed on the back it said: "Soprano Lauren Clay at 15." As if it was a shot of another historical figure or religious icon. As if she was a saint.

THIRTY-NINE

In the morning he got up and collected snow without her asking. They did pushups together before the fire and ate and drank strong tea and then burned all their garbage. She was proud of him. She felt alive again, felt good. The remoteness suited them. The house lodged no history they knew and the landscape seemed undeniably a place where they belonged. It was the dream place. It was the sound of so many voices you could not hear a single one. She looked out again at the frozen expanse drained of color. Blinding as it gleamed beneath the blue sky like the inside of a cloud cut down.

"What are we going to do today?" he asked. "Are we going to get on the road?"

"I was thinking we could dismantle one of these houses and build a boat," she said.

He stared blankly at her.

"We'll need to go to a hardware store and get some supplies."

He turned his back to her for a minute, stood completely still.

"Okay," he said finally.

They left the house and trekked up the hill to the car. While they walked he began singing "Winter Wind" distractedly, his boots crunching on the snow like a metronome, as if it were a song for hiking. His voice was a sweet tenor but it was made for laughing, not singing. He crescendoed on "sing heigh-ho, unto the green holly" and inadvertently changed key. The sun was still low in the sky, turning the bottoms of the clouds silvery orange and pink. And the bright snow reflected its glowing and held the forest's gray shadows; crisp silhouettes of trees as if they were cut into the ice moved when the wind came up, and the dark forms of birds traveled over the white land.

Their skin stung from the cold where it was exposed, and their breath rose and drifted in pale clouds about them. When they reached the top of the rise Danny stopped singing and seemed almost forlorn, and the snow glittered like crushed glass and the sun cast a golden glow across the landscape.

The car was covered with a delicate pattern of frost, a lace of white moss, and the doors were frozen shut. They stood pulling on the handles for several minutes until the driver's door opened — tearing the rubber seal, which was cracked and brittle. She knew there should be more snow there at this time of year. That the roads shouldn't even be passable. The car should be buried in a snowdrift, the gasoline should be almost frozen. Just like the Black River back home was threatening to flood, not freeze. They should never have been able to get off ON-137. Yet here they were, cold but not dead. No animals had come at night to eat them. No wind blew out their fire. No fire burned their house down with them inside it. They were the very things that warmed the land. Nothing was going to stop them.

The car turned over with difficulty and she put the heat on and they sat and waited with the engine running while ice retreated across the windshield.

"Are you okay?" he asked.

She looked over at him. "I am," she said calmly. "Are you?"

He shook his head almost imperceptibly. And she put out her hand for him to hold.

"Remember you used to sing to me on the way home from school?"

She smiled. "Of course I do."

"That was the weird thing. When you left.

366

Because suddenly there was no sound from you. And then the turntable broke. The house got really quiet when you were gone at first. And then Mom got me the computer so we could talk and I didn't have to do everything at school." He was talking really fast, almost talking to himself. "It's so quiet here," he said. "It's too quiet."

"It is." She still didn't know what was upsetting him.

"This place feels like the songs you practiced," he said, and she felt the hair on the back of her neck stand up, knew he had been to that dream place with her — or could at least see it now. Her singing and his vision of trekking across the frozen landscape, eating polar bear meat, they took place in the same world. Something had drawn them both to this frozen ground long before they ever came there.

She looked through the faint shadow of frost on the windshield at trees in the distance and nodded. He was right. If the landscape was sound it would be high and precise and white. Arvo Pärt had once called his music white light, comprising all colors. And the blending of the melody and the voice he described as one plus one equaling one. That was what she wanted. That was the equation she wanted. But she would settle for one plus one equaling none.

"I saw so many pictures of places like this," Danny said. "But being in the place is like hearing the song. It's not like a picture. I thought it was but it isn't at all, there's so much space and air and light."

She smiled at what he was saying. It was silent here but the space begged to be heard. Could not be described otherwise. She had taken them somewhere that looked most like what she held on to inside. Sounds no war, no family, no thought could reach. If she was no longer worthy of singing or hearing sacred music she could go to the land that was its mirror and get lost in its reflection.

He said, "Being here makes me think I've never actually been anywhere before. People take vacations on break from school, but we never took vacations. Plus when I was home I just ignored home most of the time. We were there but we weren't there."

She had nothing to say to comfort his anxiety and he was already gazing out the window again, humming "Winter Wind." If this was a place he couldn't ignore that was good. She'd make sure this was a real vacation, and he could see and do great things. She wanted him to be happy. Maybe she could make everything right in the next few days. Either go home, or start over there, find work, and get a place near Daryl's. Maybe nobody had to pay.

She looked at him bundled in his coat and boots, a reflective stillness so foreign to him now settled over his face, in his eyes. The car was warm at last and she backed out quite far until the road widened and she could turn around. Just a few more days, she thought. But she could only make him promises in her head. She would take him to the coast and then they would leave. She would teach him how to drive. They would see the land changing. They would break free of the things that tied people up in the spiral of their DNA, and in the demands made by blood. They would live in the future. Because the future is the only safe place to be.

She and Walker gave their casualty reports to Captain Parker. There would be a 15-6 and Parker would be the one to determine if any action would be taken.

When none was, she'd gotten her first tattoo. A wide black armband. Black blank ink suited her skin just fine. She'd gotten two more bands out of respect and so she wouldn't forget who she was.

"You gunna do that every time you gunna

end up with long black sleeves," Captain Parker told her. "Get yerself some pretty flowers like I got." He looked steadily at her and smiled. Parker had more than pretty flowers on his arms. Green-stemmed tulips and hyacinths and daffodils wound their way up his forearms and biceps through a junkyard of weird signifiers: an Irish harp, a Star Trek insignia, a dragon, a lightning bolt, the eye of Horace, the ace of spades, a Jack Russell terrier, a skull, the equation for the second law of thermodynamics, a Puerto Rican flag, Gandalf smoking a pipe, and a powder-pink heart with the words *I LOVE DEBBIE* — written inside in the same font, he'd enthusiastically pointed out to her, used for the *I Love Lucy* show.

This was the man who made decisions for them. And it was Captain Parker who told her that Camille, Daryl's wife, had moved back to Canada to live with her parents outside of Hebron.

"Tat does go nice with yer eye, though," he said. "Can you see outta that thing?"

"Yes sir, I can see fine. It's a burst blood vessel."

He grinned. "It's real sharp."

Her right eye was a deep scarlet. When the field doctor first saw it he thought she'd been hit by a chunk of safety glass from the window. But apparently it happened right after the incident, when she and Daryl were back inside the FOB in medical. Waiting.

FORTY

They got gas at the Exxon station, a grubby weathered salt-stained building with Plexiglas windows. Danny went in to pay for the fuel and was gone for ten minutes.

"What took you?" she asked.

"I used this amazing new invention called a toilet," he said. "And soap."

The town was farther away than she'd remembered, and they drove past miles of snow-covered nowhere, telephone poles and an occasional billboard flanking the highway. Out in the distance they could see narrow black roads cutting through the landscape and disappearing into pine-covered hills. Danny was full of questions about the region for which she had no answers, just anecdotes from Daryl. Finally he asked her about something she knew a little about.

"Why was Joan of Arc such a big deal?" he asked.

"A lotta reasons," she said. "Because there

weren't women soldiers back then, for one."

"But why was she a saint? Was it because she was a soldier or because she thought God was talking to her?"

"Because she led some battles in the Hundred Years War and she claimed God sent her to do that," she told him. "After the English burned her at the stake the pope declared her innocent and made her a saint, so she was like a retroactive saint."

It was getting too hot in the car with the heat on and their coats and long underwear. She turned it down and opened her window a crack, letting in a sharp gust of icy air and a crisp smell that exhilarated her and made her feel like driving forever, as far north as they could go.

"So she was executed for fighting the English?"

"She wasn't," Lauren said. "Her official crime was actually dressing like a man."

"No way."

"Seriously. They put her in a men's prison instead of a convent where she would have been guarded by nuns, so she had only men for guards. She wore men's clothes and wouldn't take off her armor because she didn't want them to mess with her. And since she wouldn't put on a dress they charged her with the heresy of cross-dressing, and the penalty for that was death."

The road before them was covered with a long patch of ice, and she slowed down.

Danny laughed. "That's fucking ridiculous."

"Yeah," she said. "It was a lose-lose situation. When she agreed to put the dress on they attacked her and took it away again and gave her only men's clothes for a second time. When she put the men's clothes she'd been forbidden to wear back on at their insistence, they charged her with heresy and burned her at the stake."

"Jesus," Danny said.

"Yeah. Not a good way to go. But the interesting thing is she hallucinated legions of soldiers behind her in battle, and sometimes it was just her and a couple of dudes she knew. She saw visions of saints too."

"Like good ol' Saint Sebastian," he said. Then he called the dog up into the front seat and put his arms around him, scratched his chest. "Looks like he's getting a thicker coat because of the cold," he said, and she laughed and nodded. Then looked away when Sebastian yawned, squinting his eyes and curling his tongue. He'd been sleeping in the back seat where he didn't exist, but now, sitting with Danny, the dog's body was clearly visible.

"Uh, what else," she said distractedly. "Right, she was a leader. That's the other reason she was a big deal — she was a teenager and she led an army."

"Like you," he said proudly. "You were all about bossing people around too, right?"

Lauren was quiet. She did not want to think about the orders she had to give and struck the images from her head, unfortunately replacing them with images of her own teenage life: years doing laundry and getting Danny from school, making the same simple dinners with frozen things, sitting beside her father while he watched TV. She thought about falling asleep sometimes before Danny did, worrying, even as she fought to keep her eyes open, that he would get hurt with no one to watch him while she slept. She thought of the slur "combat support." Because officially women weren't in combat. They just support. It was the same fucking job as every soldier she served with, but with the added downgrade in title and pay. She thought about how she was a noncommissioned officer because she didn't have the college behind her, how errors in thought metastasized, bred more errors in thought — another way the past swallowed the future.

"I'm not like Joan of Arc at all," Lauren said simply. "I was kept in a woman's prison."

She pulled over to the side of the road abruptly, handed him the keys, and then walked around to the passenger side.

"You can drive home," she said.

"To Watertown?"

"No, you bonehead, to the FOB."

He slid behind the wheel. "Are we going to build a boat?"

"Are you nuts?" she asked him. "We don't know how to build a boat."

He looked confused for a minute and then brushed his hair out of his eyes, looked at the line of trees in the distance.

She said, "All you have to do is look straight ahead. Put it in drive. Right pedal is the gas, left pedal is the brake. It's like driving bumper cars. But you have to keep your eye on the road and don't go too fast."

He put his foot on the gas and the car lurched forward and then he turned sharply to the right and she grabbed the wheel from him and straightened it out. He put on the brake and the car slid several yards on the snowy road and they were thrown forward and caught tight against their seatbelts.

"Okay," she said. "Let's give that another try."

On his second attempt he drove slowly, maybe seven miles an hour for about a hundred yards. Lauren sat beside him laughing, pretending to paddle a canoe.

"Okay," she said. "Little faster."

He picked it up to fifteen and then twenty miles an hour. She knew that video games didn't prepare people for the real world of killing, and now she knew they didn't prepare you for the real world of driving either.

His look of concentration was so funny she started laughing again.

"Shut up," he said defensively. "Nobody learns how to drive in the fucking snow."

"You do," she said.

It was a straight shot with no traffic and, apart from the icy road, a good enough place to learn how to drive. She could feel his confidence growing. She could feel his mind working and was brought along in the vicarious joy of learning something new, the feeling of mobility and escape.

When they turned off onto the narrower extension that led to their camp, they heard a hollow beating rolling sound, and then in the distance she could see a blur of tan and gray amid the rising cloud of white.

Danny put on the brakes and she took out the binoculars, spotted the source of the roiling thunder, and handed them to him. A herd, dozens, maybe tens of dozens of deer, their bodies taking up a wide swath of the flat land below the ruined houses, were running up toward the road.

They watched in a kind of terrified wonder, a resigned horror, as the deer ran directly toward the car, unstoppable: the sound of their hooves on the ground getting louder, the rush and muscle of their bodies and the fluid rise and fall of their gait over the contours of the snow, like one animal, like a thing with one mind, about to engulf and trample them.

The first several animals in the herd saw the car and diverged around it, and suddenly they were in the center of the sound; they could see the deers' labored breath pumping from their nostrils in the cold, and their eyes black as glass as they tore around the car, their narrow, bony powerful legs and hooves just missing or the staccato clang as they nicked the hood and the fenders. Then finally the rest of the herd ran past on one side and the anarchic drumming din faded back into the snow.

They stared at one another, their hearts racing, even as the land around them fell silent again.

FORTY-ONE

When he called their father from the Exxon station no one had picked up. Jack Clay didn't have a cell, and because Danny didn't have his own cell he couldn't call their mother. The number was programmed into the phone and he'd never called it manually before or bothered to memorize it.

After working out she let him drive again. He was excited that with the car he could go where he wanted and do what he wanted. If something happened, if she got any stranger, he could get them out of there. He headed out past town onto a wider paved road that was better maintained and that he assumed was built for logging. For all his excitement at getting behind the wheel, he still drove slowly and cautiously. Braking often and looking constantly in the rearview mirror, which he hadn't paid much attention to before.

They were both dirty from days without a

shower or hairbrush, putting their sweat-soaked long underwear back on after it dried from the fire. They were red cheeked from the cold, their skin chapped, and they shared a feral ambitious look, especially when smiling. Without electricity, they were not staying up long after dark these few days and they were rising early. The discipline of setting and maintaining fires and keeping warm and hydrated was a rewarding kind of obsession. And there were real conse-quences to screwing up. He thought it was like they were living on the underside of a flat earth she'd come to occupy as a soldier. She was comfortable with extremes now and this world was a counterpoint to the other, difficult and isolated and stark. But peaceful and safe.

She said, "There's no one behind us, bud. Don't worry about the mirrors now, just concentrate on what's in front of you."

The sky was bright and there was no wind. She gave him her aviator glasses and put the sun visor down to keep the glare from her eyes.

Danny gained confidence and picked up speed, and she cranked up the heat and rolled her window down to feel the cold coastal air on her face. She'd felt no fear when he was driving. Bad as he was, knowing that he was capable, that he was learning, made her feel at ease; the more dispensable she became, the lighter she felt.

The landscape was pristine: the glacial dome of the mountains, long limestone ridges that looked like chunks of the continent had been upended, and beyond that the promise of wide open land, an icy shoreline and glaciers and water with nothing to obstruct their gaze for miles. The legend of whales beneath floating ice in a warming black sea. It was waiting out there for them.

Her mother was right: She needed to go somewhere where she could relax. And that was nowhere with no one. Or almost nowhere with Danny. She would finish teaching him what he needed to know and then maybe he'd be safe enough to leave for a while. That was the whole idea after all coming from their neighborhood. A place where people lived side by side, day in and day out, with people they had abandoned. The idea was not to stick together, not to stick around, but to give someone everything they needed to be alone and strong. To never have to see you again.

Danny rolled down his window too and then began howling. Behind him Sebastian scratched excitedly at the glass. His fur blowing wildly in the wind, he held his face up majestically to the cold.

"What's he doing?" Danny asked her.

"He's just excited," she said.

Danny laughed, picked up speed, and drove up a long rise. And now they were both howling, like some grave weight that once held them down had at last been cut away. They could see the sky and nothing more in the distance, and felt the coast before them as they drove along the crest of the rise.

Then she told him to stop and they would walk the rest of the way for a bit. Better to see it without anything to get in the way, no noise of the car, no windshield to obscure the horizon.

He pulled over and they walked to the top, beneath the blue sky.

The complicated enormous mass of black metal towered before them like a witch's floating castle off the coast. Four massive columns rose from the floor of the ocean lashed by cresting waves, making the base appear to rock. The rigs were tremendous things that dwarfed the world around them and caused Lauren's knees to buckle. She fell, catching herself with her hands, and then stood mute. Hot tears in her eyes. Here it was. In the middle of all this beauty. The thing busily sucking the past up from the ground and melting the future, burning their lives before they could live them.

"I wanted you to see this," she said, her voice shaking. And she did. She wanted him to know what it all looked like. That the thing she fought for was cold metal, and money, and absolutely nothing more. In the suffocating heat or in killing cold, these industrial castles looked the same. He'd seen the forest and the deer and the sky, and now he was seeing this. And she was seeing it too. Knew she could never work there. Never get near such a thing again.

He stood squinting beside her, licked his chapped lips. "What is it?"

Her eyes were dark and liquid and she didn't look at him. But he could hear her voice clearly in his head the same way she used to say it, almost in a whisper, pointing to the page: "The Snow Queen's Castle."

Later that night he found himself wide awake, and the song played as clearly as if it were coming from a radio, like it was coming from the outside — not in his head at all. But there was no radio and he knew it was him and that he was hallucinating the worst song ever written by a band he hated more than any other band in the world. "We are the champions, my friends," the song went, "and we'll keep on fighting till the end."

He started crying. It didn't matter that he'd seen wild animals and driven a car and looked at a giant oil rig. Being stuck with little but his own mind and not even a piece of paper meant listening to Queen. Which meant that when there was nothing to entertain him, he was a shallow vessel torturing himself with things he'd mocked his whole life, not able to recall a single bar from a song he liked, or a line from a book he'd read. He was supposed to be quick and smart. But it was beginning to look like he was not quick and not smart, was actually a dumb fucking chump, hallucinating dead Freddie Mercury.

He woke her up, and he was alarmed when his own voice didn't make the sound go away. It was bitter cold and dark, and the creepy falsetto refrain was a sarcastic taunt describing their sorry state.

"What is it?" She sat up instantly, and in the dim light of the fire he could see she was holding a gun tucked in close at her side. He closed his eyes and covered them with his hands. Maybe he was dreaming. It seemed very unlikely that he was sleeping on the floor of a ruined building with no locks and few windows in the middle of winter in front of a fire made from broken furniture and cedar shingles with his sister who was holding a gun and an internal soundtrack from a gay pride parade.

When he opened his eyes her hands were empty. But everything else was the same. "Would you sing something?"

"Danny, what the hell?"

"I'm hearing music." He shook his hands around in front of him as if he were in pain, shook his head, he began crying. "Sing something!"

"I think you're dreaming, bud."

"I'm not." He felt tears running down his face and struggled to keep his voice steady. "I'm not dreaming. I've read about these things happening when there's no noise for a long time. People get songs trapped in their head and then they hear them. Could you please please sing something?"

She pulled her bag closer to his and put her arm around him.

"I don't want anything stuck in my head," he whispered.

She said, "I hear you, bud," and he felt her rough mitten on his face, rubbing the tears from his cheeks. "But you're okay, you're okay. You just had a bad dream."

He shook his head. He wanted to tell her

what was happening but he was mute from fear that he had been hearing things that weren't there, fear that she'd brought a gun on this trip and he hadn't known it. Hadn't known not to go anywhere with her because she was different now. There had to be a reason they were both losing it this way. A simple reason he was overlooking. He thought maybe they had eaten something poisonous. Maybe they were both sensory deprived, or it was confusion from the cold. Hypothermia. The thought sent a jolt through his stomach, constricted his breath. Or maybe it was all biological. Maybe their mother had left because she was going crazy and didn't want to hurt them. Maybe their father had left them on their own in the house because he was crazy. Maybe the two of them would be homeless forever, living together in this shelter beside the sloping ghosts of other houses because of something in their blood. She saw the dog for real, he knew she did. And now this was happening to him. Maybe the deer hadn't run by them at all. Maybe they had never left his room and the *National Geographic* pictures. Lauren had been the one person he was sure of, and now she was gone.

She began humming, something with no words at all, and he tried to relax, lay there looking up as the glow of flames cast shadows above them on the cracked ceiling.

He tried to breathe slowly and remember that he didn't feel like this in the mornings. He felt fine, strong. Like he knew things other people didn't know. Like he was becoming an explorer and that he was the only one who could really be with her because everyone else was shut out. She had some secret knowledge. That's why she was so confident and able to live without a phone or a computer or her boyfriend. Feeling a part of her secret world, above all the rest, made him forget he'd no choice but to be with her, that he was trapped with her. It made him want the next thing that was going to happen no matter how strange or difficult, because it would make something of him, make him more than a waiting and watching kid. He would have stories of his own. He would know what she knew. They would survive anywhere.

She sang, quietly at first. Her voice seemed more real than anything he'd ever heard. Filled with friendship and older than memories. It was like a spell that made the house seem fine, boring even, and he could see how this could simply be an evening like any other, a new kind of evening. The smell of woodsmoke, his sister's voice. Knowing that they were strong was all they had and all they needed.

"My heart's in the highlands, my heart is not here," she sang.

My heart's in the highlands a-chasing the
    deer
A-chasing the wild deer, and following the
    roe;
My heart's in the highlands, wherever I go.
Farewell to the highlands, farewell to the
    North
The birth place of valour, the country of
    worth;
Wherever I wander, wherever I rove,
The hills of the highlands for ever I love.
Farewell to the mountains high cover'd with
    snow;
Farewell to the straths and green valleys
    below;
Farewell to the forests and wild-hanging
    woods;
Farewell to the torrents and loud-pouring
    floods.
My heart's in the highlands, my heart is not
    here,
My heart's in the highlands a-chasing the
    deer
Chasing the wild deer, and following the roe;
My heart's in the highlands, wherever I go.

He could feel his own heart, feel it ease and slow as he remembered the power of the deer and the land around them. The song made it clear — the simple melody and the clear cool liquid sound of her voice. He and his sister shared some code that was twisted beyond repair and had long ago become its own new way of being. They'd been outside looking in for a long time. The world was the problem, the war that had taken her, the blank chatter-filled world he lived in alone in his room when she was gone. Maybe what they were doing was right. Even if it killed them, he thought, it was impossibly, imponderably right.

FORTY-TWO

She woke early and built up the fire and left
Danny sleeping in the house, letting the car
warm up while she took a quick run to the
end of the road and back. Then she got out
the map and found Daryl's house, which
was closer than she'd told him. She could
be there and home before Danny woke up.
Maybe bring Daryl and Camille and their
kid over to play in the snow and look
around. Or come back and get Danny and
they would all hang out for a while — give
him a chance to use their computer and
watch TV and maybe look after the little
kid while the grown-ups got caught up. And
then she and Daryl could make some plans.

She put the map on the seat beside her,
buckled up, and drove. The road to his
house did not hug the coast but rather a
small frozen lake, dotted with ice shacks,
one small green pickup truck parked on its
solid surface. She remembered the way he

had talked about Hebron, the wilderness, how much he liked his father-in-law. But mostly she remembered how he talked about Camille. The things she did with their son, Roy. The food she made. Homecoming was hard the first week, everyone knew that. But Lauren was smart enough to plan a trip and keep in touch with friends. And her backup plan was foolproof.

When she arrived at the two-story vinyl-sided colonial, the garage door was open and there was a snowmobile and a silver SUV parked in it.

Daryl's house was weighted with other people's memories. Bigger than she thought it would be but familiar to her, she'd seen the pictures from Christmas and the pictures from Roy's birthday party that summer.

The woman who answered the door was unmistakable, and seeing her in person was like seeing a celebrity. She was strong and lean looking, wearing a fleece shirt and tan Carhartt snow pants, she appeared to have just come in from the cold. There was snow melting on the mat just inside the door and two pairs of snow boots — one of them small, for a toddler. She looked tired and invigorated, her cheeks flushed, her long hair wavy and damp at the ends. Lauren felt her arms rising instinctively to embrace her. The house was hot compared to the outside and she could smell woodsmoke.

"You must be Camille," she said.

The woman cocked her head and smiled wanly at her, and then her expression slowly faded, shifted to one of recognition, and she took a step back.

"I'm Lauren Clay."

"I know who you are." She nodded. "I've seen your picture."

A little rosy-cheeked boy in snow pants slid across the wood floor in his socks and stood beside Camille, all spring and hop in his step. Lauren smiled and crouched down in front of the child.

"Hey Roy, buddy," she said to him. The boy mirrored her expression and she could see his little square teeth, his face beautiful and smooth, his almond-shaped hazel eyes like Daryl's, his thin smile the same.

"You look just like your daddy," Lauren said. The boy glanced up at his mother and she instinctively took his hand and pulled him back from the door. "Go find Grammy," she said, giving him a pat on the butt. "Scoot, Mommy's talking."

Lauren looked over the woman's shoulder into the house. It was cozy. She saw the deer head over the fireplace — might have been the animal Daryl had killed with his father-in-law on the trip he took up there when he was just eighteen.

Camille was still standing in the entryway looking at her, her face undecided. It was moving to be this close to her after only seeing pictures. Their Christmas must have been beautiful, so happy to be all together again. Lauren shrugged, tried out another smile, rubbed her hands together, and stamped her boots on the mat. "Looks like you folks are just getting in from playing," she said.

Camille shook her head. "I dropped my father at work, we needed the car today." Then she squinted, scowled, as if she didn't know why she'd bothered to speak. "Why did you come here?" Camille asked her.

Lauren laughed. "I guess you guys didn't talk about it. Daryl and I had planned for everyone to get together after the holidays. I'm staying up here near the Jeanne d'Arc Basin, brought my little brother — it's so beautiful, just like Daryl said. Must have been amazing growing up here."

Camille's eyes widened and filled with tears, and she glanced behind her into the kitchen.

"I don't want to impose," Lauren said. "I'd be happy to take everyone out in town for dinner."

Camille's face was drawn, her eyes not quite right.

"I'm Lauren," she said again. Wondering if she had somehow got the wrong house.

The woman said, "I know who you are and I don't ever want to see you again. I heard enough of you, I read enough about you in all that paperwork . . . enough about you to last me a lifetime."

Lauren was shocked.

"Do you have something to say to me?"

Lauren said, "Camille, I got back last week and I'm sure you know things can be a little rough, so I'm sorry if I've been rude, or was stupid to come here or if you want to be alone with your family. But I gotta tell you, your husband is the finest soldier I served with and he loves you so much. And he's my best friend. Well, to be honest, he might be my only friend right now."

Camille's body tensed and she started crying. Lauren reached forward and took her hand, it was vital and warm. Camille held Lauren's hand, wiped tears from her face with the other.

"Are you okay?" Lauren asked. "Is everything okay? Is Daryl out? Is he home? Can I see him?"

Camille's eyes narrowed and she began

shaking her head, her jaw tight. "What is wrong with you?" she asked Lauren quietly, her lips trembling, her face coming undone. "What the hell is wrong with you?" she shouted. "Is he home? No!" she screamed. "No. No and no!"

She felt the determination of the driver. He wanted something that was different from what she'd felt before. Daryl's voice rang out again with the promise the driver would be shot. And the vehicle seemed to pick up speed, as if the warnings were calls to hurry. She ignored the sounds of terror-stricken exuberance coming from Walker.

She adjusted her aim, emptied her lungs. A second took a year to pass and then she fired. A loud pop and tick, and the windshield blew out at about the same time as the driver's-side window. The car sped up, swerved. They hit the ground, bracing for explosives, but the car just smashed against the barricade, scraped and ground against a low concrete reinforcement, the horn blaring. She looked up at her men, felt a manic burst of laughter leave her mouth, then stood again. The car's wheels were spinning. It was not on fire, but she and Daryl knew that didn't mean a thing.

One of the car's back wheels was spinning, not touching the ground. It seemed to hang in time. Cameras mounted by the northernmost edge of the barricade should have captured more information about the driver, but the car was just out of range.

"We got another martyr over here at Jones Road or what?" Daryl asked when he radioed to get the surveillance. Jones was the boy who'd lost his arms and face, the one Walker replaced, and she'd hated the change of a numbered line on the map to a location bearing his name. She didn't feel it honored him, just made it bad luck for everyone else.

"Affirmative," she heard him say. "Sar'n Clay's work."

Daryl looked up at them. "We got two visible in the front seat. Out of range to get much more on it. One still moving but looks pinned."

They headed down and over to the vehicle. She heard the choked and feeble sound of the horn as it shorted out, gave way to another sound that made her immediately ill and then suddenly still and dead calm for whatever would be required. It was the sound of struggling, a mordant rasping whine of a thing suffering and snared. But still no kind of noise to trust. She'd felt the teleology of the driver from as far away as the FOB. Felt the resolve of their mission.

She was the first to reach the car. The sound wasn't coming from the driver. She could see through the empty frame of the windshield, what at first glance appeared to be a woman, smooth skin and shiny black hair, but then she opened the door. He was maybe twelve years old, hit in the throat, blood covering his chest, blood pooling in the seat between his legs. Beside him was the source of the sound, a woman in her thirties, pregnant, her nose broken and face bloodied, sobbing. They called for medical support. Daryl went around to the passenger side, and Lauren knelt before the boy and took his pulse. Just slightly more than nothing. She pulled him out and lay him on the ground and slipped the compress from her breast pocket, putting it over the neat hole in his throat and holding it tight. She began CPR.

She could hear the woman wailing, a congested anguished sound. Daryl was talking to her, telling her there would be help. Walker was on the radio, telling them what happened, saying there was a woman in labor. She glanced up at Daryl, who was trying to lift her gently from the car, talking quietly. The woman was gripping the door, trying to pull herself away and get to her child on the ground. He'd taken off his goggles so he could keep eye contact, his M2 hung on its strap behind him, his pistol was exposed and ready in the front holster.

"Soldier," Lauren said, gesturing with her chin that he should take the woman to the other side of the barricade where the medic would land. She turned to breathe another lungful of air into the mouth of the boy, then heard the shot and looked up to see Daryl thrown back on the ground. His jaw and cheek and top left side of his head gone, blood pouring out and down the front of his face but his other eye focused straight ahead. Before she even saw Walker, Lauren said the words, "Stand down!"

The woman was struggling to her feet still holding Daryl's pistol, dots of blood speckled her face, one hand resting on the car's hood, the front of her dress soaking wet and blood running down her legs. She dropped the weapon and hunched, clutching her stomach. Lauren felt what Walker felt but the woman was unarmed now. "Stand down," she shouted. "Stand down!"

He had raised his rifle. "Stand down, soldier, that's a direct order. Come and administer CPR to this boy. I will attend to her and Daryl. Stand down." She got up and began walking toward the woman, who was doubled over in a long contraction, holding her belly.

Walker fired from a yard away and the woman dropped straight to her knees and then, pulled by the weight of her stomach, slumped forward, landing hard, rocked there a moment before falling to the side, her bloodied face nestled close to Daryl's boots.

"That's a twofer," Walker said.

Behind him the ambulance was racing through the gate of the FOB. She could hear a helicopter and hoped it was for them.

In Medical she stood by the boy and his mother and Daryl, who was missing a chunk of his head and face and part of his brain, and whose blood was flowing freely and quickly off the table in a long thin stream. She watched them pack him in compresses. She watched them exchange looks and saw them slow their pace and then she heard herself ask, "Is he going to be okay?" The medic looked up at her, told Lauren to sit down, so someone could check her eye.

But she kept standing. Stood next to Walker, the stupid fuck they'd given her three days ago who was as sure to report her for the order she'd given as she was to report him for disobeying. She stood next to him hating him. Despising him. Together they were two killers before a silent trinity; a past present and future now blown open, and containing nothing. A ruin steeped in the oily metallic smell of blood.

The men from the helicopter pushed in to take them. She couldn't look at the boy or his mother at all. The boy's hair was shiny and black and rested just at his shoulders. He was thin, not yet an adolescent, a fraternal shadow, a mirror. She looked at the bandage at his throat and thought reflexively a thing she'd be waking to from now on. That she had not hit his head. That she'd almost missed. That she'd held in her arms the body of a child she had almost not killed.

FORTY-THREE

Danny woke up alone in the house, cold, and the fire was almost out. He had no idea what time it was — but judging by the sun it was much later than when they had usually been getting up. His sister was not there, so he restoked the fire and then walked up to the car. When he saw it was gone he stood astonished for a full minute, mute and immobile. Then he burst into tears. He kicked furiously at the snow and screamed her name. He ran to the edge of the woods, his heart in his throat. Then pushed into the thick of the trees, crashing through the branches running in a panic. He was at the middle of a great yawing emptiness. She'd left him. This couldn't be true. She could not have left him. She would not have done this.

He forced himself to stop running and catch his breath. Then he began crying again. If she would just come back he would stay there forever and not complain about it. How the hell was he going to find her? He sat down among the trees until he had calmed himself, then walked purposefully out along their running trail, looking for any signs she had been there.

Once back at the crest where the car had been parked, he turned and looked down into the hollow of the tree-lined basin and the crumbling houses and could not believe he was really there. This must be a dream — like the one where the terrible tall Snow Queen took Lauren away in her sled. His stomach lurched again and he felt his heart race. He ran down to the house. He hadn't checked to see if her things were still there. When he saw her gear and sleeping bag he calmed, laughed nervously. He tried to breathe normally and made himself sit down in front of the fire. He was not in any danger, he told himself, just alone for now.

Danny had never been alone without his phone. He had never been in a place with no people. But he was now and there was no choice and he had to suck it up like Lauren said.

He gathered snow and heated it over the fire and put in a tea bag. He did pushups while it steeped. Then drank it. Then walked slowly around the compound of little houses. Things were the same as when she was there. Nothing was going to hurt him. He went back in and heated one of the MREs and did situps and ran in place until he was very warm.

He knew she would not leave him. She would not. And if something happened to her he could run out along the main road and find someone and tell them what happened. He imagined trying to explain why he was there. How he got there. He could walk to the Exxon station — it would be a long walk and probably take most of the day, but if he started now he could get there before dark. He could live just fine. He could find her.

He ate and began packing their gear. And then he burst into tears again. How long was he supposed to wait? What if she came back and he was gone? He stood in front of the fire, immobile, stared into the flames and tried to steady himself. Tried to imagine where she could have gone or what she would be doing.

The wind blew against the house and when it stopped he heard boots on the snow and rushed to the door.

She was walking slowly down from the car. He let out a long trembling breath and then started laughing: What a baby, he must have been alone for just three hours and he had panicked. Of course she wouldn't have left him. The surge of joy in knowing flowed through his body in a great wave of relief and contentment.

He got out the pot to make them tea, but when she entered the house her face was red and swollen and her hair a mess as if it had been tangled by hanging out the car window in the wind. Her face was solemn and alert like a dying animal's. Frightening like an animal's. Her coat was not zipped and she had no hat and didn't seem to feel the cold.

He walked to her and hugged her and she rested her head against his shoulder. He could feel a sadness flow through him as if her whole body was made of it.

"Let's get something real to eat," she said finally, and handed him the keys. She stood and looked around the house, picked up the things she had left, pointed to his sleeping bag but said nothing.

He grabbed the rest of their gear, and when she nodded he knew they were finally going to see Daryl.

She let Danny drive into town so he could practice getting around in traffic — get familiar with intersections and traffic lights.

There were two intersections in the town and trucks, SUVs, and logging vehicles were the only things with wheels out on the roads. Their car stood out, shabby and salt covered with new deer dents. She closed her eyes and leaned back as he drove, holding the dog on her lap to keep her warm. He did not ask her where she had been or why they were leaving. He was a smart boy.

Danny did fine getting around, drove down Highway 1 and then pulled into the parking lot of a little diner. She handed him a Visa card with his name on it.

"Why do I have a credit card?" he asked.

"It's a debit card," she said blankly. "We have a joint bank account. Merry Christmas."

The table was sticky and the air close and heavy with grease, the smell of bacon and onions, coffee and propane. They sat at one in a row of booths that ran along the side of the building and faced a counter and round, red-topped stools. Christmas lights framed the rectangular windows, the corners of which were covered with thick patterned frost into which someone had scratched their initials.

The place was filled with men in flannel shirts drinking coffee, hunched before oval plates that were piled with pancakes and eggs and meats. The building was too narrow and bright and hot, and the sound of dishes and silverware and the number of wide-shouldered men in boots was familiar. It made her feel apprehensive about what was outside and where they were going. And it made her slightly sick looking at them, thinking today one of them was probably going to get hurt. Their big thick bodies and skulls and eyes completely unprotected. They looked naked without their helmets, hard hats, whatever they were called.

Their waitress had kind gray eyes, a small mouth, and pockmarked skin. Her smile a row of short square teeth and exposed gums, red hair pulled up into a covered bun.

Danny ordered pancakes and bacon and eggs and a piece of blueberry pie and a milkshake and a cup of coffee. This made her smile, so he ordered a Danish too. Lauren ordered coffee and drank it down quickly when it arrived. Something in her was gone. Something in her was getting lighter, disintegrating while he watched.

But when his food came she smiled again, looked almost content as he hungrily wolfed down pancakes, his wavy black hair falling around his shoulders. His cheeks were flushed and he looked healthy, purposeful, alert in an unfettered way. It was satisfying to see how much food he had in front of him, to watch him eat. She wanted him to be happy.

"So," he said, his mouth full of pancake. "Are we going to go see your friend?"

She shook her head and opened her mouth to say something but then didn't. He continued eating.

"Hey," he said, "when we go home, are you going to go to Curtis?"

A strange sound escaped her throat. "What do you know about Curtis?" she asked him contemptuously. She was shivering, and in the bright light shining through the window he could see that her dark eyes were darker still, filled with broken blood vessels. Making her face look like a mask that no one was wearing. Her strong hands were wrapped around the coffee mug, and they were chapped and worn from the cold.

He looked at her with pride. "I know everything about it," he said. "I listened to every song you practiced. I know it's harder to get into than any school in the country, I know they have an opera company. I know you got in. And I know it's free."

She looked away from him, watched to see if Sebastian was still in the car. She knew why only she could see him. She knew why she had believed Daryl was home too.

She knew what she was. A ghost and her dog, but somehow she'd forgotten that she had not returned at all. The woman she was supposed to be, was meant to be, would have been, could never exist at all now, and she was stuck dragging around this ruined version of herself. She owed it to the memory of her real self to get rid of this doppelganger that she was trapped inside, some false and foreign shadow that was no more alive than the dog.

"You said you'd go when you came back from Iraq," he said simply.

"I would have," she told him. "Believe me."

Lauren had gone to the car while Danny walked to the back of the diner to wash up. Their father answered on the first ring and accepted the charges, said, "Thank God," and was too emotional to speak. At first Danny thought he had hung up but then Jack Clay said, "Thank God" again. Then urgently: "How's your sister?"

"She's good," Danny said, pressing himself farther into the corner of the pay phone so people couldn't hear him. "We're camping outside a town called Hebron in Canada. Can you come and get us?"

"We'll have someone pick you up right now."

"No, no," Danny said. "No. You come get us. I'll hang up and I won't call again."

Danny could hear PJ talking in the background, then his father said, "Okay, buddy, let's talk about it for a minute. It's not that easy."

"Yes it is," Danny said. "We're just on a little trip. Please! I lost my phone or we would have called. Please you do it, just you. I'll try to come to breakfast every morning at the diner. There's only one diner. And then you can just run into us. And we can go home."

"Where's your sister right now?" His father's voice was so kind and slow and clear it scared him.

"She's in the car, what's the big deal?" Then, answering his own question, he said, "I have to go before she wonders where I am."

"Danny. Where outside of Hebron?"

"I don't know," he said. "I have to go. There's a motel connected to the diner and it has a blue sign with a moose on it. If you leave soon you can be here in the morning and we can all get breakfast." Then he hung up before Jack Clay could ask him anything more that he couldn't explain.

■ ■ ■ ■

She shut the passenger-side door and slid down in the seat so she could only see the sky and the telephone wires from the window. It was just another day now. Nothing had changed. The plan had always been to join Daryl and she had managed to forget what that really meant. But she would not forget again.

She let herself feel it one last time. The day she got the package from Curtis. How it gave her a sense of actually physically rising where she stood.

She had raced on her bike to Troy's office and the news had cracked his face open with such pride, and he had grabbed her and squeezed her tightly and kissed her on both cheeks, and she cried. She sat in the chair in his cramped office and she cried with relief. She could go, she could leave.

He had been right about auditioning as a soloist, and about the repertoire he had chosen for her. A simple piece in English, one in French and German and Italian, and "Lucia's Aria" — not required, but letting them know who she was, that she could do it.

He had accompanied her, sat at the piano

bench with the kind of grace and ease she'd never seen, as if he had finally brought her to his home, finally shown her where he was from, and it was not a place in this world. And she knew at last, the way he smiled, the way he looked past people when they spoke or squinted in confused amusement, he was looking at everything from this other place. He lived side by side with people but not among them. And now he had brought her here. He rolled his shoulders once and briefly rested his hands in his lap, then looked directly into her eyes so that she could tell him when to start; tell him without even nodding, without a gesture, just a thought that he could hear.

She stood beside him and felt him anchoring her. With her next breath there was no longer any distinction between her body and her voice; she existed for the next thirty minutes as sound. Troy sat beside her easily, elegant. He had shown her how to do this. Agreed four years ago to bring her there, because he knew the day he met her this was where she was from. He knew the way home.

She picked Danny up from after school and she twirled him around and around when they got out the door. They skipped along the sidewalk and she sang "Fair Robin

I Love." He knew it by heart. He sang it too in his little boy's voice, a piping warbling chirp that made her laugh.

That day she felt she could do anything. Knew she could.

She could sink into the ground and open her lungs, she could use the weight of her body to release herself from the weight of her body. She could rise, escape. She could disappear.

Lauren had two more weeks of knowing she could do anything before the first foreclosure notices came in the mail.

FORTY-FOUR

Grace was sucking her thumb again. She'd quit a year ago but since the fire she had her thumb in her mouth and was sleeping in bed with Holly. Holly looked down at her daughter's placid face. Her eyes shut, a white and yellow LEGO car clutched in one sleeping hand.

Now that she had her head clear, now that she had some time to think, her only thought was that she had almost lost Grace — not her own life but Grace's, being with Grace. Her daughter could have grown up without her.

Holly lay on her side, stroking the girl's fine hair as she slept. The Tinker Bell nightlight cast a blue-green glow about the room.

She went over it again, who was there. Who left. When it started. She was certain at first it was her fault for tossing cigarettes off the back porch, but no, not with all that rain. She'd never seen Troy at The Bag of

Nails in her life. Now the news was saying he was an alcoholic, trying to make him out as some kind of gay drug addict from the big city who once played at the Met. The phrase "played at the Met" was in almost every story. It was ridiculous. He was just some guy like the rest of them, just some guy that had fucked up and was living with it. She began to cry silently, curled herself closer to Grace and held her, smelled her skin, her baby shampoo. The tears streamed down her face and into her daughter's fine damp hair, and a deep hollow horror rose in the pit of her stomach.

She hoped Lauren and Danny were okay. Hoped that Lauren had not run away because of the fire. She was grateful for the check and she wanted her to be home and that was all. A vast sadness seized her when she thought about Lauren and she felt suddenly entirely alone. It was one thing for Holly to be fucked up, to have made some mistakes, be dealing with setbacks. It was another thing entirely for Lauren to be having trouble, changing her plans when she was finally free and could pick up where she left off. Lauren's successes had been hers too. Knowing that someone who was so much like her could achieve things, could sing, could break out of the shitty neighborhood and make money, not get stuck. Having Grace had made her like a lot of girls in the neighborhood, girls she never thought she'd understood or cared about. But she'd still been an honor student. She was still friends with Lauren Clay, which meant she could do what she wanted, even taking care of a kid. Lauren hitting Shane, taking off with Danny, lying to everyone was a thing she never saw coming and it shook her confidence, made her feel like a failure and like she'd failed as a friend, like leaving had never really been an option. She was simply there to stay. Another new year in the same place.

She kissed Gracie and listened to her wistful murmuring; her voice still carried something that felt like it came from Holly's body.

It was too much, knowing what she knew. The sense of betrayal and then feeling ashamed at her own stupidity. How could she have missed what people were saying all along? What Shane was saying, what Lauren herself had told her?

And she was ashamed that she was still there like a schoolgirl. In her childhood room with her child, her mother sleeping down the hall. She couldn't take another night of going over it all, not another night of crying. This was the worst part about having no work. Nine o'clock was not her bedtime; it guaranteed her five hours of lying awake realizing exactly what had become of her life. Every little detail she had missed while she was working or playing with Gracie.

Finally she got up and walked into her mother's room.

Bridget was reading in bed. She looked up and stretched out her arms, and Holly came over and lay her head on her mother's chest.

"You look so pretty with that haircut, Toots," Bridget said, placing her hand on her daughter's cheek. "You look smart."

Holly lay there quietly.

"Gracie sleeping?" Bridget asked.

Holly nodded. "I need to get out for a while," she told her mother. "I wanna go for a drive."

"I guess I need some errands run, now that you mention it." She picked up the box of Newports on her nightstand and rattled it.

"I won't be gone long, can you check on her?"

Bridget said, "That's what I'm here for, babe."

■ ■ ■ ■

She climbed the stairs feeling what had become of her lungs and rapped on the door of the tiny efficiency on Arsenal Street. There was nowhere else he could be now. When he opened it his face lit immediately with joy and she had to control the reflex to smile back, to hug him. He was wearing a green flannel shirt and cut-off shorts with long underwear beneath them. She smelled the liquor on his breath and the stale odor of laundry and cigarettes wafting out from the dark space behind him. Before she could say anything he swept her up in his arms and put his face against her neck and started sobbing.

She stiffened against him, waited for him to calm down.

He sniffed, his voice was tight, when he said, "I'm sorry, baby. I'm sorry, come in." He put his hand over his mouth and stepped aside so she could. "I thought you weren't going to call. I thought you were mad I didn't visit."

She took off her windbreaker. She was wearing a wife-beater T-shirt, sweatpants and rain boots; her left arm from shoulder to knuckles was bandaged with gauze and surgical tape. He looked at her body and began to cry again.

Still she felt nothing. She looked at the books piled around the little twin mattress where he slept on the floor, where he'd read to her and she'd told him her plans. His place was like some odd museum with things from boyhood, his baseball glove, a framed picture of his debate team. A little fleet of toy boats lined up on the windowsill above his mattress. It had been a sanctuary for her; providing a few stolen moments between the bar and going home to sleeping Grace when she could read or lie beside him or listen to his stories. She saw the postcards of philosophers he'd thumbtacked around the room, the framed and graying wedding photo of his parents that sat on his makeshift card-table desk along with a notebook filled with numbers that he'd alternately told her was his "work refuting Wittgenstein's *Tractatus*" or his work "analyzing chess moves," then finally and more likely the notebook where he "kept track of bets." He watched her looking around the room and braved a charming crooked smile. That roguish smile Holly knew so well, she felt it upon her own face. It was the way he acknowledged that they both loved his eccentricity, that she *got* him, knew a great secret; a world-class scholar was tucked away in a rooming house somewhere in the north country, deconstructing the whole false world while everyone else languished in their delusions. The joke was on all those sheep, the two of them were free.

"Why?" she asked.

The smile faded and he sat down on the mattress. She let the silence do its work.

He said, "I couldn't be beholden anymore. I just couldn't do it. You and me, we're not weak, babe. We had to show them. I don't need some captive audience. Some place in the material world."

"Who were you showing? Who *is* there to show? Look at what you did to me. This is *my* body." She began to raise her voice but it became too hoarse to speak. She stood before him, her arms hanging limply at her sides, and he did look at her for a long time, obediently. She watched the play of emotion on his face. The longer he looked the more it seemed he admired the scar, as if it was something she'd acquired for both of them. As if it was actually a symbol of their love and sacrifice and not her flesh.

"You're a soldier now." He said it reverently and was about to say something else but she cut him off.

"Hey," she said quietly. "Motherfucker. Guess what? I'm *not* a soldier. I'm a fucking waitress. And you're a delivery man."

He made a face, shook his head.

"Don't shake your head at me." She laughed bitterly, kicked a pile of his books to the floor. "I *know* you. I took care of you. I licked your wounds! I *loved* you! You made me feel like I could hold my head up. Like I could live here and work in a bar and still become something great. That I could be proud of this town, like coming from nowhere makes you smarter than other people, like things falling apart are really majestic. I looked *up* to you, Paddy. But all you wanted was someone to drag down with you!" She took one of his toy boats and clutched it angrily, then smashed it against the wall.

"You almost killed me, Patrick! You let another man take the blame! Your fucking war isn't our fault. It's over. It's not mine to clean up or Troy's to sit in jail for. Look at yourself, you're hiding here behind a pile of books you can barely comprehend and garbage you won't throw out and toys you were too selfish to have ever outgrown. All because you're too drunk or too tired or too lazy or too broken to have ever really lived your life."

Tears streamed down his face and he

shook his head, still smiling at her, the lines in his face deep and telling, his shoulders slumped. "None of that is true," he wept. "None of it. Baby, that is not *me* you're describing. That is not me!"

"It is, though," she said simply. "It is."

FORTY-FIVE

She checked them in under the name Daryl Green.

The room was small and dark and stiflingly hot and stagnant after having been in the open frozen house. There was a large TV and two double beds with thick ugly floral bedspreads. The floor was covered in low brown carpeting, and the place smelled like Lysol and room deodorizer.

He sat on the bed, and even though it felt good, the room was somehow far dingier than their camp with the crisp air and warm fire and smell of woodsmoke.

"Are we going to go for a run today?"

She said, "If we get separated, call Dad."

"Why would we get separated?"

"You gotta come up with contingency plans, man." She took her wallet out of her pocket and handed him four hundred dollars. "Hey, you can take a shower at least, huh? That's a good thing," she said. She was distracted, talking to him like he was a soldier, not someone she knew.

"It doesn't matter about the oil rigs," he told her desperately, a horrible feeling spreading in his belly.

She was still silent.

"There's nothing you could personally do about them," he said.

She snapped off the light on the side table and sat across from him on the other bed. "I agree with you there," she said.

It wasn't quiet that night because of the hum of electrical transformers across the road. Once she was asleep he went out to the car and found the map but not the gun. He knew there was a gun. He hadn't dreamed it. He opened the trunk and went through everything and at last found it tucked in the well with the spare. He slid it into his belt, went back in the room, and watched her sleep. Then he lay down. He'd stay awake all night and in the morning their father would meet them for breakfast and they would all go home together and they could listen to some David Bowie instead of some imaginary bullshit and he'd have good stories to tell at school, and then she'd go to Curtis and he could visit her there.

She screamed in her sleep. He jumped, was rattled as he looked over at her still body lying fully clothed, her boots still on. She looked like a corpse, a casualty from the desert transported somehow to these dingy and familiar surroundings. After a while he relaxed, turned on the TV, keeping the sound off, and watched a parade of color and garish garbage play across the screen. He flipped through channels and settled on the Cartoon Network.

When next he looked over it was because he had heard a click and she was gone. Pale light shimmered through the curtains and he leapt to his feet, crying her name.

He put on his boots and grabbed his coat and ran out to the parking lot calling for her, ran past the diner in time to see their car driving slowly, normally, just passing a green light at the only four-way intersection in town.

He screamed again. The diner was not yet open and there were still stars visible in the pale pink sky. While he was running back to the motel a blue SUV pulled up, a car he'd never seen before, an airport rental, and PJ was driving it.

"She's gone," he said, the second his father opened the passenger-side door. Jack

Clay's face, brightened by relief for one brief moment, became a mask of fear and sorrow. He went to embrace his son but Danny brushed it off. "She just left," he said, walking toward their car. "Let's go!"

"Now wait a second," his father said. Danny stared at him in disbelief.

PJ said, "Hang on, little man, we're going to head after her." He took out his cell phone and handed it to Jack, told him to call the police, then got out of the car, stretched his legs.

"Let's go, we've got to fucking go!" Danny shouted at them.

Jack walked away a few steps with the phone and began describing the situation to the 911 dispatcher and PJ was droning to him that at this point they needed more than just the three of them. Danny waited the eternity of five more seconds before he dropped PJ with a sharp kick to the knee. His father looked up in alarm and held up his hand, screaming, "Daniel, no!"

Peej lunged for him but he was already in the car.

Danny locked the doors and pulled out of the parking lot, running over a curb. The power of the car was a shock after driving the little Nissan, and the steering was so sensitive he swerved wildly, put the brakes on abruptly, throwing his chest into the wheel. Jack and PJ were running up to the vehicle as he hastily fastened his seatbelt, revved the engine and sped out, back toward their base camp. When he adjusted the rearview mirror he saw his father still running after the car, sobbing, his arms in the air, hands beckoning him back in time. He watched his father's slow defeated gait and thought if it was Low chasing him, she'd have caught the car and thrown him out of it by now.

Motherfucking Christ! What the fuck had they been waiting for? They could have called the cops from the fucking car. And he was not about to stand around describing things for the police and having them handle it. He knew where she was. She would be down in the basin, she would be taking the coastal road to the rigs. At some point she would have figured out she didn't have a gun and then she would do something stupid, something dictated by their family's faulty wiring and whatever made her scream in her sleep.

The sky was blindingly bright blue and he wished he had her aviator glasses. He drove cautiously toward the last intersection in town before the logging road and he could see troopers in their stupid tall hats. They

426

had already closed one lane and set up a checkpoint, and it was his fucking father's fault. There were two officers and both were out of their car, stopping traffic. They were leaning into the windows of the first two cars in a line of three. He drove on the shoulder of the road and pulled up beside the car that was stopped at the front of the line. When the trooper motioned for him to stop, he hit the gas. The fastest way to get them to follow.

He raced down Route 1, passing nothing but logging trucks and oil company cars, and turned, skidding and spinning onto the coastal road. He could see the tracks of another smaller vehicle that had passed this way, and when the wheels of the SUV hit gravel he sped up, panicked, and punched the steering wheel with one fist. He took the narrow seasonal road for about a mile and then turned onto the wide paved and plowed road the oil company had put down, but he knew that he was too far behind, could feel her being swallowed up by the snow.

Down in the basin before the frozen coast where the rigs were distant beacons dotting the shoreline, he saw the beat-up Nissan parked and relaxed for a moment. She must be looking at the rigs again. He had her gun, there was nothing she could do.

When he pulled up to the car she was not inside. A monstrous fear that was frozen in his chest cracked and he began to sob, looking around wildly for any sense of her. He didn't know if he was hearing sirens in the distance or imagining it.

The sun was coming up orange in the east and casting a glow upon the snow. Her tracks were small leading away to nowhere, and he could not see her walking, then in the distance he made out an olive and black figure lying flat against the snow.

His lungs ached from the cold as he ran the long yards to her, screaming her name, and through bleary eyes he realized that what he had seen was her coat. When he saw the rest of her clothes he knew she was dead and he ran even faster, unzipped his parka as he sprinted, took his sweatshirt off and was assaulted by the cold. It tore at him and he knew he was too late. Her dark hair spilled out like ink over the snow. The black bands of her tattoos against the white land made her arms look as if they'd been severed from her body.

"Low!" he shouted, but his voice was destroyed. He was terrified that none of it was real, his dead sister and the black towers of the rigs in the distance. She'd brought him to the Snow Queen's castle, where he lost his mind.

And then he thought he saw her hand move, her fingers closing as if she were clutching something. He threw his coat down around her, wrapped her head in his sweatshirt, and her legs and feet in the coat she'd discarded, pulled two hand warmers out of his pocket, activated them, and put them in her armpits, and then he pulled her up against him off the snow, grabbed her face and held it, tears streaming from his eyes and falling onto her cheeks. Her lips were blue, her fingers burned like ice where she had touched him, and he was terrified to take her pulse. Then he saw her breath white and rising above her. He clenched his teeth and held his own breath and rocked her back and forth, and then what seemed like minutes later she took another slow, shallow breath.

The sirens were getting louder at last and he took her gun from the back of his belt and fired a shot to let them know where they were, to make them hurry. In the distance he could hear the chopping reverberation of a helicopter, and then the sirens stopped. Doors slammed and bodies raced to them in heavy boots, tearing up the snow around them.

"Low," he said, holding her tight, grateful for her heartbeat. He looked out at the towers rising from the black water and the blank white coastline. And to the west the rounded mountain ranges blue and dark green with the slow life of trees. The sun was turning the sky in the east the color of flame, and all around them the snow glittered like a mirror turned to dust.

"Lauren," he said, shivering, his tears falling onto her face. The shadow of the helicopter passed above and his body was wracked with trembling.

"Low," he whispered. "Open your eyes. Open your eyes. It's beautiful here."

FORTY-SIX

Sebastian huddled down and curled his small warm body beside her, and she slipped her numb fingers beneath his collar, rested her cheek against him. She could smell his wet fur. She could feel him trembling.

The lights of the rig burned and bled to white, and before she closed her eyes, she could see the desert and the dunes out in the distance. Placid and silent and stretching on forever. She opened her eyes again at the sound of the air above her reverberating as it was beaten by the blades of the medic's chopper landing beside her. It was too bright. It was cold, not hot. There was no desert and the dog wasn't moving anymore. She tried to hold him but she was being pulled, lifted.

Then she was a part of the sky and he was small and black against the snow. She was leaving him. People stood around the dog's body, looking up. And even with her eyes shut, she knew that he was frozen. That he was gone.

FORTY-SEVEN

Time had changed. Seconds took any amount of time to pass, a week, a year. Scenes that repeated themselves did so without measure or meter. Visits lasted the duration of a remembered month. Holly and Shane stood beside her bed, their forms flickering beneath the bright fluorescent lights, talking like everything was normal but looking like they'd opened a drawer at the morgue. It made her laugh. That or whatever was in the drip. Shane bent down and kissed her mouth, and she put her damaged hands in his hair. Tasted him. He whispered something against her cheek.

People came and sat and left. At some point clocks began to measure time properly.

After a week when she could finally leave her room, she didn't want to. The sanitized brutality of the place made her feel weak. They were all warehoused there, haunting their own forms: soldiers coming back from the heat of the desert and her with her frostbite. They looked at one another in the common room and talked about the places they'd left. The people they'd abandoned. Crimes that would never be called crimes.

Troy visited weekly. First he brought the CD of her final recital, then the copies of the jury comments from her All State and All Eastern competitions. Then the full folder of her repertoire. And finally some paperwork she'd never seen before; an enrollment deferral filed years earlier, and a schedule for a fifteen-minute audition. Reading it raised the hairs on her neck and made her face flush. She looked up at him in disbelief.

"You sign here" — he pointed — "and here and here. I'll pick you up a week from Wednesday and they'll jury the Donizetti piece the following Thursday. And you owe me one hundred and fifty dollars."

He sat straight shouldered, pent up as always, with the pressure of whatever was coiled inside him dispassionately watching. He was wearing a frayed pink button-down shirt and jeans, and his hair had grown longer and unkempt. He bounced his knee as he sat in the fake leather chair, his pale blue eyes looking at her with amusement over his black-framed glasses. At the table beside them, a fit middle-aged man with a prosthetic arm was playing Scrabble with his young daughters.

"They won't want me," she said.

"Perhaps they won't, perhaps they won't now. But you don't have a lot of other options as I see it.

"What are you going to do?" he asked her. "Live upstate? Work in a restaurant? Babysit? Have you entirely forgotten who you are?" He leaned forward now and looked straight into her face. "You worked in this ghastly hole your entire life for two untalented men and a structure made of wood, plastic siding, and cement. I don't care how much you love your daddy and your little lookalike, that's literally what you did. Then you went to another ghastly hole and you worked for hundreds of men who wanted you to drive things around, kill people, and give orders to drive things around and kill people. Let's be very clear about the facts, otherwise it's not possible to make a decision, right? Do you have one small thing to show for what you've done? I say no. I say no, you don't. Nothing. Unless you count frostbite and windburn and months of your life wasted."

He reached forward and rested his finger

in the hollow at her throat. "There's no-where else to go from here, Lauren."

She was quiet, looked out the window for some time. She wanted her fearlessness back. The enormous freedom of it. A secret strength that stilled her grief, that made anything possible. But she had to sit there now without it. She'd entered into fear so completely she was at its center. The calm at the eye of the storm. To step out in any direction could mean being swept away. She thought of the stations of the cross, a new stations of the cross: ornately colored stained glass showing the flipped car, the hole in the throat, the Madonna with a broken nose, the soldier with one eye blooming dark red, the missing lanyard, the face and head of the other soldier snapping back, then vanishing in flying fleshy parts revealing exposed bone and teeth, hinges and sockets. The boy thin and dying in her arms, not his mother's, as he lay on the roadside. A narrow river of red. The still bodies and the falling bodies; the mother the son and the weight of the neverborn all pulling, blood pooling, toward the earth where Lauren stood armored, the color of desert dust, holding tight to the same kind of instrument that had cut them low.

The cathedral in her head shone with this

iconography. Light passed through these three silent bodies and also the faces and eyes of the medics, the illuminated stream of red that a mother brought forth to save the failing hope of a remaining child.

What sacred song could pass through her lips now? What choir could shield her from the sound of her own voice?

"I did terrible things," she said.

"Of course you did," Troy said calmly. "Don't let anyone tell you otherwise."

EPILOGUE

DISPATCH #217

Dear Sistopher,

I opened the link you sent where you're all dressed in black trying to smash everyone's glasses with your voice. There should be a superhero called Coloratura. When faced with danger she could shatter the glasses of her enemies. The video made Dad cry and I'm sure if Sebastian were here it would have made him howl. But seriously, Low, it made Dad cry, he was totally amazed. Then I was like, Chin up old man, it's not like she's out dying in the snow by some shitty oil rig or stuck at the VA hospital looney bin. That got him really pissed. I thought he was going to actually raise his voice.

Dad and I and Peej and Mom will be there Thursday to see your recital. You probably heard already but Mom got offered a position at St. Lawrence — a real one with medical coverage and stuff like that — and she's moving back this way. She's got a boyfriend who as far as I can tell does some kind of research on post-colonial-interlinguistic-sumarian-cryptographic-recursion theory as an aspect of primate finger painting. Not a thing he says makes sense and I'm pretty sure he's legally blind without his glasses. Dad and Peej have been helping Mom look for an apartment and she's been helping Dad paint the crappy upstairs hall, it looks good. She said she'd drive me to visit you whenever they can't but I have a feeling those cheapskates will be carpooling. All they need is a Volkswagen bus and to grow their hair out again and they'll look like the geriatric Mod Squad. It's hilarious, Low. You wouldn't believe the stories these nerds keep telling me about each other. And they play the same Jefferson Airplane album every time they're all here in the house.

School is fine. Boring but fine. I was so bored I joined track. I was so bored I learned how to build a radio. It is much much easier than you think. If I want to work in Antarctica I have to learn how to do practical things.

Dad wants to eat at that Indian place when we get to Philadelphia but I said we'd rather find a nice motel and have some MREs. And at that point he was so pissed he called me "Daniel." "What's wrong with you, Daniel? How can you laugh about these things?" And I'm like, 'Cause crying only gets you halfway there, duh. 'Cause my sister's a badass and she's alive. WTF?

Anyway, I can't wait to see you. I can't wait to hear you sing. I can't wait for us all to be there.

Low, we're safe now.

I love you.

She folded his letter and tucked it into her libretto and made her way down Locust Street to Rittenhouse Square, striding in her low heels beneath the brick, slate-roofed buildings and the gleaming sunlit steeples of downtown Philadelphia. The gutters were just beginning to fill with orange and yellow leaves. Her hair was pulled up into a bun, she wore a black sleeveless dress, carried PJ's watchcap in her little olive day pack out of habit. Soon she would be in the echoing hall and a rush of instruments and murmurs and warming voices would greet her.

She would sing her benediction, and the sound for which she was a vessel would be at last entirely clear; filling her mouth, liquid and shining, and black as the end of night. Like a cold glass bell, like a stone worn smooth. A voice like ice ready to be set alight, rising from her throat in a silent ancient refrain:

I sing now with the air I have taken from
    your lungs.

ACKNOWLEDGMENTS

I want to thank my brothers Noah and John, and our loving parents John and Kaye and Nick.

I want to thank my friends Marc Lepson, Emily Goldman, Jamie Newman, Ann Godwin, Susan Godwin, Alexis Kahn, Rebecca Friedman, Ella Meital, Sarah Knight, Kate Steciw, Karestan Koenen, Molly Lindley, Lauren Wolfe, Derek Owens, John Bryant, Joe Schmidbauer, Kelly Caragee, Franklin Crawford, Merry Whitney, Sonia Simeoni, Tommy Fritz, Liz Hand, Barb Borelli, Steve Borelli, Rachel Pollack, Ellen Klein, Annie Campbell, Harley Campbell, Johnny Fuchs, Michelle Novak, Ellen Cusick, Xan Underhill, Bianca Shannon, Selena Shannon, Marco Shannon, Sebastian Shannon, Jon Frankel, Jan Clausen, Clint Swank, Charles Hale, Rob Bass, Joe Ricker, Mitchell Sunderland, Tiffany Viruet, Will Fertman, Jacob

Bennett, Erin Kelly.

Thanks also to my students in the Bronx for their hard work and good humor, and to the Saint George Choral Society, a source of pure joy in my life. Soprano Angela Leson and Artistic Director Matthew Lewis were particularly helpful with early drafts of this manuscript.

While I studied voice when I was young, any real understanding I may have of music came from my friend and stepbrother Matthew Borelli, who was magic.

ABOUT THE AUTHOR

Cara Hoffman is the author of the critically acclaimed novel *So Much Pretty.*

Hoffman grew up in upstate New York, part of northern Appalachia, where she studied classical voice. She dropped out of high school and spent her late adolescence travelling and working as an agricultural laborer and runner in Greece and the Middle East.

In the 1990s she returned to the United States, had a baby, and found a job delivering newspapers, which eventually led to full-time work as a staff reporter.

She has been a visiting writer at St. John's University, Goddard College, Columbia University, and Oxford University, where she lectured on violence and masculinity for the Rhodes Global Scholars Symposium. She lives in Manhattan and teaches writing and literature at Bronx Community College.

The employees of Thorndike Press hope you have enjoyed this Large Print book. All our Thorndike, Wheeler, and Kennebec Large Print titles are designed for easy reading, and all our books are made to last. Other Thorndike Press Large Print books are available at your library, through selected bookstores, or directly from us.

For information about titles, please call:
(800) 223-1244

or visit our Web site at:
http://gale.cengage.com/thorndike

To share your comments, please write:

Publisher
Thorndike Press
10 Water St., Suite 310
Waterville, ME 04901